Mary Francis Cusack

**Meditations for Advent and Easter**

Mary Francis Cusack

**Meditations for Advent and Easter**

ISBN/EAN: 9783741192388

Manufactured in Europe, USA, Canada, Australia, Japa

Cover: Foto ©Andreas Hilbeck / pixelio.de

Manufactured and distributed by brebook publishing software
(www.brebook.com)

Mary Francis Cusack

**Meditations for Advent and Easter**

# MEDITATIONS

## FOR

# ADVENT AND EASTER.

BY

THE AUTHOR OF "MEDITATIONS FOR LENT," "S. FRANCIS AND THE
FRANCISCANS," "THE LIFE AND REVELATIONS OF S. GERTRUDE,"
ETC., ETC.

## DUBLIN:

### JAMES DUFFY, 15, WELLINGTON-QUAY;

AND

22, PATERNOSTER-ROW, LONDON.

1866.

DUBLIN:

Printed by J. M. O'Toole & Son,

6 & 7, Great Brunswick-street.

# Ad Mariam.

*Now ready.*

THE LIVING CRIB : a little book for ADVENT and CHRISTMAS. Price 2*d.* ; Twenty-five copies for 4*s.*

ALSO,

THE LITTLE BOOK OF THE LOVERS OF THE HEART OF JESUS CRUCIFIED. Price 6*d.* ; Ten copies, post free, for 5*s.* 6*d.*

These two little books can only be obtained from the Rev. Mother Abbess, Convent of Poor Clares, Kenmare, County Kerry.

*Orders are requested.*

# CONTENTS.

—————

## ADVENT TO CHRISTMAS.

# PREFACE ON MEDITATION.

MEDITATION is one of the most essential and important duties of the spiritual life. It is absolutely necessary for religious, it is almost necessary for seculars ; but many persons who would profit exceedingly by this holy exercise, are deterred from practising it by imaginary difficulties, by supposing that it is only intended for those who have attained a high degree of perfection, or who are aiming at great sanctity ; others, who really wish to practise medi- tation, because they think it pleasing to God, and who love Him too much to be afraid of any pains and trouble to themselves when there is a hope of doing His will more perfectly, are often in great difficulties, from not knowing how to commence the good work. Unfortunately, many of the instructions and directions for meditation are far more suited to the comprehension of those who have made it for years, than of those who need to be taught in the simplest manner.

We do not offer the following advice to those who have already made meditation for years, and from whom we would be only too glad to learn higher things ; but for those who are beginning to practise meditation, either in the world or in the cloister.

And, first, let us consider what meditation is. To meditate means to think about anything. We are medi- tating all day long, for all day long we are thinking more or less intently on some subject. If we are going on a journey, we meditate or think about it : (1) how we shall travel ; (2) about the place we are going to ; (3) about the friends we expect to meet when we arrive at our journey's end. Now, if we want to think about spiritual things, that is, to "make a meditation," we must just

act in the same way.  For example, if we wish to make a
meditation on heaven, we shall think : (1) how we can
get there most surely and safely ; (2) we shall try to
recollect all that we have heard about it ; (3) we shall
think of the friends we expect to meet there.  Ah ! those are
our best friends ; for who was ever greeted at the end of the
longest journey with one-half the love with which Jesus
and Mary will greet us, when we reach our heavenly home ?

Now, in the ordinary affairs of life, the more important
the subject is about which we are thinking, the more
carefully we employ those three powers of our mind—our
memory, our understanding, and our will.   If we are
thinking or meditating about a journey (to continue the
illustration already used), we shall use our memory, to recall
what we have read, or known from experience, about a
similar undertaking ; we shall use our understanding, to
find out how far these recollections will help us in our
present purpose ; and we shall use our will, to *will* or
determine what we intend to do.   We use these powers of
soul constantly, and in the very order above-mentioned,
every day of our lives ; yet, when we are told to use them
in meditation, we fancy it is something very difficult,
simply because the terms are new to us by which what we
have done and are doing every day is described.   See how
we may use our memory, understanding, and will, when
we meditate or think about heaven.   We use our memory
by remembering some text of Scripture, such as, " In my
Father's house there are many mansions ;" or some subject,
such as our Lord Jesus sitting at the right hand of God the
Father ; and we try to picture to ourselves, *i.e.*, to
remember, or call to mind, all we have heard about
heaven, its joys, its peace, its beauty, its everlastingness ;
then we use our understanding, by trying to understand or
learn what may be profitable to us from this meditation.
We learn or understand from it, that what happens in
time is of little consequence, because time is so short, and
eternity so long ; we learn that God has prepared such joys
for us as no human heart can imagine, and that our one

great object in life should be to prepare ourselves for these eternal joys. Then we use our will, to will or resolve, with our whole hearts, to prepare for heaven, to live for heaven, to remove every obstacle, however great, which might prevent us from getting to heaven ; and this brings us to the great end of meditation, mental prayer. To many persons mental prayer sounds as terrible and difficult an undertaking as meditation ; but as we trust meditation will no longer appear difficult, even to the most simple and unlearned, so we hope mental prayer will also appear easy and attractive. Mental prayer simply means praying in our minds. When we pray with our lips, so that a sound can be heard, we are using vocal prayer ; when we pray in our hearts, so that no one but God can hear us, we are using mental prayer; and those very persons who are frightened at the idea of mental prayer, nevertheless often make it unconsciously.

Mental prayer is the end of meditation, because prayer is that which unites us most closely to God. We meditate or think about holy things, in order that our thinking may end in praying ; even as we meditate or think about what we are going to do, that our thinking may end in doing. All the planning and thinking about a journey would never take us a step on the road, unless we acted on what we thought ; and all the acting might end very badly, if we acted without thinking or meditating beforehand. And if we should consider a person very foolish who undertook any important duty or occupation—who began to build a house, or set out on a journey, without having thought of what they were going to do—how much more foolish should we consider those who never think about those duties which are of the greatest importance—about that journey which cannot be performed a second time, to repair the errors of the first ! We cannot over-estimate the importance of daily meditation. There are few persons in the world so occupied that they could not give ten minutes every day to this duty. Ten minutes for God, leaves twenty-three hours and three-quarters for the world and self. But some may object that they hear Mass daily, and hence really cannot give more time to devotion. Why not make a little meditation at the commencement of Mass ? No one knows what the soul gains in stability of purpose and in help for daily needs, until they have tried giving even ten minutes a day regularly to meditation. It would be impossible here to enter into all the reasons for this assertion, but two may be briefly mentioned : first, it forms a habit of leading the mind to think of God; and second, the daily consideration of the various circumstances in our divine Lord's life, even for a few moments, leads the soul on insensibly to love Him more and more.

But the more beneficial meditation is to us, the more the devil will try to prevent us from attempting it ; and if we do attempt it, to prevent us from continuing it steadily. He will persuade us to omit it on any possible excuse, but we must be prepared for this, and determine not to allow excuses. He will try to distract us, to make us feel weary ; nay, even to inspire us with an utter disgust for it; so that we shall be almost amazed ourselves at our dislike, and at finding that we would rather do anything in the world than think of God for a few minutes. Further, he will allow us to enjoy devotion at other times ; but at the *precise time* when we ought to make our meditation, it will seem actually distasteful. Souls have been tried thus for years, even in the cloister, even at the times appointed for devotion to the most holy Sacrament. For this trial there is only one remedy : a firm determination to make our meditation, or our visit to the blessed Sacrament, at the time appointed, and for the time appointed. Happy they who persevere until death in resisting this temptation ! Even if the whole time of meditation is spent in dryness and distraction, there is a grace, above all, there is a strength, which may be felt, and is felt, by the faithful soul ; and even one omission, one meditation yielded to the tempter, leaves a weakness of soul that may not be recovered for many days. We shall conclude with what we hope may be useful to beginners.

### SIMPLE DIRECTIONS FOR MEDITATION.

1. Read over a part of the meditation you intend to make
at night, and try to think of it when you awake in the
morning. This is called remote preparation.

2. Fix a time for your meditation as early in the morning as possible; commence it by trying to recollect
yourself, and by saying the *Veni Creator*, or, if your time
for meditation is very short, say only one verse of that
hymn. Remember that the Holy Spirit alone can teach
you to pray, so you should be very earnest in invoking His
help.

3. Then read over the meditation carefully; when you
have done so, exercise your memory by thinking of the
subject, your understanding by trying to enter into it, and
your will by making acts of faith, hope, charity, &c.
Remember, however, that mental prayer is the great end
of meditation; and if the Holy Spirit helps you to pray at
once, do not wait to think, but begin to pray. For example, if your meditation is on heaven, when you have
read it over, or even a few lines of it, if you feel inclined
to rest, quietly, as it were, thinking how happy it will be,
how blessed it will be to see Jesus, &c., do so as long as
you feel inclined; but if the first thought makes you wish
to pray that you may love God more, who has loved you
so much as to prepare such great things for you, then pray
during the whole time.

4. When the time is nearly ended, try to form a good
resolution, and put it in the Heart of Jesus or Mary.

5. Then thank God for the graces He has given you, by
saying some little vocal prayer, and conclude all with a
very brief examination of conscience about the meditation
only; asking yourself, first, if you tried to be faithful to
the time appointed; and secondly, if you did your best to
make a good use of it.

It is very advisable, also, at the commencement of a
meditation, particularly where twenty minutes or half an

hour can be devoted to it, to offer it for some special purpose, and to request some special grace by it; such as to
offer it to our Lord to obtain the grace of patience, resig-
nation, meekness, obedience, recollection, &c., and to ask Him
to give us an increase of this grace by the meditation. But
the great thing is earnestness; to commence with fervently
imploring the help of the Holy Spirit, and with a firm purpose to resist all distractions, and not to let the time slip
over us idly. Alas! what do we not lose every day in our
devotions by want of earnestness! If ten minutes or half
an hour were given us every day to collect gold-dust, how
hard we should labour for the time appointed! Shall we
not also labour as fervently for a heavenly treasure? Do
not let us make a scruple of omitting the time of meditation, and no scruple at all of wasting it. Even in sickness,
and in very severe sickness, we might gain incalculable
benefit by a few moments' thought of God, at or near the
time when we usually made our meditation. If we cannot
think, we might say one Hail Mary, or one verse of a
hymn; and when our illness is not so severe as to prevent
us from exerting our minds a little, even though from
weakness we may be unable to meditate, we might find
great help and comfort in reading a few words of a spiritual book; nor should those who are really and constantly
suffering, make any scruple of substituting spiritual reading,
which generally ends in meditation, for the more exact
meditation which should be made under ordinary circumstances. To love God more is the end of our life; and
how shall we love Him if we do not think of Him, and
converse with Him, so as to know Him more and more?

CONVENT OF POOR CLARES,
*Kenmare, Co. Kerry,*
*Feast of the Patronage of our Lady,* 1865.

# MEDITATIONS

### FOR

# ADVENT AND CHRISTMAS,

#### IN HONOUR OF THE

#### INFANT HEART OF JESUS COMING TO REDEEM US.

———◆———

## ADVENT SUNDAY.

### THE HEART OF THE INFANT JESUS, OUR COMING LIGHT.

"Behold, the Lord cometh, and all His saints with Him; and in that day there shall be a great light." All. Ant. at Lauds.

"And the light of the moon shall be as the light of the sun, and the light of the sun shall be sevenfold, as the light of seven days, in the day when the Lord shall bind up the wound of His people, and shall heal the stroke of their wound." (Is. xxx. 26.)

*1st Prelude.*—Represent to yourself the Heart of the Infant Jesus in the womb of Mary as a flame of clear and beautiful light coming to enlighten all nations. Represent also to yourself the terrible light of the second coming, which will be open and manifest to all.

*2nd Prelude.*—Pray that you may be so enlightened by the light of the first coming, that you

B

may not be terrified by the light of the second coming.

*1st Point.*—Look at the Heart of the Infant Jesus. It lies hidden in the womb of Mary, even as his blessed Humanity will be hidden hereafter in the tabernacle. Oh, what a holy, beautiful, peaceful light is the light of the Infant Heart of Jesus! How it longs to come forth and manifest itself to all, to console, to instruct, to illuminate! Are we, also, longing to receive this light? Are we praying with our whole hearts that it may come to us, and that we may be prepared to receive it? However great our spiritual enlightenment may be, we are still, in some measure, "sitting in darkness and in the shadow of death." But the light is coming; already we can see the dawn upon the mountain. When Mary was born, the first ray of light tinged the eastern sky; when Jesus was born, the light of this mystic moon was as the light of the true sun, because of her perfect union with Him; and the light of the sun was sevenfold, as the light of seven days. The light was sevenfold; that is, the light was perfect, for it was the light of God.

*2nd Point.*—Let us beseech the Infant Jesus to enlighten us in that particular way in which we most need light. We are all "born blind" through the sin of our parents; and, unhappily, though we have obtained light in the waters of baptism, we too often, by our own fault, relapse into blindness more or less intense. Sometimes we do not wish to see the sin we should forsake, or the virtue we should practise, because it would cost us something to act upon this light; sometimes we profit so little by the light, that it is withdrawn from us, or it is not imparted in the fullness and brightness with which more faithful souls are favoured. There are souls in whom the light of God shines so brightly, that they cannot commit the shadow of an imperfection without perceiving it immediately ; there are souls in whom that light shines so resplendently, that they see even the shadow of an imperfect motive in the best action they perform. Why should we not be thus favoured ? It is not because the light is unwilling to come, but because we are unwilling to receive it.

*3rd Point.*—What shall we do to obtain this great grace ? Let us go to Mary. Let us devote our Advent to Mary. Let us consecrate every thought, word, and action to Mary during this holy season ; and then, on the blessed Christmas morning, she will herself place her Infant in our arms ; nay, rather, she will lay Him down to rest in our hearts ; and He is so obedient to His sweet mother, that He will never stir from the heart wherein she places Him, unless she comes to take Him away. Surely we will not oblige her to do so ? Advent should be a time of special devotion to Mary. Jesus again lies mystically in her womb. Again she pleads unweariedly for her people, as she pleaded in that blessed Advent when He took flesh of her flesh, and bone of her bone. Oh, let us kneel before her now as we would have knelt

before her then, and implore her to intercede for
us with Jesus, to obtain for us that He may indeed
be our light, and that we may never be of the
number of those who prefer darkness. Then, indeed, may we hope that the light of His second
coming will be a light of glory to us, and not a
light of condemnation.

*Aspiration.*—Come and enlighten us, O sweet
Infant Jesus.

*Form your resolution, and place it in the Heart of
the Infant Jesus. Examen of Meditation.*

———

# MONDAY.

## THE HEART OF THE INFANT JESUS, OUR COMING KING.

"Lift up thine eyes, O Jerusalem, and behold the mighty
King." Ant. at Magnificat.
"The Lord shall be king over all the earth." (Zach.
xiv. 9.)

*1st Prelude.*—Represent to yourself the Infant
Jesus as a king coming now to deliver, and as a
king coming hereafter to judge.

*2nd Prelude.*—Pray that you may be one of the
faithful subjects of this King, so that you may not
be punished hereafter with His enemies.

*1st Point.*—Consider the throne of this Infant
King. It is in the heart of Mary, the only human

heart in which He was ever permitted to reign supremely. Oh, how we should love that heart, how we should honour it, grander and more magnificent than the ivory throne of Solomon, "overlaid with the finest gold" (3 Kings, x. 18); fairer and more beautiful than his litter of the wood of Libanus, with "its pillars of silver, its seat of gold, its going up of purple, and the midst covered with charity for the daughters of Jerusalem" (Cant. iii. 10); for there is no charity like the charity of the heart of Mary, and there our Infant Jesus rules! Oh, let us go and adore Him there! Let us fall prostrate before Him, "the Lord, the coming King. O let us adore." Let us offer our homage to Him through the heart of Mary; let us kneel in spirit at the foot of this "ivory throne," from whence none are repulsed. Here every petition will be received; here we shall find our best and surest advocate with the King.

*2nd Point.*—But Jesus will not always remain on this fair throne of ivory. He seeks no litter of purple for His repose. Alas! has He not come to die on a couch covered with purple—the purple garment of His most precious blood? But when sweet Jesus comes forth from the heart of Mary, He will seek for other hearts wherein to reign. Shall we not offer Him ours? nay, rather, should we not implore Him to accept them? Oh, let us prepare our hearts to be His throne! He is coming forth from a heart which never gave Him a moment's pain, from a heart where all was subject to

His rule, from a heart which never caused Him to shed a tear of pain, or to breathe a sigh of anguish ; and He is coming to hearts who will treat Him with coldness, with indifference—alas ! O my God, that it should be true—to hearts who will treat Him with ingratitude, with cruelty, who will even dare to hate Him. O sweet Infant Jesus, how Thou must love us, when Thou willest to leave that gentle, tender heart for those cruel and wicked ones !

*3rd Point.*—Consider the gentleness of this Infant King. He comes as the Prince of peace. Oh! surely we will endeavour to drive all His enemies far away. How could we bear that our young Prince should be disturbed and molested ! Surely, from very love of His infant gentleness, we will use every effort to prepare our hearts for His reign, and we shall take care that He rules undisturbed. There shall be no cruel Herod to drive Him away, to seek the young Child's life. Alas ! if unhappily we should be guilty of mortal sin, we would seek His life. But we will take care that no rumour of fear shall reach Him, that no imperfection, if possible, at least that no deliberate venial sin, shall disturb Him. Alas ! if we do not permit Him to reign now in our hearts as the King of peace, He will reign hereafter as the King of vengeance. But if we are His faithful subjects now, oh, what joys and glories He will prepare for us when He calls us to heaven, His kingdom, for eternal ages !

*Aspiration.*—Come and reign over us, O sweet Infant Jesus.

*Form your resolution, &c.   Examen.*

---

## TUESDAY.

### THE HEART OF THE INFANT JESUS, OUR COMING LAWGIVER.

"He will teach us His ways, and we will walk in His paths : for the law shall come forth from Sion, and the word of the Lord from Jerusalem." (Is. ii. 3.) 1st Lesson at Matins.

*1st Prelude.*—Represent to yourself the Infant Jesus as your lawgiver.

*2nd Prelude.*—Pray earnestly that you may have grace to obey all His precepts.

*1st Point.*—Consider the office and authority of a lawgiver. It implies a power to command, and a power to enforce the execution of commands. Our Infant Jesus comes now to fulfil the former of these functions; He will come a second time to compel the latter. Jesus comes now to give us laws, to explain them, and to exemplify in His own person how we should practise them. He tells us to be meek and lowly of heart; He explains to us the nature of this meekness and lowliness, and He practises the lesson He teaches, so that we can have no excuse if we refuse to obey the law. We cannot complain that we do not

understand what has been fully explained ; we cannot complain that we are not able to do what
another has done.   And thus has our dear Infant
Jesus explained and practised every precept which
He has given.   What excuse, then, can we find for
disobedience ?

*2nd Point.*—" He will teach us His ways."   We
must not follow our own ways any longer.   The
ways of the Infant Jesus may be difficult to learn
at first, but let us remember they are the ways of
a God.   Oh! let us cry out to Him with our whole
hearts, " Teach me Thy ways."   His ways are not
like our ways.   Our ways are the ways of ignorance, the ways of sin, the ways of short-sighted
mortals ;  the ways of the Infant Jesus are the
ways of eternal wisdom, the ways of perfect holiness, the ways of an omniscient God.   Let us
weep before Him that we have so long followed
our own ways, that we have been so fearfully bent
on them, to our own destruction, had not His
mercy saved us.   But we must also " walk in His
paths."   All that He teaches us to do, He has
already practised.   The lawgivers of this world may
coldly and sternly give laws which they never intend to keep themselves ;  they may write their
laws in blood, in the blood of those whom they
drive to sin and desperation by cruel enactments—
but it is not so with Jesus.   He is the first, the
only lawgiver who keeps His own precepts before
He asks others to keep them ; and if His laws were
written in blood, it is His own Blood, His own

most precious Blood, which He has shed even while yet an Infant, to atone for the transgressions which He knew we would commit against the blessed, holy, peaceful laws He came to enact. Was there ever a lawgiver who died to atone for the sins which would be committed against His laws, who suffered death because justice must have its due, and preferred to suffer instead of the guilty?

*3rd Point.*—O my Saviour, my sweet Infant Jesus, teach me. I will try to listen meekly, to obey faithfully. My sweet little Lawgiver, I cannot bear to think that Thou shouldst suffer because I will sin—because I *will* to sin. Oh, take my will from me—my wicked will—since it causes Thee so much suffering! I give Thee up my will : oh, give me Thine in exchange! I will listen for Thy lowest whisper. I will hear and obey Thy voice in the duties of my state, in the requirements of my holy Rule, in the slightest intimation of the wish of my Superior. O my sweet Infant Lawgiver, I will be so anxious to obey Thee, that I will consider even the slightest intimation of Thy will as a treasure, above all when it contradicts my own; and I will seek for Thy footsteps, and walk in Thy paths, the paths of lowly, unasking obedience, the paths which lead to Paradise, whither Thou wilt bring me, O my Infant Love; where there will be no law but love, and where love will never be grieved or disobeyed.

*Aspiration.*—Sweet Infant Jesus, rule me and guide me for ever.

*Form your resolution, &c.    Examen.*

---

# WEDNESDAY.

## THE HEART OF THE INFANT JESUS, OUR COMING PRINCE.

" And the Lord said to me : This gate shall be shut: it shall not be opened, and no man shall pass through it : because the Lord the God of Israel hath entered in by it, and it shall be shut for the Prince." (Ezech. xliv. 2.) Response, 2nd Lesson at Matins.

*1st Prelude.*—Represent to yourself the vision of Ezechiel, and behold Mary, the closed gate through whom none but the Prince may enter.

*2nd Prelude.*—Pray that when Jesus enters into your heart, in the adorable Sacrament of His love, you may close its gate, and that none but the Prince may enter therein.

*1st Point.*—Consider the magnificence of the types which prefigure the advent of Jesus, and the glories of Mary. What more majestic, what more sublime, than this type of the Eastern gate, which the Prince alone might enter, and which was shut for all others ! Well might the holy Fathers of the Church love to linger on the grand prophetic page. Mary opens the gate of her womb, Jesus comes forth, and it is closed for ever—closed for the Prince, for the sanctuary of the All Holy may not be defiled by mortal touch. Let us approach that golden gate; let us kneel before it. The Prince is within, still mystically hidden in its embraces; but the gate, the golden gate, is always accessible, and we may speak through it to the Prince. O Infant Prince, alas! that when the golden door opens, and Thou goest forth from the shelter of that temple, it will be to suffer, to die!

*2nd Point.*—But there is also a golden door by which Jesus enters into our hearts—a golden moment when our Infant Prince asks admittance. Shall we keep Him waiting? shall we refuse to admit Him? shall we make delays and excuses? We may have done so heretofore, but now we will do so no longer. O come, sweet Jesus, come! We will have one golden gate also, by which the Prince alone shall enter. If others must have places in our hearts, they must enter by side doors, which we shall watch carefully, and seldom open; but the gate, the golden entrance of our hearts, shall be open for the Prince alone. Oh, marvel of all marvels, that He should condescend to enter therein! Oh, grief of all griefs, that we should so neglect this royal guest, whom it should be our glory and our joy to entertain with the tenderest affection and the deepest reverence!

*3rd Point.*—Let us take Mary for our model in receiving Jesus, and in entertaining Jesus. He predestinated us before all eternity to be His

own, even as He predestinated Mary to be His
mother. He prepared graces for us, even as He
prepared graces for her. And as He prepared for
her that grace of graces, to which none other
might aspire; as He made that golden gate for Himself as an entrance to the sanctuary of her body,
in which He dwelt ; so has He prepared the golden
gate of the most holy Sacrament, that He may
thereby enter into us, and abide corporally with us,
while millions are denied this unspeakable favour.
Have we ever considered what we owe to God for
His providence in permitting us to be of the number of His children, into whom He enters, with
whom He unites Himself in the adorable Sacrament? Have we ever made the thanksgiving we
ought to make for this stupendous favour? Oh!
let us try to realize what this favour is, and then
we shall be more likely to keep the golden door
closed for the Prince, to let none other even approach it; for what can be worthy of sharing our
love with God Himself? what sacrifice can be too
great to offer in thanksgiving for the honour of the
Prince's presence?

*Aspiration.*—O sweet Infant Jesus, my Prince,
enter into my heart, and close the door, that none
else may enter therein.

*Form your resolution, &c. Examen.*

'

# THURSDAY.

## HEART OF THE INFANT JESUS, OUR COMING SAVIOUR.

"But I will look towards the Lord, I will wait for God my Saviour : my God will hear me." (Micheas, vii. 7.) Ant. at Magnificat.

*1st Prelude.*—Behold the Infant Jesus coming forth from the womb of Mary as our Saviour.

*2nd Prelude.*—Pray that you may obtain the full benefit of the salvation He is about to accomplish.

*1st Point.*—Consider the meaning of the word saviour, and what it implies. It implies danger from which deliverance is needed ; it means the deliverer. The danger is sin ; the danger is eternal ruin ; and so great is the danger, that only a God can be the deliverer. Oh, how that Lord has loved His creatures ! Their danger did not lessen His security ; their ruin could not shake His stability ; and yet He cannot rest in His security, or repose in His stability, without coming Himself to save and to give rest to His creatures. Well may we "look towards" the Lord. If we were perishing in a torrent, with what eagerness would we not look towards a deliverer who appeared on the bank of the river, hastening to our assistance ! With what hope, with what love we should gaze upon him ! and if we knew that he could certainly save us, with what faith we would expect him!

*2nd Point.*—In Advent we should unite ourselves with the whole Church in expecting our Deliverer. We should offer up ceaseless acts of faith in His power, of confidence in His love, and of hope in His goodness. Perhaps our deliverance will be proportioned to our earnestness in preparing for it. Above all, we should unite ourselves with Mary. Her spotless purity, her burning love, her perfect faith, her ceaseless tears and intercedings, brought the Messiah from heaven, whom her nation had so long desired. Then let us offer our desires of deliverance in union with hers. Let us unite ourselves to her faith, her hope, and her charity in expecting Jesus. Let us beseech Him to accept her sublime acts of virtue in atonement for our coldness, and for her sake to " come and deliver us." He can refuse nothing to her prayers whose love won Him from heaven to earth. If we desire to obtain special favours and graces at Christmas, let us be devout to Mary; let us ask all through her in Advent. She is the tabernacle before which we should pray, and none ever knelt before her in vain.

*3rd Point.*—Let us endeavour to ascertain the special danger from which we should ask individually to be delivered. In the order of grace, as in the order of nature, there is some special disease to which we are predisposed, and which will prove our ruin, if we do not watch its symptoms and check its progress. How carefully and anxiously we watch the disease by which we think ourselves endangered ! how we guard against all that might excite it or increase it ! and then, if the least danger is apprehended, how quickly we consult the physician, how implicitly we abide by his directions! Would to God we were one-half as anxious about the constitutional malady of our souls. But let us begin now ; let us consult our spiritual physicians, employ the remedies they prescribe, and occupy ourselves during this Advent in imploring our coming Saviour to deliver us from this malady, whose danger He knows better than we can.

*Aspiration.*—Heart of my Infant Jesus, come and deliver me.

*Form your resolution, &c. Examen.*

## FRIDAY.

### THE HEART OF THE INFANT JESUS, OUR COMING PURIFIER.

" And one of the Seraphim flew to me, and in his hand was a live coal, which he had taken with the tongs off the altar. And he touched my mouth, and said : Behold, this hath touched thy lips, and thy iniquities shall be taken away, and thy sin cleansed."(Is. vi. 6, 7.) 2nd Lesson at Matins.

*1st Prelude.*—Represent to yourself the subject of Isaias' vision: he "saw the Lord sitting upon

a throne high and elevated, and His train filled
the temple." The Seraphim attend Him, and cry
one to the other : "Holy, holy, holy, the Lord God
of hosts, all the earth is full of His glory."

*2nd Prelude.*—Pray that you may be so purified
as to adore this God of hosts worthily.

*1st Point.*—Consider the Infant Jesus as our
Purifier. He comes that He may touch our lips,
not with a live coal from the altar of sacrifice, but
with Himself, the Victim of sacrifice. Even as the
Seraphim adored trembling, and uttering in this
marvellous vision the Sanctus, Sanctus, Sanctus,
which never ceases before the eternal throne, so
did they tremble and adore uttering the same canticle of adoration as they knelt before Mary, when
Jesus sat upon the royal throne of her royal womb.
And yet we can dare to approach that majesty
without fear and without adoration. Advent
should be for us a special time of purification.
We should purify ourselves to receive our new-
born King at Christmas; we should purify ourselves to prepare for the coming of that King, no
longer as an Infant and a purifier, but as a judge
and a dispenser of justice. Oh, let us seek to have
our lips now so purified by the Sacrifice of the
Altar, that they may be worthy of the eternal
entrance of our coming Bridegroom !

*2nd Point.*—Consider the words of this lesson :
"They cried one to another, Holy, holy, holy."
Thus, also, should we cry to each other, by our
words and our example, Holy, holy, holy. Our

God is holy ; we must be holy. Our God is holy ; we are His children ; children must be like their father. Our God who is coming to us is a holy God ; He cannot love iniquity ; He will turn away from us if He finds we are not in earnest in endeavouring to deliver ourselves from sin—from that sin from which He is coming at such a cost to release us. We must give each other good examples—examples of fervour, examples of charity, examples of devotion—crying out one to another, "The Holy One is coming; let us prepare to meet Him."

*3rd Point.*—We need two kinds of purification. When the Seraph touched the lips of the Prophet, he said : "Thy iniquities shall be taken away, and thy sin shall be cleansed." Our Infant Jesus is coming to touch our lips with the kiss of peace, that He may impart this twofold purification. First, He will cleanse all our past sins, that is, He will "take away our iniquities;" and we must prepare for this by a good confession, a fervent contrition, and worthy penance. Oh, how earnestly and specially we ought to prepare for our Christmas confession ! Jesus is coming to take away our sins ; it is but little He asks us to do to obtain so great a grace. Secondly, He will purify us by cleansing us from our daily imperfections and faults, and for this we must prepare by commencing now to observe our resolutions with great fidelity, so that our sweet Jesus may find only such imperfections as are almost inevitable to human frailty.

C

*Aspiration.*—O my sweet Infant Jesus, touch my lips and my heart, and purify me more and more. *Form your resolution, &c. Examen.*

----

## SATURDAY.

### THE HEART OF THE INFANT JESUS, THE MYSTIC DEW.

"Drop down dew, ye heavens, from above, and let the clouds rain the just : let the earth be opened, and bud forth a saviour." (Is. xlv. 8.)

*1st Prelude.*—Consider your Infant Jesus coming down from heaven as a gentle dew, to fertilize the earth; watering the earth, which is Mary, and budding forth as a Saviour.

*2nd Prelude.*—Pray that sweet Jesus may drop dew upon your soul, as a mystic earth, and bud forth salvation in your heart.

*1st Point.*—Consider the magnificence and beauty of this simile.. The dew drops gently from heaven; and by this mystic dew we may understand the Divinity of Jesus. It comes from heaven, but descends to earth. It comes from above, but it falls, like long-expected rain, into the womb of Mary. And Mary is the earth, the mystic earth, into which the Divinity descends, that by the power of that Divinity, which alone could operate so great a marvel, it may bud forth a Saviour. O thrice holy Dew ! O thrice blessed Earth ! The earth—that is, the soul of Mary—has pined, and longed, and prayed for that Dew. The ardour of her desires has brought it down from heaven. Again and again she cried as none ever had cried, or will yet cry: "For Thee my soul hath thirsted; for Thee my flesh, O how many ways!" (Ps. lxii. 2.) She thirsted for her God, not alone that her own soul might be filled, but that her people might be refreshed by the living waters. She looked out upon the world, parched and dried by the scorching fires of sin and lust, and she cried to God that He would come and deliver His people; and for her sake He came.

*2nd Point.*—As the first man Adam was formed from the earth, so the second man also would be formed from the virgin earth, Mary. He drops His Divinity, as dew, into her womb in the silence of the night, that the bud of His Humanity may germinate therein. He comes with the silence of dew. His descent into her womb was hidden and noiseless; and thus His grace comes even now, as a soft and silent dew, into the hearts of His chosen ones. Oh, how earnestly we should pray that this mystic dew of grace may descend into our hearts! How earnestly we should cry out, "For Thee my soul hath thirsted; for Thee my flesh, O how many ways!" and when the dew of grace has softened and fertilized us, then we may hope that Christ will be found within us, and that our life may become so one with His, that He may indeed be our life.

*3rd Point.*—If we desire this mystic Dew, if we
wish that Jesus should germinate in us, by assimi-
lating our life to His, let us seek this favour and
grace through Mary.   Let us seek to be like her in
our lives, if we desire in our measure to be like her in
her favours. Her heart was prepared for this Dew; it
was calm, loving, and full of desire to obtain it ; and
when the Dew descended into that virgin earth, O
how faithfully she corresponded with all the fertility
it effected !   It is the quality of dew to refresh and
fertilize ; let us pray that we may obtain all that
our coming Saviour desires to give.

*Aspiration.*—Drop down dew, ye heavens, from
above, and let the clouds rain the just.

*Form your resolution, &c.   Examen.*

## SECOND SUNDAY.

### THE HEART OF JESUS, THE FLOWER OF THE ROOT
### OF JESSE.

"And there shall come forth a rod out of the root of
Jesse, and a flower shall rise up out of his root.   And the
Spirit of the Lord shall rest upon Him." (Is. xi. 1, 2.)   1st
Lesson at Matins.

"Blessed is he that shall not be scandalized in Me."
(Mat. xi. 6.)   Gospel for second Sunday in Advent.

*1st Prelude.*—Represent to yourself the Infant
Jesus as a flower budding in the womb of Mary.

*2nd Prelude.*—Pray that you may love and

cherish this Flower, and that it may be planted in your heart.

*1st Point.*—Consider the words of the Prophet : " And there shall come forth a rod out of the root of Jesse, and a flower shall rise up out of his root. And the Spirit of the Lord shall rest upon Him." Already Mary is recorded in the prophetic page, even as she has already been predestinated in the eternal counsels as the Mother of Jesus. She is the rod of the root of Jesse, the rod which bears this mystic Flower. The stem which supports the flower always corresponds in grace and beauty to the flower which it bears. How beautiful, then, is the stem Mary, which bears the Flower Jesus. O most favoured stem ! O most holy Flower ! The stem nourishes and gives life to the flower. Humanly speaking, the stem is necessary to the flower. Mary nourishes and gives life to Jesus ; the sap of this stem, that is, the blood of Mary, forms the sacred Humanity of the Flower Jesus. How we should reverence that stem ! how we should honour it ! how we should strive to protect it from the blasts of dishonour ! how we should water it with tears of love and devotion !

*2nd Point.*—The rod Mary springs from the root of Jesse. "Of this man's seed, God, according to His promise, hath raised up to Israel a Saviour, Jesus." (Acts, xiii. 23.) Mary springs from a royal and a holy stock ; but while the progenitors usually ennoble the scion of a royal house, the scion here ennobles her progenitors. Mary need not glory that

she is of the race of David, but David will glory, to
all eternity, that Mary sprang from his root.   Oh,
how deeply this root had entered into the bed of
humility, since its branches ascend so high !   How
great its stability, since it supports a God!   How
marvellous its fertility, since it produces the Author
of creation.   Let us bow down in lowly homage
before this plant, and adore its Flower, who has
called Himself the " Flower of the field, and the
Lily of the valley ;" the flower of the fertile field
of Mary's virginity, the lily of the deep valley of
her most profound humility.

3rd Point.—Let us beware lest we should be
" scandalized " at the lowliness of this Flower.   Our
Lord Himself gives us this warning in to-day's
Gospel :   "Blessed is he that shall not be scandalized in Me."   Alas ! what fear there is that we
may take scandal at Jesus, when Jesus Himself
considered it necessary to pronounce a benediction
on those who were not scandalized in Him.   We
are scandalized in Him when we question the
wisdom of His providences and the love of His
providences ; we are scandalized in Him when we
fail to appreciate the greatness of His humility and
the beauty of His meekness.   The world of heresy
is scandalized in Him, because it will not stoop to
honour her whom He has stooped so low to exalt.
Let us beware lest we should fail, even in the least
degree, in the honour due to the stem of Jesse.
Let us pray that this Flower may be transplanted
into our hearts by her blessed hands, and let us

water it with our tears, and cherish it with our love. Then we may hope that the Spirit of the Lord will also rest on us, and fill us with His sevenfold gifts.

———

## MONDAY.

### THE HEART OF THE INFANT JESUS COMING TO DELIVER THE CAPTIVES.

"He hath sent Me to preach to the meek, to heal the contrite of heart, and to preach a release to the captives, and deliverance to them that are shut up." (Is. lxi. 1.) Ant. at Mag.

*1st Prelude.*—Represent to yourself the Infant Jesus coming as a deliverer, and the King Jesus coming as a judge.

*2nd Prelude.*—Pray that you may so prepare each year for the anniversary of His first coming, as to be enabled to meet Him at His second coming without fear.

*1st Point.*—Consider the mission of the Infant Jesus. He comes to preach, to heal, to release, to deliver. Our divine Lord Himself declared these were the characteristics and the proofs of His mission. When John the Baptist sent his disciples to ask if He was the one who was "to come," Jesus proved that He was indeed the long-expected Messiah by His works. They were to go and relate to John what they had seen and heard ; the miracles which they had seen performed; and the gospel which they had heard preached. And now our sweet Infant Jesus is coming again, as it were, on the same work, the same mission. He will preach to us by His example ; He will preach humility by His lowliness, He will preach silence by His speechlessness, He will preach charity by His surpassing exercise of that sublime virtue, He will preach love of Mary by His own conduct towards His blessed Mother. And if we are "meek" we shall hear Him and obey Him. The little Infant Jesus has not come to confound the proud, to silence the boaster, to humble the haughty ; this will be His work at another coming, when He will manifest His power. Now He comes only to manifest His mercy. Oh, let us pray for meekness, the meekness and simplicity of little children, that we may rightly hear and obey the preaching of this little Child !

*2nd Point.*—He comes to heal. O successful Physician, who is both the adviser and the remedy. We need not fear, however deep our wounds may be, however long they may have rankled and festered, the little Infant Jesus has a cure for all ; one drop of His Infant blood can heal the most inveterate and long-standing sore. Let us no longer complain of our imperfections, of our temptations, of our difficulties, of our weakness. Here is a remedy which cannot fail. All through this blessed Advent, let us kneel in spirit before Mary, the tabernacle where Jesus reposes, and pray to

Him to come and heal us, and He will come, and our healing will be perfected in proportion to the depth of our contrition, for He has come to heal the contrite of heart.

  *3rd Point.*—He comes to release the captives. Oh! let us never forget that there is another day coming—a day of exceeding fear—a day of agonizing dread; a day when Jesus will come, not to release, but to bind; not to deliver, but to shut up. And this day will be anticipated for us by the day of our death. The year is fast passing away. Can we tell if we shall live to see the close of another? Are we sure that this terrible day will not come to us before another Advent? If we have prepared for it, and it does not come, shall we be any the worse? If we have not prepared for it, and it does come, what will be our terror and dismay! Oh! let us run to our Infant Jesus, and beseech Him to release us now from sin, that we may not be bound eternally by it.

  *Aspiration.*—O sweet Infant Jesus, come and heal us, come and deliver us.

  *Form your resolution, &c.  Examen.*

# TUESDAY.

## THE HEART OF THE INFANT JESUS SENDING A MESSENGER TO PREPARE HIS WAY.

"The voice of one crying in the desert: Prepare ye the way of the Lord, make straight in the wilderness the paths of our God." (Is. xl. 3.) Ant. at Mag.

*1st Prelude*—Represent to yourself the great Prophet announcing the coming of Jesus.

*2nd Prelude.*—Pray that you may profit by all the messages of grace which Jesus sends you.

*1st Point.*—Consider the exceeding love of Jesus in sending a messenger to prepare His way. When earthly monarchs undertake a journey to a distant part of their dominions, they send messengers before them. These messengers are charged to provide for all their comforts, to remove every obstacle to their advancement, to warn the people of their approach, that they may conceal all that would prove offensive to royal eyes, to banish all semblance of sorrow, to command public rejoicings. But our sweet Infant Jesus has no such purpose in sending messengers before His face. Oh, no. His messenger is not charged to see to His comforts, for our coming King, our sweet Infant Jesus, has renounced all comforts. His messenger is not commanded to put out of sight such objects of sorrow and distress as would prove an annoyance to an earthly monarch. No; the messengers of our sweet Jesus were desired to assemble the unhappy and the miserable, to make the most unhappy and the most miserable the most welcome; for our Infant Prince is content to suffer all manner of afflictions Himself, if He can only console one of the poorest of His subjects.

*2nd Point.*—Consider the messengers whom the Infant King employs. Before His first coming He sends the Baptist; but Jesus is always sending messengers before His face, for He is always coming to His people with some new grace, some new mercy, some new kindness. How many messengers has He sent you this year, and how did you receive His messengers? When He came, was the way prepared? He sent you a messenger of warning, by the flight of time, at the close of last year; a messenger of recollection, by a short retreat; a messenger of remembrance of His passion, in Lent; a messenger of remembrance of His love, at Easter. He sent you, perhaps, messengers to say earth was not your home, by sickness and suffering, by kind trials, by temptations, by wise and loving admonitions. He sent you messengers of daily graces, which, perhaps, you were too much occupied with other things to notice, or if you noticed them, you have forgotten them. Oh, if we only profited by all the messengers Jesus sends us, how different our lives would be!

*3rd Point.*—The voice cries in the desert. Earth is a desert to Jesus, because His Father is not loved and honoured there; and yet we try to make a home of the desert, and marvel then we cannot make ourselves comfortable in it. The voice cries in the desert. Jesus is often obliged to make a desert for us, because we will not listen to His voice, or the voice of His messengers, in the crowded city. When sweet Jesus wants a soul all to Himself, and purposes to do great things in her, He leads her into the very depths of the wilderness. He takes from her all she loves; He makes earth utterly desolate; and He leaves her for a little while to know and feel the bitterness and anguish of this desolation; and then, O then, He comes to her Himself into the wilderness, and the desert rejoices and blossoms like the rose, and the rivers of waters break forth, and the soul, suspended between heaven and earth, lies upon the cross with Jesus, and lives only to love or to suffer, and suffering manifest is here only joy, and love is her reward.

*Aspiration.*—Sweet Infant Jesus, make me faithful tô the calls of Thy messengers.

*Form your resolution, &c.    Examen.*

# WEDNESDAY.

## THE HEART OF THE INFANT JESUS, THE LAMB OF GOD.

"Send forth, O Lord, the Lamb, the ruler of the earth. . . . And a throne shall be prepared in mercy, and one shall sit upon it in truth in the tabernacle of David, judging and seeking judgment, and quickly rendering that which is just." (Is. xvi. 1, 5.) Lesson at Matins.

*1st Prelude.*—Represent to yourself the Infant Lamb of God in Mary's womb, the tabernacle of David.

*2nd Prelude.*—Adore Him in that tabernacle, and pray that He may rule you from it.

*1st Point.*—Jesus is coming to us now as the Lamb. We know how gentle, how humble, how silent, how uncomplaining is that Lamb. Lambs were used for sacrifice, and Jesus is coming to be a sacrifice. One day we shall see Him as the "Lamb that was slain," and that Lamb has a "book of life," in which He writes the names of His children. (Apocalypse, xiii. 8.) Oh, let us go to Him now, and implore Him to write our names in that blessed book! Alas! that they must be written with His Blood. One day we shall see that Lamb "standing upon Mount Sion" (Apoc. xiv. 1), and with Him one hundred and forty-four thousand having His name, and the name of His Father written on their foreheads. And those blessed souls who stand near this gentle Lamb, who stand *nearest* to Him, who go *wherever* He goes, those souls who sing a canticle which no one else can learn, who are they? And why are they thus so wonderfully favoured? We know this also; they are "virgins," and the first-fruits of that most precious blood which the Lamb is coming to pour forth, that He may purchase them. Oh, how dear are virgins to Jesus, when He purchases them *first* of all the redeemed !

*2nd Point.*—But the Lamb has a throne. We are told what the throne is, and how it was prepared. The throne was " prepared in mercy." Let us look for this coming Lamb, and we shall soon see where He is enthroned. He sits in the tabernacle of David. Mary is the tabernacle of David, where the Lamb is enthroned, a thousand times more beautiful and more magnificent than the Temple of Solomon, the poor type of her perfect holiness and incomparable beauty. And if it was so honoured, and the Holy of Holies so revered, because it contained the ark and the cloud of the chekhinah, how shall she be honoured and revered who contained the Lamb of God ! His throne is " prepared in mercy." Who can ever fathom the depth of mercy which prepared Mary to be the throne of mercy, the well-spring from which the fount of mercy poured itself forth upon the whole earth.

*3rd Point.*—Jesus is coming now as the Lamb. He is coming to open the " sealed book " (Apoc. v.

5) of the Incarnation, which none other could open. The seals of redemption are opened. But when the Lamb comes as the "Lion of the tribe of Juda," He will open the seals of judgment, and pour forth the vials of wrath. Oh, let us beseech Him to come now as the Lamb, the Ruler of the earth! Let us submit ourselves to His gentle reign, lest haply we should be compelled to submit to Him as the Lion of wrath and judgment. Now He comes as the Lamb, to give us the fleece of His justice to cover us, the fleece of His merits to sanctify us. He comes to give us His blood to purify us, and His flesh to feed us. Oh, how can we ever love this gentle Lamb enough! And if we receive Him with love, when He comes hereafter as the Lion to a guilty world, He will come as the Lamb to us. If we submit to the rule of the Lamb now, the Lamb will rule us for all eternity, for those " who have washed their robes, and made them white in the blood of the Lamb," shall serve Him day and night; they shall hunger no more, and thirst no more, and the " Lamb shall rule them, and lead them to the fountains of the waters of life." (Apoc. vii. 17.)

*Aspiration.*—O come, Thou blessed gentle Lamb —come quickly.

*Form your resolution, &c. Examen.*

# THURSDAY.

### THE HEART OF THE INFANT JESUS COMING ON A LIGHT CLOUD.

"Behold the Lord will ascend upon a swift cloud, and will enter into Egypt, and the idols of Egypt shall be moved at His presence." (Is. xix. 1.) 1st Lesson at Matins.
"Behold a little cloud arose out of the sea like a man's foot." (3 Kings, xviii. 44.)

*1st Prelude.*—Represent to yourself the Prophet Elias upon Mount Carmel praying for rain, and behold this mystic cloud, the type of Mary.

*2nd Prelude.*—Pray also earnestly for the refreshment of a world already parched and desolate with sin, and ask that refreshment may come through Mary now as Jesus through her of old.

*1st Point.*—Consider Mary as the mystical cloud on which Jesus comes. At first the cloud is so small that it seems scarcely larger than a man's foot. Thus, Mary at first is hidden from the world. But she contains Immensity; and as years and centuries pass on, the cloud spreads over the whole of the eternal horizon. It refreshes, it fertilizes, it pours down torrents of grace upon the world; and as we approach the end of time, the cloud will increase more and more, and the Church will obtain yet larger blessings, yet richer graces, through the intercession of Mary. Jesus comes to us hidden in this cloud; hence it is that He gives His choicest graces through it. And those who, like the Prophet, ascend the heights of Carmel, those who are most elevated above the things of earth, who have ascended the steep mountain of perfection with toil and pain, they will the soonest perceive this mystic cloud. Thus the Church sings of Mary : *Sicut nebula texi omnem terram*—"As a cloud I covered all the earth." (Ecclus. xxiv. 6.)

*2nd Point.*—The Infant Jesus comes to us upon this cloud. It is a "swift" cloud, because of its love and desire. Oh, how swiftly Mary hastens on her path of mercy, when a soul cries out to her for relief! How she hastens to tell Jesus all its needs, and to bring Him to its deliverance ! It is a light cloud, for Mary never was burdened with the heavy weight of sin or lust. The Egypt of the world needs a deliverer. The presence of Jesus alone can destroy its idols. Alas ! do we not need His presence as much now as at His first coming ? How full of thankfulness and joy we should be that He comes again with special grace and power each Christmas ! If we only entered more faithfully and earnestly into the festivals of the Church as they recur, what increase of grace we should obtain ! Let us begin to do so now. Let us prepare for this Christmas as we should have prepared for the birth of our Infant Saviour, had we been on earth when He came, and had we been privileged to know of His coming. He will come to us as really, as effectually as He came to Bethlehem.

D

He will give us as abundant graces as if we had been present there. It is not because we were not present at the events which the Church commemorates, that we do not obtain all the graces which were then given, but because we do not prepare for these commemorations, and thus fit ourselves to receive what will be as freely given now as then.

*3rd Point.*—Jesus comes to us now in a cloud, that is, concealed in the mysteries of the most holy Sacrament. It is still Mary who brings Him to us. If she had not given Him a body in her womb, formed of her own life-blood, how could we now feed upon Him as our daily bread? It is from this mystic cloud that the manna of the most holy Sacrament is rained down upon us. We receive Jesus through Mary; let us, then, go to Jesus through Mary. Let us ask her to give us this Bread of Life; and when we receive it, let us offer Him all the love and devotion and spotless purity of His spotless Mother, in atonement for our coldness and neglect.

*Aspiration.*—Come and deliver us, O sweet Infant Jesus.

*Form your resolution, &c.   Examen.*

# FRIDAY.

## THE HEART OF THE INFANT JESUS COMING AS OUR COMFORTER.

"Say to the faint-hearted : Take courage and fear not : God Himself will come and save you." (Is. xxxv. 4.) Ant. at Mag.

*1st Prelude.*—Represent to yourself the little Infant Jesus coming as your comforter.

*2nd Prelude.*—Pray that you may be worthy of His divine comforting.

*1st Point.*—The earth was filled with darkness and desolation before the coming of Jesus. How much more dark and desolate will it be before His second coming ! It will be darker, because men will have rejected the Light ; and more desolate, because they will have rejected the Comforter. At Christ's first coming, the darkness and desolation was one of desire ; the world pined for a comforter, it longed for a guide ; and yet it knew not its needs, or knew them but vaguely. Hence, there was one deep cry of desire and expectation from all creation. There were a few who " looked for salvation in Israel ;" a few who longed and prayed for the Coming One ; a few who said in their hearts at least, " Come, Lord Jesus, come quickly." Let us unite ourselves during this Advent with them ; let us offer our sweet Jesus the tears of the

Prophets, the sighs of the Patriarchs, the blood of the Martyrs, above all, the love and desire of Mary, as our best preparation for our coming God.

*2nd Point.*—God *Himself* will come and save you. Oh, how certain and full will that deliverance be which is effected by a God! God Himself will come and save you. He sees us perishing in the ocean of our iniquities, and He will not send His saints or His angels to save us; He will come *Himself*. What a reason for holy confidence! If we are willing to be saved, we may be assured of our salvation. Since God Himself has willed to come and save us, we may know how desirous He is of our salvation, and how much confidence we may have that He will effect it! But if we desire to be saved either from eternal ruin, from an evil inclination, a long-continued imperfection, or a trying temptation, we must will our salvation with as much earnestness as God has willed to effect it. This is the reason why so many souls perish, not that God is unwilling to save them, but that they are unwilling to be saved. Yet we are unwilling in our measure when we do not use every exertion in our power to conquer sin and to attain virtue. Let us examine ourselves, and see how we are preparing for this God who is coming to save us.

*3rd Point.*—God Himself comes to save us whenever we receive the most holy Sacrament. The altar at which we kneel is another Bethlehem, at which Jesus has just been born. There we behold the Lamb of God, and there we may receive Him into our hearts. Oh, let the faint-hearted "take courage," for here they may receive the eternal strength ! Oh, let the fearful banish all their dread, for here they may receive their consolation. "God Himself" comes to save us ; and hence those who are weakest in soul and in body, need this blessed strength more than others, and can only live by this life. Jesus comes to save us through Mary ; therefore we should seek Him through Mary. Blessed are they who seek Him ever through her. Now He comes through her, and in her they will find Him. Hereafter He will come with her, and she will then be the salvation of those who seek salvation through her now.

*Aspiration.*—I am weak ; save me, O Lord.

*Form your resolution, &c. Examen.*

---

## SATURDAY.

### THE HEART OF THE INFANT JESUS THE JOY OF THE HUMBLE.

"O Lord, Thou art my God, I wilt exalt Thee, and give glory to Thy name : for Thou hast done wonderful things, Thy designs of old faithful, amen." (Is. xxv. 1.) 1st Lesson at Matins.

*1st Prelude.*—Represent to yourself Mary singing her canticle of joy, "My soul doth magnify the Lord," and exulting in her Saviour, her Redeemer,

and the Redeemer of her people. Then behold
Eve expelled from the Garden of Eden, and
mourning in unutterable anguish the ruin caused
by her sin.

*2nd Prelude.*—Pray that you may be enabled to
rejoice with Mary, by imitating the penitence of
Eve.

*1st Point.*—Consider the faithfulness of God.
Five thousand years have elapsed since He made
the promise, "She shall crush thy head." Even
when it was uttered, Mary was present in the mind
of God, and every type which prefigured her coming
was ordered in marvellous succession and wisdom,
from the miraculous fruitfulness of Sara, to the mystic vision of the golden gate in the temple shown to
Ezechiel. But how many saints of the old dispensation lived and died before Mary came! The
unbelieving doubted, and the scoffer scoffed; but
the word of the Unchangeable was written in
"the Book," in the book of Scripture, and in the
book of the eternal purposes, "She shall crush
thy head." The demon had deceived and ruined
the human race through the woman; through the
woman the demon is now deceived and ruined.

*2nd Point*—How great is that woman, for whom
above five thousand years was not considered too
long a preparation! How fearful was the sin for
which woman suffered such terrible punishment!
Until Mary came, woman was at best the servant,
but more often the slave of man. "I will multiply thy sorrows and thy conceptions," was the

awful sentence of the Judge. And the sorrows of woman were, indeed, multiplied, until she came whose sorrows were concentrated on One, whose conception was limited to One. Henceforth, where-ever Mary was known and honoured, woman was free. Even those who refuse to honour Mary, gain the advantage of her advent, though they will not honour her as the restorer of woman. Hence-forth barrenness is no longer a reproach to her, nor is she obliged to conceive in anguish. The deliverer has come; and while "marriage is honour-able in all," there is yet a more excellent way; and the Queen of virgins has made virginity the highest privilege of woman and her noblest praise.

*3rd Point.*—How powerful is that woman, to whom God Himself gave authority " to crush the serpent's head "! The head is the emblem of power; crushing signifies not merely victory, but that the vanquished can no longer exert his power, that he cannot rebel again. The ancient enemy lay crushed beneath the feet of Mary, when she accepted the will of God that she should become His mother. Well might the " dragon be angry against the woman " (Apoc. xii. 17), and make war with her spiritual seed, since he has failed so utterly in making war with her. Well may he endeavour to prevent devotion to Mary, knowing as he does her power. If we desire to overcome the dragon, to crush the serpent, let us seek her aid, whom God Himself has declared should accomplish this work.

*Aspiration.*—O Mary, crushing the serpent's head, crush his power in me.

*Form your resolution, &c.    Examen.*

---

## THIRD SUNDAY IN ADVENT.

### THE HEART OF THE INFANT JESUS COMING TO DELIVER US.

"The Lord is nigh.  Be nothing solicitous : but in every-thing by prayer and supplication with thanksgiving let your petitions be made known to God." (Phil. iv. 5, 6.) In-vitatory at Matins and Epistle for the day.

*1st Prelude.*—Represent to yourself the Infant Jesus in the womb of Mary preparing to come forth and deliver us.

*2nd Prelude.*—Adore your coming King with joy and thanksgiving.

*1st Point.*—This is the Advent Sunday of joy. The Mass commences with joy.  "Rejoice in the Lord always ; and again, I say, rejoice." And what is the cause of our joy ?  "The Lord is nigh." He is near in the commemoration of His first coming.  He is near in the hope of His second coming.  He is near, we know not how near, in that swift, sudden coming, which shall be to us the end of time and the commencement of eternity.  How many causes, then, we have for joy !  When a great prince is born, what rejoicings take place, what long preparations are made even before the birth of a royal child! The nobles prepare gifts, the monarch prepares feasts, his subjects prepare rejoicings. Shall we not also prepare gifts, and feasts, and rejoicings for our coming Prince? Let each have a gift to offer Him; some daily practice of virtue, some little daily thanksgiving for His love in coming to redeem us, some little daily self-denial. And when the day of His birth has come, we can gather our thanksgivings and our devotions in one, and lay them at His feet, or, better still, place them in the hands of our Mother to present for us to her Son. The touch of her blessed hand will beautify them, even if her love does not prompt her to add to them from her own treasures.

*2nd Point.*—"Be not solicitous." Why? Because "the Lord is nigh." What should we think of the heir to a kingdom, who was always fretting about trifles, who, even when all his necessities were supplied to-day, began to weep because he feared they would not be supplied to-morrow? What should we think of the son of a king, who gave himself up to anxiety about his temporal affairs, because he had some difficulty in managing them in his father's absence, when he knew that father was even then coming to deliver him from every embarrassment? O Christian soul, you are the heir of a kingdom, the child of a King. He is "nigh": why be solicitous? What is there on this earth worth five minutes' anxiety? Or if you must be solicitous, be

solicitous for God, and it will not destroy your
peace, or hinder your sanctification, as being solicitous for yourself will most assuredly do.  Be
solicitous for His interests; be solicitous for His
glory; be solicitous to prepare a welcome for Him;
and let it be more in prayer and thanksgiving than
in restless, busy work.

*3rd Point.*—But if we are commanded to be
"nothing solicitous," we are not commanded to be
indifferent.  We are not told not to work for God
in our daily duties, or our spiritual employments;
we are not told to use no foresight, or care, or holy
thoughtfulness, how our work, spiritual or temporal,
may be done best : on the contrary, we must work
as if all depended on our labour; we must occupy
ourselves earnestly with plans for God's glory and
our own sanctification, according to our circumstances and state of life ; but we must *not* be solicitous ; we must not give ourselves up to undue
anxiety, to repining if we fail, to fretting cares.
Why?  Because "the Lord is nigh." He is coming;
He will soon be here ; and we shall see that His
providence arranged all things, even our contradic-
tions and disappointments, for the best.  We must
be nothing "solicitous," because we can "pray;"
and if "our requests are made known to God," do
we wish that He shall give us what He thinks best,
or what we think best?  Are we not sure that He
hears what we say to Him, and that He will do
what He knows is best for us.  What reason, then,
can we find for being solicitous?

*Aspiration.*—The Lord is nigh ; O come, let us adore Him.

*Form your resolution, &c. Examen.*

---

## MONDAY.

### THE HEART OF THE INFANT JESUS THE CORNER STONE.

" Behold I will lay a stone in the foundations of Sion, a tried stone, a corner stone, a precious stone, founded in the foundation. He that believeth, let him not hasten." (Is. xxviii. 16.) 3rd Lesson at Matins.

*1st Prelude.*—Consider the Infant Jesus as the foundation stone of Sion, the Church of the living God.

*2nd Prelude.*—Pray that you may be placed as a precious stone on that foundation.

*1st Point.*—The corner stone of a building is always proportioned to its strength and magnificence. It is this stone on which all the others rest, and without its support the edifice would soon fall into ruin. Behold the Stone on which the Church of God is founded ! That Church is destined to endure to eternity, and hence the foundation stone is the Rock of ages; that Church is to be magnificent in its sanctity, and hence it is founded on the King of saints ; that Church is to surpass all that the human mind can conceive in its beauty, and hence it is founded on the Eternal Beauty. Let us offer our most fervent thanksgivings to the Infant Jesus, for having chosen us to be stones in this mystic building. How many has He passed by to choose us, and who could He have chosen so unworthy? Have we ever thanked Him enough for the gift of faith? If we have not, let us begin to do so now, when He is about to manifest Himself to the Gentiles, and to those who knew not His name.

*2nd Point.*—This stone is a tried stone. O sweet Infant Jesus, Thou comest to be tried and fashioned by the rude tool of suffering, and we desire to be stones in this building without any fashioning that can give us pain. When Solomon was building the temple, which was both the type of Mary and of the Church, the workmen were required to cut and hew the stones at a distance, "so that there was neither hammer, nor axe, nor any tool of iron heard in the house when it was in building." (3 Kings, vi. 7.) We must also be cut and hewed here for the eternal temple, since no sounds of pain can be heard therein; since into whatever shape we are fashioned now, we shall continue for all eternity. Oh, how ardently we should desire the hammer and the axe : the axe of purification, that every evil may be cut away; the hammer, that we may be refined and polished, that our virtue may be perfected by suffering !

*3rd Point.*—"He that believeth, let him not hasten." Let us not desire that hours of suffering should pass quickly; for we believe they are hours of purification, of preparation for our place in the eternal temple. Let us not desire that they should hasten, lest we should be less fit for the place for which we are destined, or less "precious" than the Heart of Jesus designs to make us. Alas! if, by our murmurs or impatience, we should deprive ourselves of the least touch of that purification which He is giving us daily with His own wounded hand! Alas! if, by our petulance or pride, when reproved or advised by our superiors, we should deter them from admonishing us, and thus lose a brightness perhaps transferred to a more perfect soul.

*Aspiration.*—O sweet Infant Jesus, come and prepare us for Thy eternal kingdom.

*Form your resolution, &c. Examen.*

---

## TUESDAY.

### THE HEART OF THE INFANT JESUS COMING TO ENLIGHTEN US THROUGH MARY.

"And the light of the moon shall be as the light of the sun, and the light of the sun shall be sevenfold, as the light of seven days, in the day when the Lord shall bind up the wound of His people, and shall heal the stroke of their wound." (Is. xxx. 26.) 3rd Lesson at Matins.

*1st Prelude.*—Represent to yourself the beauty of Mary as she longs each hour with deeper desire to behold her Child and her God.

*2nd Prelude.*—Pray that you may also become spiritually beautiful by your ardent desire of Jesus.

*1st Point.*—Mary, the moon which enlightens the Church, becomes every hour more beautiful. Her light was the one bright spot on a dark earth, when Jesus beheld it from His Father's throne, and came down into her womb. But her light was hidden, for the time of its manifestation had not yet come. Nor will Mary's light be fully manifested until this prophecy has its full accomplishment at the second coming of Jesus. How, indeed, could we bear the fulness of its glory, when even its rays are dazzling to our sinful eyes. But at the moment of the Incarnation the light of the moon did indeed become as the light of the sun. The Sun had concealed Himself in Mary's womb, and henceforth she shines with His light. Her light was indeed clear, and fair, and beautiful ; but now she shines with the light of God, she sees in the light of God, she lives in the light of God.

*2nd Point.*—Hence it is that those who are most devout to Mary know Jesus best. They see Him with and in her light, and her light is His. Oh, if we need light to see our imperfections, let us go to Mary, and ask her to show them to us ! She sees them in God's light, she sees in what manner they are most offensive to Him. She sees the little specks and motes which we could never discern, because her light " is as the light of the sun," which manifests what is hidden to every light less penetrating. If we need light to discern our path of duty, let us go to Mary. She sees all things in the light of the Sun of justice, for He abides in her. She will point out to us the shadows of self-deceit. She will shine upon our path in the fulness of heavenly beauty ; and when all earthly light fails, if we have the light of Mary's love, we shall never lose our road.

*3rd Point.*—The light of the sun fertilizes, and brings the fruits of the earth to perfection. But it also has the power of scorching and destroying. Mary is now as a mystical sunlight, fructifying the people of God. Jesus has come " to bind up the wound of His people," and He has made the light of His Mother's love a principal instrument in effecting this blessed end. When the sunshine of Mary's love is turned upon a soul, what graces it obtains, how rapidly it ripens, how marvellously it fructifies, what knowledge it attains ! Oh, let us beseech her to look upon us ! Her look is life. Once again her divine Son will come, and then this prophecy will have its perfect accomplishment— " the wound " of God's people will be healed eternally, and the light of Mary will shine with an eternal glory. But there will be another light—a light of fear, a light of destruction. The light of the Sun of justice will be sevenfold ; magnificent to His chosen, destructive to His enemies. Oh, let us pray now that the powerful light of Mary may illuminate and fructify our souls, lest the destroying light of the last awful day should scorch us for eternity !

*Aspiration.*—Mother of Jesus, be my mother. *Form your resolution, &c. Examen.*

---

## EMBER WEDNESDAY.

### THE HEART OF THE INFANT JESUS SENDING HIS ANGEL TO ANNOUNCE HIS COMING.

" The Angel Gabriel was sent from God into a city of Galilee, called Nazareth, to a virgin espoused to a man whose name was Joseph, of the house of David ; and the virgin's name was Mary." (Luke, i. 26, 27.) 1st Lesson at Matins. Gospel at Mass.

*1st Prelude.*—Represent to yourself the scene of the Annunciation.

*2nd Prelude.*—Pray that you may receive all God's messages with the humility and deference of Mary.

*1st Point.*—As Christmas approaches, the Church leads us on deeper into the mysteries of this holy season. This day, in ancient times, was one of great devotion and special observance. Alas ! that the coldness of our love should have occasioned the withdrawal of so much that might help us heavenward. But a special Mass and Office is still left to us. Let us try to enter into the Church's designs. Perhaps if the Advent is a short one, Jesus will come to us in a few days. How can we prepare ourselves better, than by uniting ourselves with Mary ; by joining in spirit with her as she hears the Annunciation; by uniting our preparations for our coming Saviour to her preparations for His Nativity; by joining, with all the love of our hearts, in this the Church's special commemoration of the Annunciation.

*2nd Point.*—But we must think also of another purpose for which this day is appointed. Alas! that we do not think more prayerfully of the ember days, as they recur at each season of the year. God does not need our prayers; but in the designs of His providence, He is pleased to act as if He were influenced by them. And what more momentous subject of prayer could we find than that which should be uppermost to-day? If the pastors of the flock are not faithful and holy, what will become of the sheep? To-day hundreds are preparing for the solemn rite of ordination. They are to be God's messengers. Like the Angel Gabriel, they will be "sent from God" to His virgin spouse, the Church, to announce the tidings of salvation. Theirs is a high commission, an awful dignity, and an untold honour; nay, they are even honoured far above Gabriel, for he but brought the message of God to Mary, but they will bring God Himself to His people. How clean of hands and pure of heart should those angelic messengers be! Can we pray sufficiently for them?

*3rd Point.*—Consider the manner in which Mary receives this message. Meditate on her profound humility, her meek attention, her prompt obedience. Do we thus receive the messengers whom

E

God sends us? Is our answer *always* an *Ecce ancilla?* Would to God that we did not even utter a refusal or a murmur. Let us learn from Mary how to reverence our priests and superiors, and how to obey their message. God sends us countless messages all day long—messages which are whispered in our hearts, but which we are often too busy to hear—messages of love, of warning, and of counsel. Let us examine ourselves as to the manner in which we receive those favours. Let us resolve earnestly, for the future, to receive them like Mary. Let us always be as handmaids, loving, gentle, thoughtful handmaids of our beloved Jesus, watching for His messages, however secret, and ready to say meekly, *Ecce ancilla, Domine.*

*Aspiration.*—Behold the handmaid of the Lord; be it done unto me according to Thy word.

*Form your resolution, &c. Examen.*

## THURSDAY.

THE HEART OF THE INFANT JESUS SENDING A
MESSAGE TO MARY.

"Hail full of grace, the Lord is with thee : Blessed art
thou among women." (Luke, i. 28.)
"And there shall be faith in thy times, riches of salvation, wisdom, and knowledge." (Is. xxxiii. 6.) 2nd Lesson
at Matins.

*1st Prelude* as yesterday.

*2nd Prelude.*—Pray for grace so to imitate Mary,
that Jesus may abide with you also.

*1st Point.*—Consider the angelic salutation, "Hail
full of grace." If Mary was full of grace before
Jesus was conceived in her womb, how she must
have overflowed with grace when the Fountain of
grace abode within her! O immaculate Mother,
may some of the overflowings of thy grace descend
into our poor hearts! O most pitiful Mother, the
fountain is at thy disposal. Thou hast the key;
open, oh, open its treasures to us, for we are parched
and thirsty. Consider the words, " full of grace."
Mary was so full of grace, that there was no room
for self, and no room for creatures. Self and
creatures are the two great obstacles which prevent
us from receiving the measure of fulness of grace
which God desires to give us. Let us ask our
immaculate Mother to teach us the secret of empty-

ing ourselves, that we may be filled with God.
Let us begin this blessed work now. Jesus is
coming very quickly; shall we not do all we can
to make room for Him in our hearts?

*2nd Point.*—Let us try to ascertain the special
obstacle which prevents us from receiving the
fulness of grace. Let us beseech our divine Lord
to purify our intentions, our actions, our purposes,
our life. Mary had no end but God, and hence
she was ever full of God. But we have so many
ends, that He cannot find room in our hearts.
Until a soul has watched herself very closely,
and has received great light from God, she will
have no conception how imperfect and how mani-
fold are the motives of her very best actions; and
when she is trying to do well, why should she not
try also to act purely? God will thereby be so
much more glorified, and our merit so immensely
increased.

*3rd Point.*—Consider the words, "the Lord is
with thee." He loves to dwell in the humble
heart. His delights were with the children of
men long ere He came to die for them to win their
love. And if the Lord was "with" Mary before
He became incarnate in her womb, how much
more really was He with her when He took flesh
of her! He was with her before the Incarnation,
but now He is in her. Oh, what a union between
a creature and a Creator! Oh, what a union
between flesh and spirit! Oh, what a union
between man and God! Jesus is also with us and

in us when we receive Him in the most holy Sacrament of His love. When the priest utters the *Ecce Agnus Dei*, it is a second Annunciation. When he gives the body of Jesus, it is a second Nativity, in which Jesus is born in us and of us anew. He is born of us when we manifest Him to others by living His life, by speaking His words, by acting His acts; and thus in our measure we may be blessed with Mary, whose highest blessedness was that she did the will of God in all things.

*Aspiration.*—O sweet Infant Jesus, come and deliver us.

*Form your resolution, &c. Examen.*

---

## FRIDAY.

### (DECEMBER 17TH.)

THE HEART OF THE INFANT JESUS COMING AS THE ETERNAL WISDOM, AND CHOSING HIS MOTHER TO MANIFEST ITS EXERCISE.

" O wisdom which proceedeth from the mouth of the Most High, reaching from end to end, and disposing all things with power and sweetness; come and teach us the way of Providence." Ant. at Mag.
" And whence is this to me, that the mother of my Lord should come to me."(Luke, i. 43.) Gospel for Ember Friday.

*1st Prelude.*—Behold the Mother of God inspired by and containing the Eternal Wisdom, hastening to fulfil His desires by her visit to Elizabeth?

*2nd Prelude.*—Pray that the Infant Jesus may thus sweetly and powerfully dispose all things for your salvation.

*1st Point.*—Consider how the Eternal Wisdom orders all things for the good of His elect. He orders them "with power and sweetness." With power, because none can withstand the fiat of His omnipotence; and when to our short-sighted wisdom His plans seem to fail, or His purposes appear to be contradicted and defeated, then, as we shall see hereafter, He has acted with most power and authority, and those who imagine they resist Him, only accomplish His will. He orders all things "sweetly," and this we shall also know hereafter, if our love is too feeble too realize it now. All that has seemed most severe in His conduct towards His chosen ones, has been not only wisest but kindest. Happy are they who have passed through deep trials, which, at the time, seemed more in judgment than in mercy, and yet have known and acknowledged that the tenderest love had ordered all.

*2nd Point.*—But if the Eternal Wisdom orders all things in regard to His creatures with power and sweetness, how much more must He not have ordered all that concerned His only beloved Son! His choice of the time of His Incarnation must have been most perfect. The events which immediately preceded the Nativity in the world's history, were all overruled with a view to the divine birth. But, above all, oh, how wise a choice was the choice of the Mother of God ! Can we imagine any subject connected with the Incarnation of higher importance? Can we suppose any subject in regard to which the Eternal Wisdom would manifest itself more plainly? With what deep and lowly homage we should reverence this mother, chosen by the light of Eternal Wisdom that to all eternity He might manifest His power in her and through her. Hence she is the *Virgo potens* of the Church. Hence the first miracle in the order of grace is worked through her in the sanctification of John the Baptist; hence the first miracle in the order of nature is performed through her at Cana of Galilee. Chosen by the sweetness of the Eternal Wisdom, she is the *Virgo clemens* of the Church, and by her, with surpassing sweetness, every favour we ask is granted. Her sweetness moves her to visit Elizabeth, as the first spiritual charity of the new dispensation; her sweetness moves her to implore the supply of wine for the wedding feast, as its first temporal charity.

*3rd Point.*—Consider the words of Elizabeth, the type of all true lovers of Mary. Far from fearing lest she should pay her too much honour, she trembles lest she should pay her too little. "Whence is this," she exclaims, "that the Mother of my Lord should come to me?" Ah ! let us leave it to the cold worldling to be like the wedding guests, who never thanked Mary for the wine; we will rather imitate the saintly Elizabeth; we will cry out at each favour granted to us through her interces-

sion, "Whence is this to me, that the Mother of
my Lord should come to me?" We shall be
amazed that she can vouchsafe even to listen to
our entreaties, even to speak one word for us to
her Son.

*Aspiration.*—Mother of Jesus, plead for me with
Jesus.

*Form your resolution, &c. Examen.*

---

## SATURDAY.

### (18TH DECEMBER.)

### FEAST OF THE EXPECTATION.

THE HEART OF THE INFANT JESUS REJOICING IN
HIS MOTHER'S ARDENT DESIRES OF HIS BIRTH.

"O Adonai, leader of the house of Israel, who appeared to
Moses in the burning bush, and gave him the law upon
Sina ; come and deliver us with an outstretched arm." Ant.
at Mag.

*1st Prelude.*—Represent to yourself the Mother
of Jesus praying and longing with ineffable desires
to behold her Infant and her God.

*2nd Prelude.*—Pray with your whole heart that
you may as ardently desire Him.

*1st Point.*—The burning bush, which was not
consumed, even while surrounded with flames, is a
type of Mary's conception. She brings forth a Son,
but her virginity remains inviolate ; nay, she is

even purer from conception, as fire purifies and refines what it does not destroy. But what is this mystic fire which causes so great a marvel? "How shall this be, angel of God," exclaimed Mary, in the words of the divine office for the Saturday of this week (Ant. at Benedictus)—"how shall this be, angel of God, for I know not a man?" "Hearken, O Virgin Mary; the Holy Ghost shall come upon thee, and the power of the Highest shall overshadow thee." And well might she hearken to such a message; well might she ponder it in deep and awful reverence; well might she treasure it a secret which none might know until God Himself revealed it.

*2nd Point.*—The Holy Ghost, then, is the fire which burned Mary, but did not consume her. How awful was her nearness to that Spirit which is called in Scripture a consuming fire! how unutterably pure she must have been to bear such nearness unconsumed! She is penetrated, permeated by Him into her very inmost being, body and soul, and yet she does not die. O Spouse of the Dove, who art so dear to Him, what words can describe thy awful greatness, thy surpassing purity! We must put off our shoes even to approach that flame, and yet thou abidest in it. O Spouse of the Dove, pray for us, for thou canst obtain from Him what thou wilt; and ask that we may be purified for the coming feast, that we may be inspired with longings for the divine birth, in some manner, at least, like thine.

*3rd Point.*—Consider how Mary longs for this birth, and let us unite our desires to hers. How she implores that this Leader of the house of Israel may appear. Do we not also need His presence and His deliverance? Oh! let us ask Him to come with an outstretched arm. It is not by stretching out His arm to destroy that He will effect this deliverance. Alas! it is by stretching out His arm to suffer. It is by stretching out His arm that His hands may be nailed to the tree. It is by using the very opposite means to those which human wisdom would suggest. He delivers by suffering and by patience. Let us also learn to help others, and to assist in our own deliverance by stretching out our hands to suffer. One day our sweet Jesus will come with an outstretched arm of power; but He has stretched out His arm first to suffer, and even on that day He will bear the marks of His agony. If we desire to reign with Him then, and to be delivered by Him from eternal woe, we must suffer with Him now.

*Aspiration.*—Sweet Infant Jesus, come and deliver us.         .

*Form your resolution, &c.  Examen.*

## FOURTH SUNDAY.

### (DECEMBER 19TH.)

"O root of Jesse, who standest for an ensign of the people, before whom kings are silent, and the nations offer their homage ; come and deliver us, and do not tarry." Ant. at Mag. "I am the root and stock of David, the bright and morning star." (Ap. xxii. 16.)

*1st Prelude.*—Represent to yourself the Infant Jesus elevating His standard, and inviting all the faithful to place themselves under His protection.

*2nd Prelude.*—Pray that you may ever march faithfully under the standard of this great King.

*1st Point.*—The root of Jesse is still hidden in the mystic earth of Mary's womb ; but even now He is preparing to come forth. As the first man was made of virgin clay, so is the second; but woman is now honoured in Mary beyond all that her heart could have hoped and desired. The first woman was formed from man, and hence owed him a debt of gratitude, which she, alas ! repaid with evil. The second man is formed of a woman, and from the moment of the Incarnation, the evil which woman had done to man was more than compensated, and man owes a debt of gratitude now to woman. O Mary, who shall tell us how to repay all we owe thee ! The mystic ark still contains the hidden manna; but even now He is preparing to come forth and feed His people. O Mary, what hast thou not given to us !

*2nd Point.*—When Jesus comes forth from the Tabernacle, from the Holy of Holies, where He reposes, He will raise His standard, that all nations may assemble beneath it. He invites us with smiles and tears. He assures us that in the war to which He summons us, He will bear the hardest share ; and that, however many our defeats, if we only rise up after each and invoke His help, we shall be counted as having won the day. He promises to bear the brunt of the battle, and assures us that He will endure all, and more than all, which the meanest soldier in His camp may suffer ; nay, more ; He promises that our wounds shall shine resplendent as suns, and prove no small part of the magnificent adornment He is preparing for us. Who would not desire to enlist under such a leader ? Alas ! that any should be led astray by the deceitful promises, the false protestations of His enemies.

*3rd Point.*—Let us beseech Him to come and deliver us ; let us implore Him not to delay, lest our weakness should prove our ruin ; let us ask Him to shine upon our souls as the morning star. One day He will come, and angels will display His standard in the heavens. Oh, how many will desire to flock beneath that banner then, who are ashamed to appear even near it now ! But it will be too late. That ensign will be a protection to the people of God, but it will be a destruction to the enemies of God. That sign of the cross, which they have despised, or viewed with indifference, will be no protection when enemies assail them; but it will be the very mark of the elect, and the token of their being under the protection of the great King.

*Aspiration.*—O sweet Infant Jesus, come and deliver us, and do not tarry.

*Form your resolution, &c. Examen.*

•

---

## DECEMBER 20TH.

### THE HEART OF THE INFANT JESUS THE KEY OF DAVID.

"O key of David, and sceptre of the house of Israel, who openest and none can shut, who shuttest and none can open; come and lead us forth from our prison-house, where we sit in darkness and the shadow of death." Ant. at Mag.

"Behold I am living for ever and ever, and have the keys of death and of hell." (Ap. i. 18.)

*1st Prelude.*—Represent to yourself the Infant Jesus coming to offer the keys of the kingdom of heaven to the pastors of His Church, that all who desire it may be admitted therein.

*2nd Prelude.*—Pray that the golden key of mercy may open its doors for you, through the merits of the coming Saviour.

*1st Point.*—The key is the emblem of power. He who possesses the keys of a palace, is master of the palace. The keys of a city are placed in the hands of its conqueror. Our sweet Jesus comes, as the key of David, to open to us the royal treasures of that royal house. But we may refuse them; we

may prefer our poverty ; we may imagine the treasures of earth greater and better than the treasures
of heaven.  Let us not forget that many, that multi-
tudes do thus deliberately prefer the treasures of
earth.  Alas ! if we should in any measure be so unhappy as to act thus !  We prefer earth to heaven,
when we prefer the pleasures of sin or sense, however
trifling, to the boundless treasures which we might
obtain by mortification.  We prefer earth to heaven, when, even in trifles, we occupy our time with
what pleases us, instead of with what pleases Jesus.
We prefer earth to heaven, when we fail in earnestness of purpose, in purity of intention, in at-
taining that nearness to God to which He is calling
us, because we do not like the trouble of constant
watchfulness over self.

*2nd Point.*—Consider the power of Him who
holds this key.  A conqueror may win the keys of
a mighty city to-day, and to-morrow they may be
wrested from him.  A prince may hold the keys of
his palace to-day, and to-morrow the monarch
Death may strike his hand, so that he can no longer
hold them.  But who can snatch the keys from
the hand of our Infant Jesus?  If He opens the
door of the prison-house, who can close it?  If He
frees the captive, who can bind him again, unless
he wills to resume his chains?  If He opens the
golden gate of the palace of David, the "many
mansions" of the Father's house, who can close its
portals against us?  But we must remember, also,
that if He shuts none can open.  Oh, how we should

fear, how we should weep before Him! how we should beseech this gentle Infant that the gates of mercy may never be closed on us! And if we fear that these gates are well-nigh closed because of our sins, let us have recourse to Mary. Jesus has hidden the golden key of mercy in her blessed heart, and she can never refuse to use it for poor sinners; and even if Jesus is obliged to take the key from her, lest she should admit such vile creatures as we are, if we only kneel and weep at her feet, she will kneel at the feet of Jesus, until He gives her the key again; for He can refuse nothing to her, who never refused anything to Him.

*3rd Point.*—But if we desire to obtain all the privileges of the key of David, if we desire to possess the key of the sacred Heart of Jesus, we must give Him the key of our hearts. Our sweet Jesus asked S. Gertrude for the key of her heart, that He might take away from it what He pleased, and place in it what He pleased. But when that saint of love asked Him what was this key, He told her it was her good will! Oh, let us hasten to lay this key at the feet of our Infant Jesus, or rather to place it in His little hands! Let us ask Him to keep it, and never more give it back to us. He will forgive many a fault and many an imperfection to the heart which with true good will seeks to be His alone.

*Aspiration.*—Sweet Infant Jesus, come and open the door of mercy to sinful men.

*Form your resolution, &c. Examen.*

## DECEMBER 21st.

### FEAST OF S. THOMAS, APOSTLE.

#### THE HEART OF THE INFANT JESUS COMING AS THE ORIENT FROM ON HIGH.

" O Orient, Splendour of eternal light and Sun of justice ; come and enlighten us sitting in darkness and the shadow of death." Ant. at Mag.

"The Orient from on high hath visited us. To enlighten them that sit in darkness, and in the shadow of death : to direct our feet into the way of peace." (Luke i. 78, 79.)

1st *Prelude.*—Represent to yourself the splendour of this glorious Sun coming forth as the light of morning to illuminate a dark and sinful world.

2nd *Prelude.*—Pray that we may be truly enlightened by His coming.

1st *Point.*—The special sin for which Jesus condemns the world is its rejection of light, because, by rejecting light, they rejected Him. This, He says, is the "judgment" or condemnation of men ; " light is come into the world, and men loved darkness rather than the light." Why ? " Because their works were evil." (S. John, iii. 19.) If they had received the light, they would have perceived their darkness. But theirs was a deliberate rejection of light, and a deliberate choice of darkness ; for the word " preference " implies a choice between two objects. Do we ever prefer darkness? Do we ever wilfully blind ourselves to the light of truth? Do we ever try to hide from ourselves what we can scarcely help seeing, lest we should be obliged to act against our evil inclinations. Oh, let us pray fervently for grace to be " children of light." How noble, how beautiful a title! Jesus says of Himself, " I am come a light into the world ;" and asks us to be His children, " children of light." (S. John, xii. 36 and 46.) The children of light are full of light ; they are all openness before God and before men. They do no deeds of darkness, because they have nothing to conceal.

*2nd Point.*—Since Mary is the mother of light, she must be its most fruitful source. More enlightened than the Prophets, more enlightened than the Patriarchs, more enlightened than all the Saints, Mary is filled with light, because she contains its Author. Hence those who are most truly devout to Mary, will be most enlightened in divine things. As a mother will impart all the knowledge she possesses to her children in proportion to their age and advancement, so does Mary impart the light of God to her spiritual children in proportion to their spiritual necessities. Happy they who are favoured with the least ray of this light ! It will not fail to guide them to the eternal day. Let us beseech this kind mother to enlighten us, to teach us all we need for our perfection and sanctification, to impart to us the necessary light for our respective duties.

F

*3rd Point.*—Jesus is coming as the Sun of justice. Oh, let us beseech Him to ripen the fruits of grace in our souls: alas! perhaps the little plants of grace have hardly yet commenced to germinate. But, beneath the rays of this powerful Sun, they will shoot forth and multiply rapidly. Let us beseech our sweet Infant King to come quickly, and illuminate us "sitting in darkness and the shadow of death." Let us beseech Him to enable us to reflect His light on others, like the great Apostle of to-day. Let us beseech Him to enable us to overcome our doubts and unbelief, and in our measure to evangelize even until death. How many thousands are sitting in darkness whom we might lead forth into light by our prayers, if not by our words! "Sitting," because the darkness is so intense that they fear to move. "Sitting," because they are paralyzed by the chill shadow of death.

*Aspiration.*—Come, sweet Infant Jesus; come, and be our souls' light and love.

*Form your resolution, &c.    Examen.*

## DECEMBER 22ND.

### THE HEART OF THE INFANT JESUS COMING AS THE DESIRE OF NATIONS.

"O King and Desire of nations, corner stone which unites both in one ; come and save man, whom Thou hast formed from clay." Ant. at Mag.

" O poor little one, tossed with tempest, without all com-fort, behold I will lay thy stones in order, and will lay thy foundations with sapphires, and I will make thy bulwarks of jasper : and thy gates of graven stones, and all thy borders of desirable stones. All thy children shall be taught of the Lord : and great shall be the peace of thy children." (Is. liv. 11-13.)

*1st Prelude.*—Represent to yourself Mary and Joseph on the road to Bethlehem, despised by all, and yet bearing the King and Desire of nations.

*2nd Prelude.*—Pray for grace to discern Jesus in His Saints, lest you should unhappily despise Him by slighting them.

*1st Point.*—Consider our coming King as the Desire of nations. How ardently we should desire Him as our Deliverer, as our Saviour, as our Friend, as our Brother! With what anxiety we desire the moment when a friend shall arrive after a long journey. How carefully we prepare for his recep-tion ! how fondly we anticipate the moment of meeting! But we shall never welcome such a friend as Jesus. Let us begin to-day to increase the

earnestness of our preparations. It is time to get
the little crib ready in our hearts, where we pro-
pose to place Him at the moment of His birth.
How shall we honour so royal a guest ? How shall
we be able to console Him for the neglect and indifference of the creatures He comes to save ? What
reparations shall we make to Him for being driven
to the cold stable at Bethlehem, for being sent
by His creatures to live with beasts ? Alas ! the
poor beasts were better than many of His creatures,
for they had never sinned.

*2nd Point.*—Consider how we may best prepare
this little mystical couch for the Infant Jesus. Let
us cover it with the purple of charity. Let us commence to-day by offering every beating of our
hearts, in union with the beatings of the Infant
Heart of Jesus, to the Eternal Father, as an act of
homage and love to our coming King. How
many acts we shall have made before Christmas
night ! Then we might offer the first beating of
our heart, after we receive our Lord, in union with
the intention of the first beating of His Infant
Heart, when He came forth from Mary's womb.
Oh, what a concentration of love that pulsation
manifested! ·We know how our poor human hearts
beat high with desire and affection for those who
are dear to us. Who shall even imagine what
the Heart of Jesus felt and desired, how ardently
it throbbed with love for us, with desire of our
salvation ?

*3rd Point.*—There is nothing Jesus desires from

us so much as love—love to Him and love to the brethren. He knew there would be a great diversity of stones in the spiritual temple of His Church; and He knew also that this diversity, which ought to have produced increased beauty, might, on the contrary, produce disagreement and discord; so He comes as the Corner Stone, that He may both support and unite those mystical stones, that they might be " laid in order," that they might be " desirable stones." He comes to unite the Jew and Gentile, that both may be one in Him. He comes to unite the rich and poor, that the one may give of the abundance of their temporal wealth, and the other of the abundance of their spiritual treasures. Oh, let us seek and pray to be united in Christ Jesus to all! We may well bear with what He bears with. The stone that appears so unsightly or so disagreeable to us, rests upon the Corner Stone, on which we also rest: how, then, can we choose but love it?

*Aspiration.*—Heart of my Infant Jesus, unite me to all Thy beloved ones in Thee.

*Form your resolution, &c. Examen.*

## DECEMBER 23RD.

### THE HEART OF THE INFANT JESUS COMING AS OUR KING AND LAWGIVER.

"O Emmanuel, our King and Lawgiver, the Saviour and Expectation of all people; come and deliver us, O Lord our God." Ant. at Mag.

"Now all this was done that it might be fulfilled which the Lord spoke by the Prophet, saying : Behold a virgin shall be with child, and bring forth a son, and they shall call his name Emmanuel, which being interpreted is, God with us." (Matt. i. 22, 23.)

*1st Prelude.*—As on yesterday.

*2nd Prelude.*—Pray earnestly for this coming God, that He may indeed abide with you.

*1st Point.*—Consider the words, "Now all this was done that it might be fulfilled which the Lord spoke by the Prophet." How many things are done, the purpose of which we, in our ignorance and blindness, fail to discern ! Who would have supposed that a heathen emperor would issue an edict for his own advantage, in order to prepare the way for the fulfilment of a prophecy. Thus it has been since the world began. Man acts with a view to his own ends and interests, and God over-rules to His own eternal glory. Oh, with what submission we should accept all the decrees of Providence ! How careful we should be not to question their wisdom or their love ! We only see

man's end now, hereafter we shall see God's end.
All the varied events and circumstances of our lives
have been ordered and overruled that some purpose,
not indeed spoken by the mouth of the Prophets,
but designed by the God of Prophets, might be
fulfilled.

*2nd Point.*—Consider the great purpose now on
the eve of fulfilment, the birth of Emmanuel. Because we refused to dwell with God when He offered
us His love and His company all day long in the
Garden of Eden, God has come to dwell with us.
And even while He is, as it were, obliged, for our
punishment, to withdraw from us the sensible
manifestations of His presence, which we might
have enjoyed there, He comes to change Himself,
as it were, into our nature, that He may be
able to abide really, though invisibly, with us.
Oh, let us beseech Him to come as our Emmanuel, to abide with us as our God! Alas!
that our desires of His presence should be so
cold, our love so feeble. Jesus is coming as our
Saviour, and we scarcely desire to be saved; or
we desire it rather to escape the company of demons, than to enjoy the company of our God.

*3rd Point.*—Consider the exceeding compassion
which moves the Heart of our Infant Jesus, and
how ardently He longs to commence the work of
our salvation. O sweet Infant Jesus, it is well
for us that Thou didst desire to save us more than
we desired to be saved. It is well for us Thy purposes of assisting us are more steadfast than our

purposes of amendment. It is well for us that Thy love is the noble love of a God, the unchangeable love of the Majesty of heaven, for no other love would bear the coldness and contempt of Thy creatures. Sweet Jesus, Thou mightest well have expected some little preparation for Thy birth, since its time and place had been so plainly predicted by the Prophets. Sweet Jesus, Thou mightest well have hoped to find some few hearts hastening to welcome Thee to this poor dark world with all their love. But not one came to Thee. Thou hadst to call the shepherds by angelic messengers, and the kings by a star, but none came uncalled. Sweet Jesus, how shall we love Thee, what reparation shall we make to Thee !

*Aspiration.*—The Lord is at hand ; O come, let us worship Him.

*Form your resolution, &c. Examen.*

## CHRISTMAS EVE.

### THE HEART OF THE INFANT JESUS COMING TO SAVE US.

"In the evening you shall know that the Lord hath brought you forth out of the land of Egypt: and in the morning you shall see the glory of the Lord." (Ex. xvi. 16.)
"To-morrow the iniquity of the earth shall be done away, and the Saviour of the world shall rule over us." Versicle at Mass and Office.

*1st Prelude.*—Represent to yourself the arrival of Mary and Joseph at the stable, after they have vainly sought room in the inn.

*2nd Prelude.*—Pray that you may never drive your sweet Infant Jesus from your heart.

*1st Point.*—Already the Church has commenced her Christmas office. Now she implores her dear Lord to come in His Divinity, crying out, "Thou that sittest upon the cherubim, appear;" and now she implores the advent of His adorable Humanity, exclaiming, "He is as a bridegroom coming out of His bride-chamber." Yes; Mary is the mystic bride-chamber, and the one true bride; and He comes forth from her to run His course. Alas! that the end of that course should be blood and death! Alas! that the children of the bride-chamber should conspire to slay the Bridegroom, in all the beauty of His love and manhood! O

sweet Jesus, how many and how mystical are the
treasures of Thy Church's words and office : "To-
day ye shall know that the Lord will come, and
to-morrow ye shall see His glory"!   O sweet Jesus,
how happy shall we be if we truly know that Thou
hast come !  If we know it with a saving knowledge
in the day of life, we shall, indeed, see Thy glory
in the day of eternity.

*3rd Point.*—Let us take care lest we murmur at
sweet Jesus, when He brings us out of the land of
Egypt.   The road through the wilderness is not a
pleasant one, and there are many things in the
Egypt we have left which seem attractive.   We
cannot expect, as pilgrims to Canaan, to have every
comfort and convenience on the road.   When
Moses uttered these words to the children of Israel, it was to tell them of the manna, the heavenly
bread, which on the next day was sent to them.
And Jesus comes now, also, to let us see His glory.
To-morrow He will give us the living bread.   To-
morrow He will feed us with His flesh and blood,
of which the manna rained from heaven was but
a feeble type.   He knows how much our spiritual
life will need this sustenance.   Oh, let us never
loathe this holy Bread, as the children of Israel
loathed the manna, and asked for other food than
that which God had given them !

*3rd Point.*—To-morrow sweet Jesus will come.
Oh, how blessedly near is His advent !   To-day we
are decking our houses for His divine visit ; let us
not forget to deck our hearts.   Let us sweep out

every imperfection, every imperfect disposition, every wandering thought, with the besom of penance, and adorn ourselves with the fair bright flowers of contrition and love. To-morrow our Infant King will come. Are we prepared to receive Him? Have we all the love ready for Him we should like to offer Him? If we have not, let us ask our mother Mary to give us a share of hers. Bethlehem would never have seen Jesus, had Mary not brought Him there. Her love was the fullest atonement any creature could make for the world's coldness. Oh ! if we obtain but one little spark of that love, we shall be rich ; and if we ask, Mary will not refuse us.

*Aspiration.*—Sweet Infant Jesus, come—come quickly.

*Form your resolution. Examen.*

---

## CHRISTMAS DAY.

"She brought forth her first-born son, and wrapped Him up in swaddling clothes, and laid Him in a manger." (Luke, ii. 7.)

"While all things were in quiet silence, and the night was in the midst of her course, the almighty word leaped down from heaven." (Wisdom, xviii. 14.)

"Open to me, my sister, my love, my dove, my undefiled : for my head is full of dew, and my locks of the drops of the night." (Cant. v. 2.)

*1st Point.*—To-day we can have only one thought and one subject ; our prelude is our meditation, and our meditation our prelude. "She brought forth her first-born son, and laid Him in a manger." O sweet Mary, bring Him forth to-night also, and lay Him in the little manger of our hearts. They are very lifeless and very cold, but thou wilt try to warm them for Jesus, for thy first-born. We have tried to prepare a lodging for Him, and, poor as it is, we know He will accept it if thou wilt come with Him. We must try to make reparation to thee also, sweet Mother, for the unkindness of thy children, who keep the warm house for themselves, and drive thee to the stable. Alas! sweet Mother, how many there are now who are as cold and as cruel to thee! And as thou didst tell S. Gertrude that we are all thy children, that Jesus is called thy first-born, rather than first-begotten, because thou willest to include us all in thy family, and give us all a share in thy maternal love, we must act towards thee as children, and thou wilt act toward us as a mother.

*2nd Point.*—Consider the time at which Jesus comes. In the night, when all things were in "quiet silence." Yes, Jesus always comes to us in the night of sorrow, and when our hearts are still. But our silence must be a *quiet* silence, if we desire to entertain this gentle Child, for He cannot bear the rough noise of unquiet men, or the busy talkativeness of a heart exteriorly silent, but inwardly full of commotion. Oh, if we will but quiet our hearts and open them wide, He will "leap from His royal throne" into the midst of them, so

great is His haste to come and save us! Nay, He
even asks us to open them for Him; and who could
refuse anything to the little Babe of Bethlehem? He
calls us "His sister and His love," He even tries to
persuade Himself we are His "undefiled;" and He
comes with His head full of dew, full of the rich
dew of the graces of His Divinity, that He may
fertilize our souls; but, alas! He comes also wet
with the drops of the night, with the griefs and
tears of His adorable Humanity. O little Babe
of Bethlehem, come, leap into our hearts to-night.
We will treasure the dew Thou bringest, and we
will try to wipe away the "drops of the night"
from Thy baby brow, and we will shut the doors
of our hearts so close when Thou comest, that
Thou wilt never be able to leave them again.

*3rd Point.*—Let us try to enter into the spirit
and intentions of the Church in celebrating the
adorable Sacrifice three times on this great festival.
She commemorates thereby the threefold salvation
He has come to effect: 1. He saves those who
were before the Law; 2. He saves those who were
under the Law; 3. He saves those under the Gospel.
And further, three spiritual nativities are comme-
morated: 1. the eternal nativity of Christ, born
before all time, from eternity, of His Father; 2.
His nativity in time from the womb of Mary; 3. His
spiritual birth by grace in the souls of His children.
Hence, we might do well to offer the midnight
Mass in thanksgiving to God for the eternal generation of His only begotten Son—offering to the

sweet Infant Jesus all the love and sanctity of
those who lived and served Him faithfully before
the Law, and praying specially for all who are in
mortal sin. The second Mass, at break of day,
in thanksgiving for His love in coming down into
the womb of Mary, in thanksgiving for her perfect purity, offering Him all the love and devotion
of those who served Him faithfully under the Law,
and praying for those whom He is leading from
darkness to light, that their entrance into the
Church may be hastened. Lastly, we may offer the
Mass at midday in thanksgiving for all His love to
us and to all whom He has permitted to live in the
full light of the Gospel, in thanksgiving for His
exceeding love in abiding with us in our very
souls, praying fervently for all the just on earth.

*Aspiration.*—O my sweet Infant Jesus, I love
Thee ; and because I love Thee, I am sorry that I
have offended Thee.

*Make a Christmas offering of your best resolution to
the little Babe of Bethlehem.   Examen.*

.

# DECEMBER 26TH.

## FEAST OF S. STEPHEN.

### THE HEART OF THE INFANT JESUS COME TO OFFER HIMSELF TO THE ETERNAL FATHER TO SUFFER.

"Then said I, Behold I come. In the head of the book it is written of me that I should do Thy will." (Ps. xxxix. 8.)

*1st Prelude.*—Represent to yourself the Infant Jesus at the moment of His birth offering Himself to the Eternal Father to do His will.

*2nd Prelude.*—Pray, through the merits of this sweet Infant, that you may offer yourself up entirely to the divine will.

*1st Point.*—Consider the words, "Behold I come." They are the words of one who comes willingly, of one who comes authoritatively. Jesus comes willingly, because He desires our salvation more than we can possibly imagine ; He comes with authority, because He comes as God. But how does He come ? Let us look at the crib and we shall see. He comes not as a mighty king or a victorious conqueror; He comes not as we would have expected a God to come. His appearance so little betokens His greatness, that it is a stumbling-block

and a scandal to His people, even as His hidden-
ness in the blessed Sacrament still continues to be;
He comes as a little Child, to teach us humility
and to win our love.

*2nd Point.*—For what purpose does He come?
He tells us Himself: "In the head of the book it
is written of Me that I should do Thy will." This
is the one purpose of Jesus in the Incarnation, and
this should be our one and only purpose in life.
In proportion as we have no other purpose, will
be the degree of our sanctity and the measure of
our reward. Oh, how grand, how noble is the soul
which has only this one purpose in life! We see
every day what great things men can effect who
concentrate their energies on one occupation, who
give themselves up entirely to one study. We
see, alas! too often, what men gain for earth who
never allow themselves to be diverted from their
end, who employ every moment of time and every
faculty of mind for this end. We see how ingenious they become in converting the most opposite
and unlikely circumstances to their own advantage. O sweet Infant Jesus, make us as wise and
as ingenious in concentrating all our energies on
one end, in employing all our faculties for one
purpose.

*3rd Point.*—We cannot do the will of another
without sacrifice; and this is precisely the reason
why so many fail in this oneness of purpose necessary for the attainment of great sanctity. Jesus
did not accomplish His Father's will without sacri-

fice. He has already begun to suffer; in a few days He will even shed His Blood sooner than fail in the accomplishment of that will. How can we bear to see an Infant bleeding beneath the knife of circumcision, in obedience to an ordinance which He came to abolish, while we cannot bear to do what causes us a little inconvenience, even to fulfil a momentous duty? The truth is, we are unwilling to sacrifice *ourselves;* and until we are willing to do God's will in self-sacrifice, we cannot be like our Infant Jesus. But it is not necessary that we should *like* self-sacrifice. Humanly speaking, Stephen did not like the stones which sent him to heaven, but he liked God's will better than his own; it was God's will that he should be stoned, and Stephen preferred being stoned, not because he liked it, but because it was God's will. Oh, let us only bear the rough stones of pain and adversity because it is God's will, and we, like Stephen, shall see heaven open, and Jesus waiting there to crown us.

*Aspiration.*—O sweet Infant Jesus, help me to do Thy will.

*Form your resolution, &c. Examen.*

## DECEMBER 27TH.

### FEAST OF S. JOHN THE EVANGELIST.

#### THE HEART OF THE INFANT JESUS TEACHING US HOW TO BE HIS FRIENDS.

"You are my friends, if you do the things which I command you." (S. John, xv. 14.)

*1st Prelude.*—Behold the little Infant Jesus in the manger asking us to be His friends.

*2nd Prelude.*—Tell Him, with your whole heart's love, that you love Him, and that you have no words to tell Him how much.

*1st Point.*—But there is even a higher degree of love and perfection than that of merely submitting to the will of God. No doubt we shall be very perfect if we submit to the will of God; but we shall be very saintly if we love it. S. John loved it more than any human words can tell, when he knew that Jesus willed him to suffer all the pains of martyrdom, and then, when he had suffered all he could suffer, saved him, by a miracle, from temporal death. Oh, what tears S. John wept upon the Heart of Jesus, when he found himself so near heaven, and yet forbidden to enter it! But his tears were the tears of burning love. There was no unwillingness to accept the will of his Beloved, for he and Jesus were friends, such friends as never had been, as never will be. O blessed John, plead for us with thy friend Jesus, that our wills may become one with His, even as thine.

*2nd Point.*—S. John knew what he was sacrificing, when his friend Jesus said he must not go home after that martyrdom which almost opened the gates of heaven for him. He knew the long life that was before him ; he knew that many, many years must pass before he could lie again upon the bosom of Jesus, as he had once lain ; but John wished what Jesus wished, because they were friends ; and if earthly friends can not only act contrary to their inclinations to please each other, but even scarcely know when they sacrifice themselves for each other, how much more must it be possible when Jesus become so united to a soul, that it ceases to have a will, and sacrifice becomes a joy ! The friendship between Jesus and John was perfect ; it was the nearest love to the love between Mary and Jesus. Jesus lay on the bosom of Mary, and John lay on the bosom of Jesus ; and as he had once lain there corporally at the last supper, so to the end of his life he lay there mystically, and hence could not choose but prefer the will of his friend Jesus, whatever that will might be.

*3rd Point.*—Let us pray to the blessed Evangelist to obtain this perfect love for us. The love of submission is very holy, but the love of union is the most sublime perfection. The love of submission kisses the hand of Jesus, and accepts whatever He sends; but the love of union lies in His bosom, it feels the pulsations of His Heart, it knows His will almost by instinct; because its will is so mysteriously its own, that is has ceased to have an individual will or instinct; and even if the hand that caressed it struck it to the very soul, and pierced a thousand swords into its very inmost being, it would still have no will but to accept and to prefer all the will of its Beloved.

*Aspiration.*—O blessed John, lying upon the bosom of Jesus thy friend, pray for us, that we also may be His friends, by doing whatever He commands us.

*Form your resolution, &c.    Examen.*

---

## DECEMBER 28TH.

### FEAST OF THE HOLY INNOCENTS.

"A voice in Rama was heard, lamentation and great mourning; Rachel bewailing her children, and would not be comforted, because they were not." (Matt. ii. 18.)

*1st Prelude.*—Represent to yourself the grief of the mothers on earth, and the joy of the children in heaven.

*2nd Prelude.*—Pray that you may be ever ready to adore the designs of Providence, however mysterious.

*1st Point.*—Consider the anguish of those poor mothers, who can see nothing in the designs of God but a dark, cold, dreadful severity. They would not be comforted; and hence there could be but little, if any, submission in their grief. They are compelled to submit to the will of God, perhaps because they would only submit by compulsion; and yet, even for them, this compulsion is mercy and love. They know now what their children have gained by being sacrificed for Jesus. His Infant blood has been shed for them, and they are the first-fruits of the virgins and martyrs purchased by that blood. Oh, could those mothers only see the end as well as the beginning of their course, would they not almost offer their children themselves to the sword of the destroyer? But there is another Mother already preparing to offer her Child to the cruel knife of suffering, freely, generously, even while her heart is wrung with anguish; and by that offering she will make reparation for the sin and rebellion of many a mother who refuses to give God the treasures for which He asks.

*2nd Point.*—Consider how awful a thing it is to oblige God to compel our submission. We cannot hinder the accomplishment of His divine will, even in the very slightest matter; hence submission is our wisest as well as our holiest course. If we cannot submit because we believe that all which He ordains is ordered for us with the tenderest love, as well as with the most consummate wisdom, at least let us submit beneath the mighty hand of God. But O sweet Infant Jesus, we will rather submit for love—nay, we will not even talk of submission ; for who that loves ever names that word when there is question of the desires of those they love being accomplished by them, however painful ; we will rather unite our wills so entirely to Thine, that we shall cease to have wills of our own ; and hence there will be no need of submission to what we ourselves desire.

*3rd Point.*—God never takes anything away from us without some purpose of exceeding love. All we want for our peace of mind is to believe that "God is love." Alas! that it should be so necessary to try and persuade ourselves of it, even at this blessed season, with the Infant Jesus so near us. Were not those tried and afflicted mothers incomparably more favoured by God than other mothers whose children were left to them, and who, when they grew up, cried out, "Crucify Him! crucify Him!" and, perhaps, helped to slay their Lord in act as well as in will? If the mothers who "would not be comforted" loved God as every creature should love Him, they would not have refused to be comforted, for He would have been their comfort, even while they wept, as Jesus permits us to weep when He sends us anguish and affliction.

*Aspiration.*—Heart of my Infant Jesus, hide me in Thee.

*Form your resolution, &c.    Examen.*

# DECEMBER 29TH.

## THE HEART OF THE INFANT JESUS RECEIVING THE ADORATION OF THE ANGELS.

" And suddenly there was with the angel a multitude of the heavenly army, praising God, and saying : Glory to God in the highest : and on earth peace to men of good will." (Luke, ii. 13, 14.)

*1st Prelude.*—Represent to yourself the night of the Nativity, and behold the angels appearing in the sky, chanting their glorious hymn.

*2nd Prelude.*—Pray for the grace of thankfulness, that you may truly glorify God in every circumstance of your life.

*1st Point.*—Let us consider the words of the angels, " Glory to God in the highest." The first thought, the first desire of those blessed spirits, is the glory of God. Their own interest and their own glory never for a moment occupies their minds. Hence, so that God is glorified, they do not concern themselves further. Their love is the love of union, and they know no will but God's will. His interest is their interest ; His glory is their glory. It matters not to them that the fallen angels are left in chains and darkness, and that Jesus has passed by their nature to redeem and save ours. No thought can occupy these blessed spirits for one moment but the great one of God's glory. They only desire what glorifies Him most, and they know that He is most glorified by the salvation of man, because He has willed it so. When shall we learn to imitate their noble disinterestedness? When shall we attain this perfection? When shall we be content, nay, even give thanks to God, when others are advanced, either temporally or spiritually, and we are passed over?

*2nd Point.*—Peace is the necessary consequence of this love of union, which only desires God's glory ; and it is men of good will alone who truly desire it. Oh, let us pray for a good will, a loving will, a perfect will. Let us ask to have a will like the will of the little Infant Jesus. He came because His Father willed it ; He is man because His Father willed it ; and every action of His adorable Humanity is done purely and simply because His Father wills it. Above all things, we need pure wills and simple wills. A pure will is like a sparkling stream of crystal water flowing from its source to its end ; a simple will is like the line of beauty, beautiful because of its simplicity. How full of fervour are those souls whose wills are pure and simple ! They have no self-interest to disturb their tranquillity, for we are seldom disturbed unless by some self-interest. Even if they suffer, they are full of peace. No amount of interior trial, however harrowing, no amount of dark temptations, no distressing thoughts, perhaps one of the keenest trials of some souls, can for a moment really disturb their peace ; for they will to suffer, because their Beloved wills it, and hence they are not disturbed or disquieted.

*3rd Point.*—We never lose our peace, unless we desire to possess something which we have not got, or to retain something which we are afraid of losing. But the soul which has advanced to the love of union, neither wishes to possess or to retain. She is content to be deprived of all but her love and her God ; and even this she does not ask to possess sensibly. Oh, how full of God, and how dear to Him, is a soul thus advanced in sanctity ! Truly she is full of peace, because she is absolutely united to the God of peace. If we desire this perfection, let us ask it of the Heart of the Infant Jesus ; let us offer His dispositions to the Eternal Father, that ours may be renewed and perfected ; let us constantly offer ourselves to God, in union with the oblation of the Infant Jesus.

*Aspiration.*—Heart of the Infant Jesus, unite me wholly to Thyself.

*Form your resolution, &c. Examen.*

## DECEMBER 30TH.

### THE HEART OF THE INFANT JESUS RECEIVING THE VISIT OF THE SHEPHERDS.

" And they came with haste : and they found Mary and Joseph, and the Infant lying in a manger." (Luke, ii. 16.)

*1st Prelude.*—Represent to yourself these good and holy shepherds listening to the music of the angels, and then hastening to Bethlehem to adore their Infant King.

*2nd Prelude.*—Pray that you may be so holy and so simple, as to merit that God may confer such spiritual favours on you as may be necessary for your salvation.

*1st Point.*—How good and holy these dear shepherds must have been, whom our Lord selected, in preference to all others, for this vision of angels and this marvellous announcement! We may well believe it was not without a special design of Providence. Perhaps it was because the poor and the unlearned are always more ready to believe than the rich, who are hardened by their riches, or the learned, who are blinded by their pride. Perhaps it was because Jesus came to preach the " Gospel to the poor," as the fittest subjects for the eternal kingdom. Who can imagine their simple joy, their lively faith, their ardent devotion ! Those who have been privileged to be much with the poor of a truly Catholic country, can best imagine and realize what these shepherds did and said that Christmas night. They caught the accents of the angels, " Glory to God !" and they handed down that sublime song of praise to those who came after them, that they might utter it, even to the end of time, in circumstances of the deepest suffering.

*2nd Point.*—Consider the haste of the shepherds. They did not pause to consider whether their flocks would be safe if they left them. Ah, no ! the Lamb of God was dearer to them than the little lambs and sheep, which were their worldly all. They did not stay to consult whether the vision of angels was an imagination or a reality. They simply believed, and believing they loved, and loving they hastened ; and they had their reward ; for they found Mary and Joseph, and the Infant, and it was all they desired. They had their reward ; for they were privileged to be the first to behold and adore their new-born King. Oh, with what love the sweet Infant Jesus greeted them ! how He stretched out His little hands to welcome them and bless them, while Mary told them all that Jesus wished her to say!

*3rd Point.*—Perhaps the shepherds represented Christ's priests as well as His poor, and that He called them first as the pastors of His flock were called to minister to His people. How we should honour and love those shepherds ! how we should respect their absolute self-renunciation ! They also leave their flocks, that is, all their earthly wealth and convenience, to minister to the Lamb of God in the persons of His sheep. They most truly honour the Incarnation of the Son of God by their continual oblation of His Body and Blood; and, like the shepherds, they spend their lives in making known His wonders and His love. O sweet Infant Jesus, we would come also with the shepherds to Thy crib. We would come with the poor and simple, and believe with them and like them. May we also find Mary and Joseph, and the Infant, and may they place Thee in our hearts to abide therein for ever.

*Aspiration.*—O my sweet Infant Jesus, I love Thee; and because I love Thee, I am sorry that I have offended Thee.

*Form your resolution, &c.    Examen.*

---

## DECEMBER 31ST.

### THE HEART OF THE INFANT JESUS ENLIGHTENING HIS BLESSED MOTHER IN ALL THE MYSTERIES OF HIS LIFE AND HIS LOVE.

"But Mary kept all these words, pondering them in her heart." (Luke, ii. 19.)

*1st Prelude.*—Represent to yourself the tender and reverential love with which Mary watches every movement of her Infant Son, and considers every circumstance connected with His life.

*2nd Prelude.*—Pray for grace to ponder on the things of God, like Mary.

*1st Point.*—" Mary kept all these words, pondering them in her heart." In order to ponder on the words of God, we must " keep them." Now keeping implies guarding closely in a secure place. We must, then, treasure up the words of Jesus in our hearts, we must have a large space there to lay them up in, and in order to find room for them, we must expel all other words—all idle words, all curious words, above all, every sinful word. Let us commence the new year by imitating our blessed Mother in this. If we keep the words of God like Mary, we shall also ponder them in our measure like Mary. How reverently and carefully we should ponder all the circumstances of the life of our divine Lord ; how we should linger over every word He uttered! Those who devote themselves to thus keeping and pondering on those things, will learn a thousand secrets of love which will never be manifested to the thoughtless, and those who are less occupied with God.

*2nd Point.*—Let us consider Mary as the first model and example of the practice of holy meditation. The first meditation on the life of Jesus was made by Mary in the stable of Bethlehem, beside the crib ; and hence it is, that those who are most devout to her attain a special grace of knowing and understanding the mysteries of the life of Jesus. How simple and how sublime was that meditation! The creature adored and meditated upon the

Creator, and the Creator poured forth light and
love into the heart of the creature. This is the
essence of all true meditation. If we were more
simple we should find less difficulty in practising
it. Meditation on our side is thinking about
Jesus as we would think over the words and acts
of a friend we love very much ; and mental prayer,
which should always accompany meditation, is
asking the friend we love for what we want.
Even in the sublime prayer of the love of union,
the soul asks love instinctively, though the voice
of the soul has ceased to make itself heard. Meditation on the part of God is a pouring forth on us
of light to know, and of love to do His will, and
this is given in proportion to our earnestness. Souls
who live very near God, and think of Him constantly, are ever receiving this light and love, which
guides them and purifies their intention in a marvellous manner, even in the most trifling actions.

*3rd Point.*—O Mary, pondering at the crib of
Jesus, teach me how to ponder upon His love and
His mercies; teach me how to ponder on all the favours and graces He has granted me during the past
year, until the flame of thanksgiving breaks forth
in my heart, and manifests itself in songs of love
and adoration. Teach me how to ponder on all
my sins and ingratitude, on my wicked misuse of
His mercies, on my sinful neglect of His inspirations, on my evil failure in corresponding with the
countless lights He has given me, on my frequent
refusal to listen to the murmurs of His love, on my

neglect in observing the sweet practices of devotion He has taught me. Teach me to pour forth my whole soul in tears of grief and love upon my Infant God lying in thy arms, and ask Him to forgive me, for He can refuse thee nothing. Obtain for me the grace to give up my whole being to His service, and to make a solemn consecration of myself to Him for the new year in the stable of Bethlehem. Oh, may the angels who witness my oblation, obtain for me grace to keep my promise !

*Aspiration.*—Heart of my Infant Jesus, have mercy. Mother of Jesus, be my mother.

*Form your resolution, &c. Examen.*

## JANUARY 1st.

### FEAST OF THE CIRCUMCISION.

"After eight days were accomplished that the child should be circumcised, His name was called JESUS." (Luke, ii. 21.)

*1st Prelude.*—Represent to yourself the devotion of Mary at this ceremony, and the tenderness with which she tries to console her suffering Child.

*2nd Prelude.*—Pray that you may be ever ready to sympathise in the sufferings of Jesus by meditation, by your own sufferings, and by compassionating the sufferings of others.

*1st Point.*—Let us begin the year with our little Jesus, even though He should ask us to suffer with

Him.  Let us begin it by offering Him a new year's
gift of all our love.   Let us salute Him the moment
we awake in the morning, and wish Him, for His
new year's joy, the conversion of countless souls, and
the increased sanctification of all His elect.   To-day
our dear Lord receives the sweet name of JESUS.
Let us salute Him by His new name continually.
He has already revealed to S. Gertrude that however great the unworthiness of those who utter
aspirations of love, He is pleased with them, since
,a vase of sweet perfumes gives forth its odours, no
matter how vile the stick which may be used to
stir it up.   Oh, let us stir up the perfumes of love
in the Heart of our little Jesus all day long with
the tenderest ejaculations !

   *2nd Point.*—If we would be the children of our
sweet Infant King, we must be content to be like
Him.   He was made in all things "like unto His
brethren." (Heb. ii. 17.)   Are we content to be
made like our Brother Jesus ?   Do we wish to be
made like our Brother Jesus ?   Do we desire more
than we desire anything else in the world, to be
made like our Brother Jesus ?   O sweet Jesus,
we do desire it !   But we have seen the knife with
which our Brother was wounded, and we shrink
back in fear.   Oh, help us, sweet Jesus ; we desire
to be like Thee, but we shrink from suffering,
although we know that unless we suffer we cannot
be like Thee !   Thy life commences with suffering,
with, we might almost say, unnecessary suffering ;
for the circumcision was not necessary for our

salvation, since one drop of Thy blood could save us, but one of the many mysteries which we cannot "know" here, but which we shall "know hereafter" (S. John, xiii. 7), is the mystery of what seems to us unnecessary suffering. The life of Jesus is full of this mystery—thrice blessed are they whose lives are made like His in this also ; for though even the most saintly must say, and say truly, "and we indeed justly, for we receive the just reward of our deeds, but this man hath done no evil" (Luke, xxiii. 41), yet there are souls who seem to suffer more than others, perhaps as the highest reward of a more than ordinary sanctity.

*3rd Point.*—But there is a special kind of suffering, of which Mary is the great exemplar. Jesus is the cause of her sufferings as well as the cause of her joy. Thrice blessed are they who are privileged to follow her in this mystic path of sanctity ! This grace is given, in its highest degree, to those favoured souls who suffer purely for Jesus, who are privileged to share in the mysteries of His passion, and, in a lower degree of sanctity, in the sufferings of His daily life. It is also granted, in a certain measure, to those who suffer for or on account of others. In whatever degree this privilege is granted to us, let us unite ourselves to Mary. We may never be permitted to share, however little, in the pains of Calvary, but we may in our measure share in the suffering life of Jesus. Let us commence the new year with a

H

generous offering of ourselves to bear all His love may ask.

*Aspiration.*—Heart of my Infant Jesus, be my home for the coming year.

*Form your resolution, and make a generous offering to do and to suffer the will of God during the new year, in union with the suffering and obedience of the Infant Jesus. Examen.*

## JANUARY 2ND.

### THE SUFFERING HEART OF THE INFANT JESUS.

"I bear the marks of the Lord Jesus in my body." (Gal. vi. 17.)

*1st Prelude.*—Consider the great Apostle of the Gentiles as the model of the faithful followers of Jesus.

*2nd Prelude.*—Pray that you may be at least willing, if not desirous, to bear the marks of the Lord Jesus in your body.

*1st Point.*—Our divine Lord commences the year and His human life with bodily suffering; shall we not also commence our new year with bearing in our bodies, in some degree, " the marks of the Lord Jesus," and, like S. Paul, glory in our privilege ?  Suffering, under the old dispensation, was usually a sign of God's anger, and inflicted as such. The Jew was promised temporal favours, long life, abundance of this world's goods, a numerous offspring, and victory over his enemies, as a reward for his virtues; but in the Christian dispensation the case is reversed. The promise now is—future reward for present suffering. If we suffer with Him, we shall also reign with Him. But the difference between the rewards of the two dispensations, is founded on the difference in the relationship between God and the human race in each dispensation. In the older covenant, as a general rule, the people of God were treated as servants; hence, they received circumcision as a token of servitude, as well as of admission into the family of God. They were rewarded as servants, with temporal favours and prosperity. But the children of the new covenant are admitted into their relationship with the Father by a painless rite, that they may commence a life of voluntary suffering, and receive eternal recompense.

*2nd Point.*—Our divine Lord submitted to the rite of circumcision to teach us to love the fulfilment of the least intimation of His will, even though it may not be an actual obligation, and even should it cost us suffering; hence, this mystery in the life of our blessed Lord should be one of the greatest consolation and instruction to religious, since they are all called to special spiritual circumcision, both for their own sanctification and the good of others—in some orders by prayers, fasts, and other penitential practices, and in others

by active labours; in all, they commence and
continue their holy state in union with Jesus
suffering from His birth to His death.

*3rd Point.*—Our divine Lord obtains His name
Jesus, and His office of Saviour, at the moment
when He first experiences keen, exterior suffering,
inflicted by others. And if we desire to imitate
our sweet Jesus, we must also be content to suffer
in proportion as we desire to promote His glory,
His kingdom, and His salvation in the hearts of
others. Above all things, we must be content to
bear sufferings from others. We must suffer either
in body by penitential austerities, if our life be
purely contemplative; or if we are engaged in
active duties, we shall receive countless bodily
mortifications in the pursuit of our works of mercy.
Shall we not seek to sanctify them all, by uniting them to the sufferings of our dear Lord in the
stable of Bethlehem?

*Aspiration.*—Suffering Heart of my Infant Saviour,
sanctify all my sufferings by union with Thine.

*Form your resolution, &c. Examen.*

## JANUARY 3RD.

### THE SILENCE OF THE HEART OF JESUS.

"They found Mary and Joseph, and the Infant lying in a manger." (Luke, ii. 16.)

*1st Prelude.*—Represent to yourself the Infant Jesus lying silent in the manger.

*2nd Prelude.*—Pray for grace to understand and practise this blessed silence.

*1st Point.*—Consider the silence of Jesus. How sublime, how noble, how beautiful is the silence of Jesus! He who has created speech, is speechless; He who has devised language, uses no words; He who knows all things, appears as if He knew nothing; and we, who are ignorance itself, not only talk but teach, and are seldom silent, even when silence would be our truest wisdom. A broad, deep river rolls on in majestic stillness to the ocean, while the shallow rivulet may be heard dashing over the stones, even at a distance. Let us learn to practise silence that we may be wise, if we will not practise it that we may be holy. Let us look at Jesus, an Infant in the manger, and study each virtue which He practises, as far as it may be given to our weakness to do so, until we learn

to love what we have studied, and to imitate what
we love.

*2nd Point.*—Consider the threefold silence which
our sweet Jesus practised in His Incarnation : 1st,
the silence of preparation ; 2nd, the silence of
action ; 3rd, the silence of suffering.   How solemn
and mysterious was His long silence of preparation!
For thirty years we do not hear that Jesus either
preached or taught.   Men passed Him by as one
unnoticeable.   No one thought of asking His opinion
on any subject.   How many conversations He must
have heard, in which the grossest errors were advanced, the most absurd statements asserted, the
truth denied or misunderstood !   But Jesus was
silent.   His silence was a preparation for speech.
He would teach us that there is a time when silence
is wisdom, even though the truth should be assailed
and denied in our presence.   He would teach us .
that if we would desire to speak for His glory and
the good of others, we must prepare for speaking
by a long novitiate of silence.

*3rd Point.*—But there is a further lesson which
our sweet Jesus teaches us in this mystery.   He
would teach us the silence of preferring, when
speech is necessary, that others should speak instead of ourselves.   It was necessary that S. Joseph
should be told of the danger which threatened the
"Child and His mother," when Herod sought to
slay the Infant Jesus ; and we might naturally have
supposed that Jesus would tell Joseph or His blessed
Mother of this danger, and how they would best

avoid it. But no ; Jesus is silent. Had we been placed in similar circumstances, we should have had a thousand fears, which would have suggested a thousand excuses why we ought to speak. Would Joseph believe the angel, when the Lord of angels remained silent? And if Joseph doubted the angel —though Jesus, as God, could save Himself from future suffering, by miraculously escaping present danger—yet, might not the great designs of God, in the flight into Egypt, be frustrated? Thus we might have reasoned, and thus we do reason—alas ! too often—when we think so much depends upon our speech, and our pride helps us to break the silence which true humility would find the safest as well as the holiest course. Oh, let us pray very fervently to our sweet Jesus, to teach us the silence of preparation, that we may be able to speak well and wisely when duty requires it—that we may know how to distinguish between the pride which urges us to speak to display our knowledge, and the pride which would keep us silent when it might be a duty to speak!

*Aspiration.*—Heart of my Infant Jesus, silent in the manger, teach me when to speak and when to be silent.

*Form your resolution, &c. Examen.*

## JANUARY 4TH.

### SECOND MEDITATION ON THE SILENCE OF JESUS.

*Preludes, &c., as on yesterday.*

*1st Point.*—Consider the second silence that Jesus practises in the Nativity—the silence of action. The more we meditate on this mystery of love, the more we must see its marvellous silence of action. The greatest event which has occurred in the world's history, is manifested in one simple act which has few details. Jesus is born in Bethlehem. He lies in the manger, silent as regards speech, silent as regards action. Had the Infant God acted as men would act, how different would have been all the circumstances of His birth! How loudly His glory would have been proclaimed to the whole world! How manifestly His power would have been displayed by signs and prodigies! But we do not hear that Jesus worked a single miracle in His infancy or in His childhood. We have only the tradition of the destruction of the Egyptian idols. Thus is He silent in act; and by this silence He prepares for the sublimest actions the world has seen, or can ever see. How different from the heathen, alas! how different even from the Christian idea of greatness!

*2nd Point.*—But Jesus practises another silence, if possible more sublime and more meritorious than the silence of speech or of action, and this is the silence of suffering. With all the full powers of an intelligent human being, with all the faculties and senses of a man, He still maintains absolute silence as to all He suffers. We may sometimes practise silence of speech under trying circumstances, we may practise silence of action under great provocation to act when action would be wrong; but we seldom attain to the sublime perfection of the silence of suffering. It is as natural to us to express and to complain of the pain we endure, as it is to utter an exclamation when we are suddenly hurt. Do we ever meditate on the silence of Jesus in regard to all He suffered at Bethlehem, remembering that He was not like other infants, who cannot exercise the power of speech, and feel no inconvenience or mortification in not exercising it?

*3rd Point.*—Consider how we may imitate our sweet Infant Jesus in the blessed lessons He teaches us. Let us learn to imitate His silence of action, by restraining our impetuosity, eager to do so much, without considering whether we may not be wasting time by doing too much, as some waste it by doing too little. Let us be very sure that our actions, when we ought to act, are the actions God demands from us, and not the actions of our own choice. Alas! how many spend their lives in busy restlessness, and dignify their impetuosity with the name of zeal! But we will try to learn from our dear Lord, as one of our lessons at the crib, how to act and when to act, so that we may neither out-run nor lag behind the designs of Providence in our regard. Let us also pray in our measure for the grace of the silence of suffering. Let us try to bear suffering as Jesus bore it in the manger, mani-festing it as little as possible by our exterior, either in word or manner. Oh, how blessed and holy are those souls, who, like the Infant Jesus, soothe and comfort all who come to them by their gentle sym-pathy, while they bear in silence the deepest mental and the severest bodily suffering! If we may not attain such heights of sanctity, at least let us try to ascend a few steps towards its attainment.

*Aspiration.*—Heart of my Infant Jesus, suffering in the manger, teach me to suffer.

*Form your resolution, &c.    Examen.*

---

### JANUARY 5TH.

#### THE SHEPHERDS FIND JESUS.

"They found Mary and Joseph, and the Infant." (Luke, ii. 16.)

*1st Prelude.*—Represent to yourself the anxiety with which the good shepherds seek Jesus until they find Him.

*2nd Prelude.*—Pray that you may ever seek thus anxiously for Jesus, until you also find Him in every place and in all circumstances.

*1st Point.*—Let us meditate on the shepherds finding Jesus. This should be the one great object of our lives—to find Jesus. But if we desire to find Him like the shepherds, we must be willing to sacrifice ourselves like the shepherds. The moment they hear where Jesus is to be found, they forsake their flocks and herds, and hasten to Him. They seek Him at a sacrifice of their worldly goods and their worldly comfort. They are equally content to risk the safety of their flocks and the comfort of their night's rest. And they have their reward ; for they find Mary and Joseph, and the Infant. Probably this was not the first sacrifice these good men had made for God, for great favours are seldom vouchsafed to any who have not in some degree merited them by great sacrifices.

*2nd Point.*—They find Jesus. We may also find our dear Lord as really as the shepherds found Him, and with less personal inconvenience. On every altar in God's Church we may find Jesus, and every sanctuary may be to us a Bethlehem, where Jesus is born again in holy Mass for His people. Do we meditate sufficiently on the close connexion between the mystery of the altar and the mystery of the Incarnation ? It is true the first great purpose of Mass is the renewal of the sacrifice of Calvary; but it also renews the birth of the Lamb of God, for His priests cause Him once more to be born, as it were, anew, when the bread and wine is changed into His body and blood. Then, when we approach to receive Him, and hear the words, *Ecce Agnus*

*Dei*, we may embrace the little Babe of Bethlehem even more closely than if we took Him in our arms, for we receive Him into our hearts.

*3rd Point.*—Our divine Lord also hides His glory in the Sacrament of the altar, as He hid His glory at Bethlehem. It seemed there as if He came into the world by a mere ordinary generation; it appears here as if the priest alone officiated. There His glory was hidden under the garb of our Humanity, and men saw only an Infant, and refused to believe in the Divinity which was not openly manifested; here His glory is hidden also under corporeal appearances, and men, who see only the accidents, refuse to believe in the hidden Deity. Let us, then, offer our tenderest homage, at this holy season, to our hidden God; let us try to console Him for the unbelief which refused alike to adore Him as God at Bethlehem and on the altar; let us endeavour to be of the happy number of the faithful few who seek Him constantly and at all sacrifice; and then we shall find Him eternally with Mary and Joseph, with the angels and the shepherds, with the Father and the Holy Ghost, where His glory will no longer be hidden, and where those who have not seen, and yet have believed, will receive eternal rewards of unimagined glory.

*Aspiration.*—Heart of my Infant Jesus, I adore Thee hidden in Bethlehem, and in the Sacrament of the altar.

*Form your resolution, &c.  Examen.*

# THE EPIPHANY.

## THE ADORATION OF THE MAGI.

"Behold, there came wise men from the East to Jerusalem, saying: Where is He that is born King of the Jews? For we have seen His star in the East." (Matt. ii. 2.)

*1st Prelude.*—Represent to yourself the holy anxiety with which these wise men enquire for the new-born King.

*2nd Prelude.*—Pray that you may be always ready to come to Jesus whenever and however He calls you.

*1st Point.*—Consider the faith of these wise men. They do not come to ascertain if there is such a person born as one calling Himself the King of the Jews; they do not come to make scrupulous and captious investigations about the revelation they had received : no, their faith is sublime in its simplicity; they believe, and they worship. They believe the revelation, therefore they act on the revelation. How happy should we be if our faith were equally practical! But, alas! we believe coldly, and hence we act coldly. We give a careless assent to the most important truths, and hence they have but little influence on our daily conduct. Oh, let us pray with our whole hearts for a lively faith. Let us employ ourselves constantly in making acts of faith. Repeated acts will strengthen a habit, whether for good or evil, more than all the reflections we can make; and these reflections are only of value in helping us to produce such acts. Let us, then, reflect on the faith, that we may be led to act on the faith, and by acting on it to become confirmed in it.

*2nd Point.*—To-day we shall consider especially the great value and importance of the gift of faith. No considerations of ours can possibly impress us with its importance ; no words can explain its value. Faith alone can teach us to estimate faith, since all that is of faith can only be appreciated by a supernaturally enlightened mind. Let us, for a moment, suppose that God had not called the Gentiles to the light of faith, and that He had come only or especially for the salvation of the Jews, His own chosen people; let us suppose, even though the treasures of faith have been opened to all, that we had been born heathens ; let us suppose that we had been born even of Christian parents, and yet not in the true Church : might we not have been placed in any of these circumstances, if God had ordered our position in life other than it has been ? and have we ever been sufficiently thankful to God for all He has done for us ?

*3rd Point.*—Our lives should prove our thankfulness. The Magi showed their thankfulness for God's call by their fervour in obeying it. Do we live as if we had the gift of faith ? Are our lives the lives of those who believe in God ? Alas ! are we not every day acting in direct opposition to our faith ; living as if we believed this life to be our only concern, while we say daily, " I believe in the life everlasting ;" living as if temporal things were our great object, when we believe that in a few short years they will have passed away, and a long eternity will open on us, when the things of time will be as unimportant, except as regards their relation to the things of eternity, as a second to a century ? Do we not believe that to receive the body and blood of Jesus is the greatest grace, the most stupendous favour which can be conferred on any mortal ; and, alas ! do we not act, again and again, as if the merest trifles were far more important ? Do we not fret and distract ourselves about the trifles of every day, although we know that we shall only remember the greatest afflictions hereafter as the light shadows of a summer day ? Oh, for more faith—more real, earnest faith ; or, rather, oh, for more love of Jesus, and less love of self ; and then we should soon live lives of greater faith ; for if we believe we shall love, and if we love we shall act on our belief.

*Aspiration.*—Heart of my Infant King, help me to love Thee, and to live for Thee.

*Form your resolution, &c. Examen.*

## JANUARY 7TH.

### ON DIVINE INSPIRATIONS.

"And seeing the star, they rejoiced with exceeding great joy." (Matt. ii. 10.)

*1st Prelude.*—Represent to yourself the joy with which the Magi beheld the star standing over the stable of Bethlehem.

*2nd Prelude.*—Pray for grace to imitate the fidelity and constancy of these holy men.

*1st Point.*—The star which guided the Magi may be considered as emblematic both of the light of faith and of the special attraction of grace which God gives to every Christian soul. The Magi were particularly devoted to the observance of the heavenly bodies, and this natural attraction to a science is made a means of grace to their souls. Thus our divine Lord usually suits His special graces to the natural disposition of the soul. This special attraction is usually given in the ordinary path of duty, and we are seldom required to leave or alter our position in life in order to follow it. A few souls are guided by it, even as the star guided the Magi to the distant land of religion, where, in a special manner, a manner not vouchsafed to all, they find "the Child, with Mary His mother;" but most persons can and ought to carry out this attraction of grace in their respective positions in life. This attraction is usually such as is most likely to help us, if we follow it faithfully, to correct that evil passion or inclination, which, like the glare of a deceitful meteor, would lead us astray. If we have not yet ascertained the special attraction of grace which God has given us, and the sin or evil to which we are most prone, we should endeavour at once to know it. If we have this blessed knowledge, let us be more earnest in profiting by it.

*2nd Point.*—This attraction, like the star, moves as God guides it. If we neglect it, or turn away our eyes from it, the light becomes dim, and is altogether obscured; above all, we lose it if we are not earnest in endeavouring to correspond with the grace which it brings. We must look on this attraction as a special call from God to bring us nearer to Jesus, as a light to help us to find Him better than we should do otherwise; and if we neglect this means, prepared for us in mercy, we may not find any other way which will bring us so near to God. For example, should God have given us a special attraction to prayer, we may not find Him if we do not occupy ourselves in prayer as much as He designs we should do. If He attracts us to active charity towards the poor, our faith will grow cold, and our love to Him will sensibly decrease, if we do not warm it by special acts of benevolence.

*3rd Point.*—This light is sometimes hidden from

I

us to try our faith, as well as to punish our infi-
delities. Who can tell how great a trial of faith
the Magi endured, when they came to Jerusalem,
and found that Jesus was not there, and that no
one knew anything about Him? How amazed
they must have been that their enquiries " troubled
Herod, and all Jerusalem with him," instead of
being a cause of joy! How perplexed they must
have been that the people of this new-born King
knew nothing of Him, and even His priests could
only tell them where He would be born, but never
concerned themselves to ascertain had His birth
taken place! The light of the star, too, is hidden
from them, and heaven and earth seemed combined
to try their faith. Many would have returned to
their own country, and enquired no further. Oh,
let us pray for a faith like theirs, that we may
obtain a reward like theirs also; and, after the
long night of intense earthly trial, we shall indeed
be led where we shall find the "young Child and
His mother," where we shall never be separated
from the company of Jesus and Mary.

*Aspiration.*—Heart of my Infant King, guide me
to Thee by Thy love and Thy providences.

*Form your resolution, &c.    Examen.*

## JANUARY 8TH.

### HOW THE MAGI FIND JESUS AND MARY.

"And entering into the house, they found the Child with Mary His mother." (Matt. ii. 11.)

*1st Prelude.*—Represent to yourself the arrival of the wise men at the crib of Bethlehem, and behold them adoring Jesus.

*2nd Prelude.*—Join in their adoration, and adore the Creator of Mary in the arms of Mary.

*1st Point.*—Behold Jesus in the arms of Mary. Here He receives the first homage of the Gentile race. And it is fitting it should be so. We receive Jesus from Mary; therefore, we should adore Jesus in the arms of Mary. One day Jesus will present Mary to the world as His mother and His queen, and compel all men to render her the homage which too many now dare to refuse. Then, indeed, the faithful, who have honoured her aright, will rejoice greatly, for she will repay their homage with the love of a mother and the protection of a queen. Blessed are they to whom God gives, as their special attraction of grace, an unbounded trust in Mary; they will not need to travel far to find Jesus, for where the mother is, there also is the Child; and when they "enter into the house," the type of God's Church, they shall have all they

desire : Mary, who will lead them to Jesus, and
Jesus, who will teach them how to love and honour
Mary.

*2nd Point.*—Consider Jesus lying in the arms of
Mary as the model of devotion to her. Happy
those souls who lie with childlike confidence in her
arms, and trust all to her keeping. How safe, how
secure they shall be in time and in eternity! The
Infant Jesus trusts all to her. He hears the noise
of the advancing troop of the wise men, but He lies
unmoved in Mary's arms, and confides Himself to
her protection. He knows their state and high
condition, but He leaves all the duties of receiving
them suitably to her. He knows their doubts, per-
plexities, and trials, but He will employ Mary to
comfort and instruct them. Such confidence has
Jesus in His Mother. And how could it be otherwise? Mary is ever listening for the lowest whisper
of the will of the sacred Heart of Jesus ; she reads
its desires intuitively; there is no need of spoken
words where union is so perfect, so unbroken.
Hence, Jesus can trust Mary to the utmost, for He
knows His will is hers.

*3rd Point.*—Let us lie, like Jesus, in the arms of
Mary. How happy we shall be if she will only permit us to do so! She will whisper to us every desire of her Beloved, and obtain grace for us to
fulfil it. She will protect us in every danger, and
obtain for us the peace of trusting hearts. Let us also
learn to look on our superiors as the representatives
of Mary, and to obey and trust them as Jesus

obeyed and trusted Mary. Let us offer our obedience to them, to our Infant King, in union with His obedience to Mary. Let us learn from Him not to disquiet ourselves about what does not concern us, but to lie still in the calm strength of obedience. Alas! what hindrances we prove to those whom we should obey, by our restlessness and our needless anxieties! What cares we add to cares already too many! And if we did but imitate our sweet Jesus in the arms of Mary, lying still, except when obedience moved us, and praying for our superiors, as Jesus prayed for Mary to His eternal Father, how rapidly we should advance in holiness, and how we should strengthen and assist those whom God has appointed to guide us, who are to us what Mary was to Jesus, the earthly representatives of God's authority and love!

*Aspiration.*—Heart of my Jesus, lying in the arms of Mary, teach me how to resign myself without reserve to those whom Thou hast appointed to guide me.

*Form your resolution, &c. Examen.*

## JANUARY 9TH.

ON TRUE WORSHIP.

" And falling down, they adored Him." (Matt. ii. 11.)

*1st Prelude.*—Represent to yourself the love and zeal with which these holy men prostrated themselves before the Infant Jesus.

*2nd Prelude.*—Endeavour to imitate their example by fervent adoration of the Word made flesh.

*1st Point.*—Consider the example of the wise men : "And falling down, they adored Him." How sublime is their faith ! They see only a poor mother and a poor Child, yet they never hesitate for a moment, nor make outward circumstances an excuse for unbelief. How the Heart of the Infant Jesus must have been consoled by this adoration ! What favours and graces He prepared to reward these good kings ! How Mary thanked them in her heart, and how she rejoiced that even a few of God's creatures came to pay Him homage ! Already our dear Lord foresees the mockery of His long night of trial, when the knees of His creatures will be bent to Him, not to honour Him, but to revile Him. Already He beholds the crowds through which He will pass, where none will offer Him the least mark of respect. Already He beholds the faithful before His tabernacle, cold and careless, as if God were not present there ; and the faithless mocking and blaspheming in His very presence. But with all this knowledge, He lies still in Mary's arms, and never even breathes one desire to return to His Father's courts, where millions upon millions of angels adore Him, and love as they adore. What a lesson to us of perseverance in well doing, through all discouragements !

*2nd Point.*—Let us try to imitate the example of our sweet Jesus. We measure our success too much by what appears exteriorly, and too little by the judgment of God. Hence, we are easily discouraged, if our plans are thwarted or fail; whereas we should continue our work, whatever it may be, waiting for God's time of prosperity, should He will it to prosper, or more than content with failure, if He wills it to fail. How little we know the real meaning of the words failure and success! Did not the Incarnation look like a failure at Bethlehem and Calvary ? Does it not often look like a failure now, when we see so little fruit from it ? And yet it is the masterpiece of eternal wisdom, of wisdom which can neither fail in design or in execution.

*3rd Point.*—Let us try to console our sweet Jesus by offering Him the adoration of the wise men, and by our own adorations. Whenever we hear the words, so often repeated by the Church at this holy season, let us prostrate in spirit if not bodily, and adore our Infant King. How much we lose by performing such acts of adoration mechanically and without a special intention! We kneel before the blessed Sacrament many times in the day, without a thought, without a definite purpose. If each time we knelt we had the intention in our minds of offering the action to console the Infant Jesus for the neglect of His creatures, how it would gladden His divine Heart! If we offered it to atone for the neglect of devotion to the blessed Sacrament, what reparations we might make! Even if we failed to remember our purpose each time through human frailty, it would at least be very consoling to our dear Lord to see we have the intention. Christmas is a season of the richest graces ; do not let it pass without obtaining all our new-born King is willing to give.

*Aspirations.*—Sweet Jesus, I adore and I love Thee for all who adore Thee not and love Thee not.

*Form your resolution, &c. Examen.*

## JANUARY 10TH.

### ON GIVING OUR TREASURES TO GOD.

" And opening their treasures, they offered Him gifts."
(Matt. ii. 10.)

*1st Prelude.*—Behold the wise men prostrate
before Jesus, opening their treasures to give Him
all they possess.

*2nd Prelude.*—Pray that you also may have grace
to open your treasures, and give Jesus all you have.

*1st Point.*—The first great act of Christian worship is adoration, the second is sacrifice. Adoration without sacrifice is but the worship of the
lips ; but if our adoration be from the heart, words
will not satisfy us, for mere words can never satisfy
love. The wise men adore Jesus, and hence they
are willing to offer sacrifice to Jesus. Alas ! do
we adore Jesus, or ourselves, or the world ? We can
make sacrifices for ourselves, we willingly renounce
one good to attain a greater, we make sacrifices for
the world—oh, what great sacrifices !—and we
scarcely think of them as sacrifices, so bent are we
on worshipping the things of time and sense ; but
when there is question of adoring Jesus, and making
sacrifices for Him, how many wise calculations we
make to how much we can save and how much
we *must* give ! Oh, let us begin to-day to adore

our God as we ought to adore Him; let us examine ourselves as to our worship, and see whether the world or self is the idol of our hearts, to the exclusion of its rightful King.

*2nd Point.*—" And opening their treasures, they offered Him gifts." This is the real difficulty ; we do not like to offer our *treasures.* We are content to give what we do not value much, or what will not cost us much ; but when there is a word about our treasures, far from opening them, we try to hide them away. And it is just these treasures of ours that our Infant King wants. It is not because He wishes to deprive us of anything that would be of use to us ; oh, no ; He would far rather deprive Himself of everything, than leave us without a trifling convenience. He has proved His willingness to sacrifice Himself for us far too plainly to doubt it even for a moment ; but He wants our treasures, either because it will do us some great harm if we keep them, or because He intends to give us other treasures in exchange, which will as far surpass them as the pure diamond surpasses the shell from which it is extracted.

*3rd Point.*—Sweet Jesus, we are going to fall before Thee now, and open our treasures, and offer them to Thee. There are some who wait until Jesus takes their treasures ; and if they give them freely even then, they are indeed happy souls. But there are others who cannot wait for Jesus to take them ; they love Him too much for that ; and so they take the treasures themselves, and put them into the Heart of their Beloved; and, if it were possible, they would even try not to let Him perceive they had made a sacrifice, for they know the love of His human Heart is so immense, that He can scarcely endure that His creatures should suffer the least pain. These souls lie on the bosom of Jesus with the disciple of love; they love with the love of union like him; and hence, they scarcely even know themselves when they are making a sacrifice, for love blinds them to their own interest, or, rather, they have no interest but the interest of their Beloved.

*Aspiration.*—Heart of my Infant Jesus, I adore Thee and I love Thee.

*Form your resolution, &c. Examen.*

---

### JANUARY 12TH.

"And opening their treasures, they offered Him gifts; gold, frankincense, and myrrh." (Matt. ii. 11.)

*Preludes as before.*

*1st Point.*—What are the treasures which Jesus asks us to offer Him? We must all, indeed, offer the gold of our charity, the frankincense of our prayers, and the myrrh of our mortification. But there is some special treasure which each Christian soul must offer to her King, if she would worship Him truly; and this treasure differs as widely as the feelings and interests of human hearts.

Once in our lives, and in some lives more than once, Jesus asks us for some great treasure, and perhaps our salvation, at least our sanctification, may depend upon our giving it freely. Sometimes the treasure is the life of one who is very dear to us ; and Jesus wants that treasure, either because we love it so much that we have little love to spare for Him, or because He wills to have all our love (happy for us if He prizes us so highly !) ; and He knows if He takes this treasure, we shall be obliged to turn all our love to Him. Sometimes He asks us for the treasure of our bodily health, and offers us a suffering life, a life quite different from other lives, a life that never knows for an hour the freshness of health and the exhilaration of strength. But this is because He loves us very much ; He wants to give us the treasure of constant privation of the enjoyment of health, and the treasure of constant suffering, in exchange for the treasure of health. We shall know in heaven which treasure was best for us.

*2nd Point.*—But Jesus does not ask a great sacrifice or constant suffering from every soul. There are very pure and holy souls whom He does not seem to try very keenly ; and we may not judge in this world whether the souls who suffer most have this treasure because they love most, or because they need a purification which holier souls may not require. But there is one treasure which our sweet Jesus asks from every soul; it is the treasure of their own will ; and He asks that treasure to give them in return the treasure of His will. There are souls who are "opening" this treasure all day long, and "offering Him gifts; gold, and frankincense, and myrrh." How beautiful is the gold of their charity, how pure the fragrance of their frankincense, how touching the perfection of their myrrh! All day long they sacrifice their will to the will of their Beloved, and drop little pearls into the casket of the sacred Heart from the casket of their treasures.

*3rd Point.*—Jesus only needs to whisper to those souls the least intimation of His will; He is not obliged "to take," for they are ever opening their treasures, only too full of joy when they find a gift to offer Him. Now it is a little act of charity which causes them some personal inconvenience; but the treasure is no sooner seen than it is dropped down into the Heart of the Beloved. Now it is some fervent, thoughtful prayer for some poor sinner whom no one else thinks of, some sinner whose sin every one talks of and no one pities; but the soul knows how Jesus loved it, and she prays for it with tears which also drops like jewels into that blessed Heart. Now it is some act of mortification, some suffering borne in silence, which no one has even imagined, some mental anguish which she could not impart to any human ear, some sickness which has so often recurred, that it seems as if it should be endured even from habit, and yet is as fresh suffering every hour as the first time it was felt; but each offering is hidden and dropped one by one, in silent love, into that Heart where each will be remembered and rewarded long after the soul has herself forgotten the offerings she made.

*Aspiration.*—Heart of my Love, I will offer Thee all my treasures if Thou wilt only take them.

*Form your resolution, &c.   Examen.*

---

## OCTAVE OF THE EPIPHANY.

### THE RETURN OF THE WISE MEN.

"And having received an answer in sleep that they should not return to Herod, they went back another way into their country." (Matt. ii. 12.)

*1st Prelude.*—Represent to yourself the wise men preparing for·their return, and praying for divine guidance on their journey.

*2nd Prelude.*—Pray that you may never undertake any important duty without special prayer, lest you should be led astray.

*1st Point.*—It is evident, from the words of Holy Scripture, that the Magi had prayed for guidance as to their conduct in regard to Herod. He had expressly desired them " to bring him word again," when they had found the Child, that he might come and adore Him. No doubt, the wise men, in their simplicity, believed the crafty king, and, perhaps, their charity prevented them from even seeing why he did not seek the young Child himself, if he really wished to worship Him. Thus they might easily have been led astray, had they trusted to appearances. The serpent was matched against the dove, but the dove had a resource of which the serpent knew not. Let us learn from the wise men how to act in our dealings with others. If charity will not allow us to suspect motives which appear doubtful, let holy prudence teach us that we are never safe unless we are guided by divine Providence in all our ways, and if we pray like the wise men, we shall be guided as they were.

*2nd Point.*—Consider the manner in which the wise men received the divine direction—it was "in sleep;" perhaps as a symbol to us of the mystic sleep of prayer, in which the spirit alone is wakeful, and the body lies dormant—of that sleep which causes us to close our eyes to all worldly distractions, and listen for heavenly voices. Prayer is the mystic sleep of the spouse, during which she reposes in the arms of her Beloved. The depth of this sleep will be proportioned to the depth of her love. If she seeks nothing but Him, she will be unconscious of all besides; in proportion as she only seeks Him in part, will be her distraction and her wakefulness. Oh, let us pray for this mystic sleep. If we desire to enjoy it to the utmost, let us give ourselves up to God with unbounded confidence, for nothing disturbs and hinders this sleep more than want of confidence. Let us desire only the fulfilment of God's will in all our daily duties and actions, and we may be assured, when danger impends, that we shall "receive an answer in sleep," that we shall be warned in some manner what to do and what to avoid.

*3rd Point.*—Consider the return of the Magi to their own country. Extraordinary manifestations of God's power and providence are the exception, not the rule of Christian life. Hence, we must be prepared, after receiving any special favour, to return again as it were to the ordinary ways of spiritual life, and to walk in them faithfully. The wise men must have desired exceedingly to remain with Jesus and Mary. How many reasons and excuses they might have pleaded for prolonging their stay at Bethlehem! But they knew the will of God only to obey it. He who called them from their country desires them to return to it, and they go back "another way." They do not return as they came, for they have learned lessons they can never forget. They go back "another way," for henceforth life has other objects and desires than it had when they came to Bethlehem. O sweet Jesus, may we go another and a holier way for the rest of our lives, after having spent this holy season at Thy crib, and learned there so many and such blessed lessons!

*Aspiration.*—Heart of my Infant King, I love Thee, and because I love Thee, I am sorry I have · offended Thee. Mary, Mother of my King, be my mother also.

*Form your resolution, &c.    Examen.*

# PART II.

---

# MEDITATIONS

FROM

## EASTER SUNDAY TO TRINITY SUNDAY,

IN HONOUR OF

## THE HEART OF JESUS GLORIFIED.

---

### EASTER SUNDAY.

#### THE HEART OF JESUS RISING FROM THE TOMB.

"Jesus said: I am the resurrection and the life."
(S. John, xi. 25.)

*1st Prelude.*—Represent to yourself the sepulchre now no longer sealed, the guards overthrown in terror and dismay, and the sweet Heart of Jesus rising glorious and triumphant.

*2nd Prelude.*—Pray that, by His strength, and in the power of His grace, you may also rise triumphantly over sin in this world, and obtain a glorious resurrection in the life to come.

*1st Point.*—Consider the grave where Jesus lay.

K

A moment before the midnight hour a body lay therein ; a human Heart, once full of life, but now cold and inanimate ; a face pale and ghastly with the hues of death and the stains of blood, calm in its majestic sorrow, and yet, oh, how sorrowful ! a wasted frame—wasted with three and thirty years of hourly suffering; worn by long fasts and protracted vigils ; alas ! worn by the cruel wrongs of creatures who were loved so much, and who loved so little.    Oh, let us give one glance of burning love and one tear of heartfelt sorrow to our dead Jesus, ere we turn from meditations on His sufferings, to enraptured contemplations of His risen glory ; and, amid our Easter joys, let us remember, at least for a brief moment, how dearly they have been purchased for us !

*2nd Point.*—But the midnight hour is heard. Jesus was born at midnight; at midnight He will come to judge the world; at midnight He rises gloriously a conqueror from the tomb.    He *is* the resurrection; therefore He needs no power save His own to resuscitate His Humanity.    Oh, let us shout to Him, with shouts of joy, Alleluia ! Alleluia !    The courts of heaven are ringing with His praises, Alleluia ! Alleluia !    The Church on earth has scarcely words to express her joy ; for how can the joy of the bride be fully told in the absence of the Bridegroom ?    O Jesus, our life, our love, we have no words to tell our gladness. Thou hast risen.    The winter of suffering is past, the springtime of sorrowing is over, the autumn fruits are gathered in—Alleluia! Alleluia! Thou *canst* not suffer more; and if this thought alone has enabled us to bear close and constant contemplation of Thy sufferings, how shall we not joy therein when we meditate on Thy resurrection glory!

*3rd Point.*—Consider how we may best worship and glorify the risen Heart of Jesus. 1. Let us run with the holy women to His tomb. There we may contemplate His wonders and adore His power; there we may offer our most fervent congratulations on His joyful resurrection. 2. Let us return with the women to declare what we have seen; let us tell "the brethren" of His risen love; let us manifest to all that His resurrection is also ours, and invite all to share in it by our words and our example. 3. Let us also rise with Him. We have sought during the past season of penance to die with Him; now let us rise again. He is *the resurrection and the life;* and when we receive Him into our hearts to-day, in that adorable Sacrament, of which He has said Himself, *He that eateth Me, shall live by Me,* let us implore Him, by the love of His risen Heart, to give us life—life that becomes more strong and vigorous every day and hour until it becomes immortal.

*Aspiration.*—Sweet Heart of my risen Jesus, may I rise with Thee!

*Form your resolution, and place it in the Heart of Jesus glorified. Examen.*

## EASTER MONDAY.

### THE HEART OF JESUS MANIFESTING HIMSELF
### ⸦ TO PETER.

"The Lord is risen indeed, and hath appeared to Simon."
(Luke, xxiv. 34.)

*1st Prelude.*—Represent to yourself the love with which the ardent Peter gazes upon and adores his risen Lord.

*2nd Prelude.*—Pray for the grace of a like love and ardour, through the merits and intercession of this great apostle.

*1st Point.*—Peter was one of the first to visit the sepulchre. Even when the rest of the apostles considered the words of the women as idle tales, he "rose up and ran to the sepulchre." Thus does our sweet Jesus reward His faithful ones. They may fall, but they repent quickly. Their love may need many a trial before it becomes perfected, but still they love; their faith may waver for a moment in times of trial and desolation, but soon it burns brighter and stronger than before. They love, and sweet Jesus only asks for love. He will bear with many faults for sake of a little love. Oh, why are we so cold, why so slow to give what will cost us nothing, and what our risen Jesus desires so much? Better to be impetuous, better even to be unwise in our love, than not to love at all. Had Peter stayed at home to consider whether the words of the women were true or false, had he hesitated and doubted instead of "running" to the sepulchre, perhaps he would not have been vouchsafed this special visit of his risen Lord.

*2nd Prelude.*—Let us consider the words of the holy Gospel: "He appeared to Simon." Yes, it is to superiors, to those whom God has specially appointed to instruct and guide others, that Jesus appears. We know not what passed between Jesus and Peter when he was favoured with this blessed apparition, and we may not ask or seek to know why our superiors give certain directions, refuse certain permissions, or grant certain dispensations. It is enough for us that Jesus appears to Simon. We are not worthy to know and to see what they know and see. We are not worthy to be enlightened as they were enlightened; and even if we were worthy, sweet Jesus teaches us through others, and through others only can we know His will in questions of obedience. And yet even for superiors the risen Heart of Jesus has an instruction. They may not despise the message "of the women," they may learn in hidden ways from the feeblest and the poorest of their charge ; and, like Peter, they also should rise up quickly, examine carefully, and consider prudently, if they hope like him to decide truly on what may be a divine inspiration.

*3rd Prelude.*—Consider how we may glorify the risen Heart of Jesus appearing to Peter. Let it be by faithful and humble submission to our superiors, by promptness in disclosing to them all that concerns our spiritual state, even as the women related the message of the angels to the apostles. This done, let us rest in peace. The risen Heart of Jesus loves us far better and far more wisely than we can love ourselves, and we may well abandon ourselves utterly and unreservedly to His keeping.

*Aspiration.*—Risen Heart of my Jesus, enlighten and guide our holy Father the Pope, and all superiors, especially our own.

*Form your resolution, &c.    Examen.*

## EASTER TUESDAY.

### THE RISEN HEART OF JESUS APPEARING TO MAGDALEN.

"But He rising early the first day of the week, appeared first to Mary Magdalen, out of whom He had cast seven devils." (Mark, xvi. 9.)

*1st Prelude.*—Represent to yourself the garden and the new tomb where Jesus had lain.

*2nd Prelude.*—Pray that Jesus may visit you also at this blessed paschal time, however sinful your past life may have been, and however unworthy it may have rendered you of such favours.

*1st Point.*—Who but Jesus would have appeared first to one out of whom He had cast seven devils? Courage, poor soul, overwhelmed with fear at the

remembrance of past sins, and almost despairing
at present imperfections! Oh, take heart! Jesus
came to save. He came to seek out the souls who
would not come to Him; He came to save the
souls who seemed not to care for their salvation;
He came to save the most worthless and wretched
of His creatures; and yet we might well have supposed that after they had killed Him, after they
had treated Him as an enemy, after they had done
their worst to injure Him, that now, at least, He
would deem something due to justice, and close the
long-open account of mercy. But no; the risen
Heart of Jesus—blessed be His sweetest name!—
loves poor sinners as fondly, and tenderly, and
unreservedly as the crucified Heart had loved them;
and He appears *first* to Mary Magdalen, out of
whom He had cast seven devils.

*2nd Point.*—Let us consider how many devils
sweet Jesus has cast out of us. Alas! have we
allowed Him to cast out seven? Have we never
invited them back after He has freed us from them?
And if we are so happy as to have preserved our
baptismal innocence, to have kept ourselves in all
the purity of our first communion, or our solemn
consecration to God; are we keeping those evil
spirits not only out of our souls, but also at a distance from them? How often we permit them to
linger near us, to walk round us, when by one
heartfelt ejaculation, one earnest act of love, one
fervent act of contrition, they might be driven from
us, perhaps for ever! Oh, let us endeavour, at this

blessed Eastertide, to be faithful to our risen Love.
He will appear to us ; He will console us ; He will
strengthen us by His spiritual visits, in the Sacrament of His Body and Blood, and the whispers of
His grace, only let us drive far from our hearts
those enemies whom He has conquered for us.

*3rd Point.*—Let us consider how we may glorify
the risen Heart of Jesus appearing to Magdalen.
Let it be by imitating her fidelity.   She remained
by the tomb of Jesus weeping, when others returned
to seek rest or consolation in their homes.   O true,
loving-hearted one, O faithful Magdalen, obtain
for me a rich share in thy fidelity and thy love.
May I ever remain with thee by the tomb of Jesus,
finding more pleasure in His lonely sepulchre than
amid crowds of friends or social joys.   Some are
willing to remain with Him on Thabor ; some few
blessed souls stay with Him on Calvary ; but they
are most blessed and most faithful who remain
also by His tomb, weeping His absence, content to
be without all consolation until His return—whose
excessive love binds them to the very stone which
hides Him from them, when He can no longer be
found elsewhere.

*Aspiration.*—Risen Heart of my Jesus, drive far
from me all Thy enemies.

*Form your resolution, &c.    Examen.*

## EASTER WEDNESDAY.

### THE RISEN HEART OF JESUS CONSOLING MAGDALEN BY A VISION OF ANGELS.

"Now as she was weeping, she stooped down and looked into the sepulchre : and she saw two angels in white." (S. John, xx. 11, 12.)

*1st Prelude.*—Represent to yourself the faithful Magdalen weeping because she can no longer find Him who is her only joy.

*2nd Prelude.*—Pray that henceforth you may only weep for and with Jesus, and that you may seek Him alone in all places and occupations.

*1st Point.*—The disciples go home when they find the sepulchre empty ; even the faithful Peter and the loving John are content with "looking in and seeing the linen clothes ;" but Magdalen stands without weeping. If she cannot see Jesus, she will at least remain where she knows He has been. Oh, how fondly earthly love treasures the relics of the departed, loves to stand where they have stood, to sit where they have sat, to keep what once was kept or cared for by them ! And why may not the faithful Magdalen treasure as tenderly the grave-clothes or the tomb of her only Love ? And those who stand weeping and watching for Jesus through the long night of life, shall surely find Him for whom they have wept and watched, in the brightness of eternal day.

*2nd Point.*—Let us consider how we may imitate the example of Magdalen. Oh, let us stand weeping by the tabernacle where Jesus truly lies buried in the adorable Sacrament of the altar. We may not feel conscious of His presence; we may not see Him; our night of weeping may be long, but the morning of joy shall surely come. Neither angels nor apostles could comfort Magdalen in the absence of her Lord. If we would imitate her, and share in her rewards, let us not seek comfort from any but Jesus. Let us prefer remaining near His sepulchre weeping, to enjoying the gladdest of earthly delights apart from Him; and from time to time, as we stoop down and look in, as we make acts of humiliation and burning love, we shall see angels sitting, we shall receive holy inspirations, holy consolations, and passing glimpses of eternal joys.

*3rd Point.*—Let us consider how we may glorify the risen Heart of Jesus consoling Magdalen by a vision of angels. Perhaps we may do so most effectually by endeavouring to increase in fervent devotion to Jesus in the adorable Sacrament of the altar. The angels are never absent for a moment from the tabernacle; their life is one perpetual act of adoration and praise. Let us try to imitate them; let us carry all our griefs, and trials, and anxieties to Jesus; and if duty calls us for a few moments to His presence, let our first thought be of Him. Let us seek to have some special inten-

tion each time we kneel before the altar, on return-
ing to or leaving the choir. Now we may offer our
genuflection in reparation for the outrages of the
passion; now in atonement for the insults of
heretics; now for the souls of the faithful departed. Love is fertile in suggestions, and Jesus
will Himself teach us how to adore Him best.

*Aspiration.*—Sweet Sacrament, I Thee adore;
Oh, may I love Thee more and more.

*Form your resolution, &c. Examen.*

## EASTER THURSDAY.

### THE HEART OF JESUS APPEARING TO MARY MAGDALEN AS THE GARDENER.

"She turned herself back, and saw Jesus standing; and
she knew not that it was Jesus." (S. John, xx. 14.)

*1st Prelude.*—Represent to yourself Jesus appearing as the gardener.

*2nd Prelude.*—Pray for grace to seek Him in
every place with the same love as Magdalen.

*1st Point.*—Magdalen had been conversing with
angels, and they had inquired the cause of her
grief; but as they had not told her where her
Lord was, she turns back from them. Even angels
cannot satisfy the soul which seeks the Lord of
angels. Even the purest, the holiest of spiritual

joys, is not enough for the soul which pines for God alone. Oh, thrice happy and thrice blessed shall we be, if we thus seek our Lord. Oh, let us "turn back" from all that hinders or tempts us, however good it may appear, when we are seeking Jesus. Oh, let us never rest until we find Him. The joy of that finding will be proportioned to the earnestness and love with which we have been seeking.

*2nd Point.*—" She knew not that it was Jesus." How often we know Him not, even when He is nearest to us. He speaks to us, but we do not recognize His voice ; He appears to us, but we do not discern Him. We blame the unfortunate accident, the trying delay, the unkind action, the thoughtless word, the little neglect, the apparent or real slight, the want of consideration for our feelings ; and we say, if this had not happened, if that person had not been so neglectful, if those plans had not been crossed, how much better it would have been ; and we know not that it is Jesus, sweet Jesus, the truest, tenderest, gentlest Lover of our souls. He is standing by us, quite near, but we think it is the gardener ; He is watching us closely, but we are too absorbed in our trial or vexation to notice Him ; nay, even when we are seeking Him, seeking earnestly and faithfully, we often know Him not when He is nearest to us ; for the trial He has sent so absorbs us, that we forget to recognize His hand in its every circumstance, and to believe in His love through all its pain.

Oh, if we only "knew that it was Jesus," how differently we should act in many circumstances, in every trial; and yet, are we not well aware that He who has numbered the hairs of our head watches over and appoints each, and even the most trivial, circumstance of our daily lives?

*3rd Point.*—Let us see how we may glorify the risen Heart of Jesus appearing as the gardener. Let it be by confiding our souls entirely to His care. He is, indeed, the Gardener. Let us give Him a full and unreserved charge of the mystical garden of our souls; let us ask Him to plant, and to water, and to prune as He wills; let us offer Him the flowers of our love and the fruits of our sacrifices. It is true He can take them if He chooses; but why should we lose the merit of offering them to Him ourselves? Why should we deprive Him of the glory which we may give Him by the generous exercise of our own free will? When we are suffering, and dejected, and disappointed, let us say also, it is the Gardener; but let us remember who that Gardener is. In summer and winter, in heat and cold, early and late, He toils and labours, and He waters the plants He has set with blood. Oh, shall we ever again distrust His love or doubt His care?

*Aspiration.*—Risen Heart of my Jesus, I give Thee the flowers of my love and the fruit of my sufferings.

*Form your resolution, &c. Examen.*

## FRIDAY IN EASTER WEEK.

### THE HEART OF JESUS CONVERSING WITH MAGDALEN.

"Jesus saith to her : Woman, why weeepest thou ? whom seekest thou ?" (S. John, xx. 15.)

1st *Prelude.*—Represent to yourself the garden, and Jesus standing and addressing Magdalen.

2nd *Prelude.*—Pray for grace always to hear the voice of Jesus whenever, wherever, and however He may address you.

1st *Point.*—Jesus speaks to Magdalen ; but although she seeks Him so earnestly, she discerns Him not. Is not this often the case with us ? Unexpected trials come ; we forget they are from God, and their suddenness takes us off our guard. We pray for some special grace, and God sends some special suffering : we do not see the answer to our prayers. Some affliction comes to us, apparently through our own fault, or through the fault of others : we do not see the hand of God. Oh, there is no peace like the peace of those who see God in *everything;* no love like the love of those who trust God in everything. Our Lord told S. Gertrude that those who conquered nature should be as a pillar on which He would repose. Who would not desire to attain this honour—to receive this favour? O Christian soul, trust, trust, trust!

*2nd Point.*—Consider the manner in which Jesus makes Himself known to the faithful soul. He has spoken to her, and she knows Him not. He says but one word, and she falls at His blessed feet in an ecstacy of adoring love—"Mary." He calls her by name, and by the name dearest to His risen Heart — "Mary." He will not add Magdalen, for Jesus seldom reproaches; and we know how He overwhelms the souls who seek Him faithfully and constantly, with the tenderest caresses and the deepest love. "Mary!" The Heart of Jesus never changes. He loved the penitent one on earth, and He loves her still in heaven. O Jesus, sweet Jesus, when wilt Thou call us also by our names in heaven, as Thou hast so often and so sweetly called us upon earth? "Mary!" O dearest Lord, say but that word again. The voices of angels have sounded in the ears of Magdalen, and their music might well soothe and banish every earthly care; but to her no voice but one could satisfy, and that voice has spoken and called His sheep by name. O our risen Love, call us also, for we have sought Thee, we have longed for Thee, we have wept for Thee. We also will say Rabboni. Whatever happens, it is the Master; whatever tries us, it is Rabboni's good pleasure; whatever gladdens us, it is an echo of Rabboni's voice; and so we also will answer at all times, in all places, under all circumstances, Rabboni. Our utterance may be broken by tears, but it will not be the less loving nor the less trustful; it may not be heard or known by mortals, but the listening ear of Jesus treasures our every accent, and He will reward a thousandfold our faith, and love, and trust.

*3rd Point.*—Let us see how we can best adore our risen Love conversing with Magdalen. Perhaps we might do so in two ways: first, by an unbounded trust in our Master's love, whether He manifests Himself to us openly, or tries us in hidden ways; by saying Rabboni under every trial; by remembering that the Master is our Father, our Brother, and our Friend; by submitting lovingly to His will, however manifested to us: and secondly, by learning, from the example of Jesus, the tenderest charity to others. It is no business of ours whether our neighbours' sufferings are sent in judgment or in mercy; let us only seek to soothe and console them in the kindest manner. Let us call them by the name they love best to hear; let us offer the consolations and attentions which will please them most; let us learn that thoughtful love which divines the wishes of others, and offers a kindness, not in the way most pleasing to ourselves, but in the way most pleasing to them.

*Aspiration.*—Rabboni.

*Form your resolution, &c. Examen.*

## SATURDAY IN EASTER WEEK.

### THE RISEN HEART OF JESUS APPEARING TO HIS BLESSED MOTHER.

" My beloved to me, and I to Him, till the day break, and the shadows retire." (Cant. ii. 16, 17.)

*1st Prelude.*—Represent to yourself the patient and ecstatic love with which Mary waits for the first apparition of Jesus.

*2nd Prelude.*—Pray that she may obtain for you the grace of a glorious resurrection, and of beholding the countenance of Jesus gazing upon you with love and mercy.

*1st Point.*—Mary had no need to watch " over against the sepulchre," for Jesus lay in her heart in the adorable Sacrament of the altar, according to a pious tradition, from the moment she received Him at the last supper until the hour of His resurrection. And even were it not so, her union with Him was inseparable—a union closer than the love of bride and bridegroom—a union incomparably beyond the closest union of the highest saint. The flesh now glorified, had been formed in her pure womb; the human life now exalted to the right hand of God, had its first pulsations in her immaculate bosom; the Word which was made flesh, and dwelt amongst us, first dwelt and was made flesh in

L

Mary's womb.  Oh, how glorious, how triumphant
was His resurrection for her!  Now her joys were
consummated, and her sorrows consoled, in proportion to their greatness.  The first'public appearance
of Jesus is to the forgiven and loving Magdalen, but
the first secret embrace of His love was surely for
His own faultless Mother.

*2nd Point.*—Consider how Mary had longed for
that apparition.  She knew He would come.  She
had no doubt of the resurrection on the third
day; but the shadows of Calvary lay dark and heavy
upon her soul, until the dawn of that Easter morning.  Her night had, indeed, been one of awful
fear and untold agony.  The demons of doubt and
unbelief could not for a moment shake the firm
confidence of her pure soul, but it may be they
wreaked their vengeance on it all the more because
of the very impotence of their mightiest efforts.
Perhaps nothing but the vision of Jesus risen could
have removed the painful image of Jesus dead,
stereotyped in her heart.  But the day breaks, and
the shadows retire.  The day of Mary's power
commences, the day of grace, in which she enables
us to rise victorious over sin and demons.  Behold
how she " cometh forth as the morning rising, fair
as the moon, bright as the sun, terrible as an army
set in array :" fair as the moon to console us,
bright as the sun to fructify us, terrible as an army
to defend us.

*3rd Point.*—Let us consider how we may glorify
the risen Heart of Jesus appearing to His blessed

Mother. Oh, let us ask and pray that our Beloved may be "to us, and we to Him," until the day break, and the shadows retire ; that we may seek nothing, desire nothing, look for nothing, but Jesus crucified, until the day of eternity breaks, when we shall share His resurrection glories in proportion to our fidelity to His cross and His sepulchre. The shadows of earthly grief, and care, and disappointment, will soon pass away ; one glance of His love will turn them all into unchanging brightness and beauty. O Mary, by thy joy in the resurrection of thy sweetest Jesus, obtain for us the grace to live ever with eternity in view.

*Aspiration.*—My beloved to me, and I to Him, till the day break, and the shadows retire.

*Form your resolution, &c.    Examen.*

---

## LOW SUNDAY.

### THE HEART OF JESUS SAYING TO HIS DISCIPLES : PEACE BE TO YOU.

"And after eight days, again His disciples were within, Jesus cometh, the doors being shut, and stood in the midst, and said : Peace be to you." (S. John, xx. 26.)

*1st Prelude.*—Represent to yourself the disciples assembled in the upper room, and conversing lovingly of their dear Lord.

*2nd Prelude.*—Pray for the grace of great devotion to all religious exercises in which you are united with others.

*1st Point.*—Jesus comes when the disciples are within, and the doors are shut. He knoweth our " sitting down and our rising up," and He watches for the moment when His grace can be given to us with the greatest advantage. If any of the disciples had been late, they would have missed that blessed Pax ; if they had been absent without real necessity, they would not have seen Jesus. Oh, let us be fervent and punctual in our duties, whatever they may be, lest our risen Lord should come seeking for us, and we should lose His blessing and His presence ! Jesus comes when the doors are shut. If we desire the visits of our dearest Lord, we must be " within," that is, we must not only be at the post of duty, but we must also have our thoughts at home, fixed on God, and on the employment in which we are engaged for Him. If our thoughts are straying and wandering, we are not " within ;" and we must have the "doors shut," and locked with the golden key of love and a pure intention, for our enemies, the Jews—our self-love, our sinful inclinations, the demons who seek to destroy us, or at least to injure our work—are prowling without, and our hearts are the "upper room" where Jesus would abide always, if we admitted none but Him therein.

*2nd Point.*—" Jesus stands in the midst." Let us ask Him to come to-day into our hearts in the

Sacrament of His love, and to stand in the midst. He stands as a Judge, to decide our difficulties, and to enlighten our ignorance. He stands as a Ruler, to govern our thoughts, and words, and actions. He stands as a Master, to teach us all we should know, and He will have patience with our ignorance, if we are only willing to learn. He will pardon our slowness of apprehension, if we only manifest a good will ; He will supply even for our deficiencies, if we submit humbly and lovingly to His instructions. He stands as a Friend, to warn us of every danger, to assist us in every difficulty ; nay more, He stands as a Bridegroom, to pour forth on us the unutterable effusions of the love of His risen Heart.

*3rd Point.*—Consider how we may glorify the risen Heart of Jesus standing in the midst of His disciples. Surely, it will be by inviting Him into the midst of our hearts to-day in the most holy Sacrament, or at least by a spiritual communion ; by closing the doors of our hearts to every worldly care and distraction, and by submitting to all His instructions. Listen to the words He addresses to His disciples : " Peace be to you." When Jesus stands in the midst there must be peace ; and peace of heart is a Christian privilege, a resurrection gift, of which none can deprive us unless we wilfully deprive ourselves of it. We may be tried, tempted, suffering, disappointed, dejected, but none of these things can deprive us of peace. We lose it when we murmur under trial, when we become

impatient in suffering, when we question God's love
in disappointments and crosses; because then we
have forbidden our sweet Jesus to "stand in the
midst;" and when He is gone, or even partly
withdrawn from us, we can no longer have perfect
peace.

*Aspiration.*—Risen Heart of my Jesus, give me
Thy peace.

*Form your resolution, &c.    Examen.*

---

## SECOND MONDAY AFTER EASTER.

### THE RISEN HEART OF JESUS INSTRUCTING THOMAS.

"Then He saith to Thomas: Put in thy finger hither, and
see My hands, and bring hither thy hand, and put it into
My side." (S. John, xx. 27.)

1*st Prelude.*—Represent to yourself the awe and
amazement with which Thomas beheld His risen
Lord.

2*nd Prelude.*—Pray for the grace to know Jesus
more and more by the marks of His wounds.

1*st Point.*—Thomas was absent when Jesus came
the first time to visit His disciples. The holy Gospel
says, "Thomas was not with them when Jesus
came." Alas! is not Jesus often present, and we
are absent? Is He not constantly present in the
adorable Sacrament of the altar, and are we not
often absent from His presence without real neces-

sity? Does He not come frequently to visit us in the holy communion, and we are absent? Absent, perhaps, because we have preferred other company to the company of Jesus, not, indeed, deliberately, for we would rather die than act thus, but we are absent because we have preferred the indulgence of an imperfection, the commission of a fault, the folly, perhaps, of a scruple, a miserable want of confidence in our best Friend—to Himself, to our loving Jesus. Alas! are we not also absent sometimes, though present in body, when our thoughts, desires, and anxieties, are occupied more with others than with Jesus? O risen Jesus, come and visit us; we are waiting for Thee, pining for Thee, longing for Thee. O our Love, our Life, do not tarry; we cannot live without our Life, we shall die without our Love; come, and by Thy grace we will not be absent either in body or in spirit.

*2nd Point.*—Consider the burning love of the risen Heart of Jesus. Thomas was absent when Jesus came, so Jesus must needs come when Thomas is present. Our risen Love is still the same kind Jesus He always was. He is not changed. Oh, let us only believe it; let us try to convince ourselves of it. He is not changed since He spent the long, weary day trying to win poor sinners to love Him, the long, weary night praying for sinners to come to Him. If we would only believe this, how glad He would be, what glory we should give to His risen Heart, and what peace and strength we

should obtain for our own souls. Jesus comes
when Thomas is within. If sinners will come to
Him, He will come to them. He watches the
moment when He can assist us best ; shall we not
endeavour to correspond with His generous and
unwearied love ?

*3rd Point.*—Consider how we may glorify the
risen Heart of Jesus instructing Thomas. Let it
be by our endeavours to be always prepared for
His visits, by seeking to correspond faithfully with
His love. We may always know where and how to
find Jesus, by "the print of the nails ;" we may
always discern Jesus when He visits us, by "putting
our fingers into the place of the nails." Even in
His risen glory our Lord still retains the tokens of
His sufferings ; and those wounds which were so
painful and humiliating, are now His glory and His
honour. Let us learn from this to love suffering,
to love duties, employments, trials, which are
marked with "the print of the nails." Let us
put our hand, that is, our whole intention, into
them, and accept them with special love. Such
duties and trials will be the most profitable for our
own souls, will give God the greatest glory, and
will benefit our neighbour most ; and in such we
shall most surely find our risen Lord.

*Aspiration.*—Risen Heart of my Jesus, teach me
true fidelity.

*Form your resolution, &c.   Examen.*

## SECOND TUESDAY AFTER EASTER.

### THE RISEN HEART OF JESUS SENDING MAGDALEN TO HIS DISCIPLES.

"Go to My brethren and say to them : I ascend to My Father and to your Father, to My God and your God." (S. John, xx. 17.)

*1st Prelude.*—Represent to yourself our divine Lord addressing Magdalen, and the humble love with which she listens.

*2nd Prelude.*—Pray for grace to bear the messages of Jesus faithfully to others.

*1st Point.*—Consider the messenger whom Jesus chooses. It is Magdalen, out of whom He has cast seven devils—Magdalen, the notorious public sinner. Ah! but it is the same Magdalen who could spend her wealth in ointment to anoint her Lord, and pour forth her tears in floods to wash His feet. But it is a woman whom Christ chooses as a messenger to His apostles, to the men who are to found His Church, and to govern it, until He comes again in glory, in the persons of their successors. True, it is a woman ; but the Head of the Church honours in her the person of women, for the love of that one woman through whom we have obtained a Redeemer. Let us learn also from this to beware how we despise others, and think ourselves righteous. One who has sinned deeply, may repent nobly; one who has fallen low, may rise to a place with princes; one who has become a reproach among men, may yet be honoured by God. How much more, then, should we not be charitable in our thoughts, in our words, and in our manner, to those who have led good lives, and yet, through human frailty, or in the inscrutable designs of Providence, may be permitted to fall suddenly and grievously. Perhaps in their restoration and humiliation they may give more glory to God, and obtain a higher place in heaven, than you who have never sinned so openly.

*2nd Point.*—Consider the message of Jesus : "Go to My brethren." Yes; even after we had slain our Brother Jesus, He calls us His brethren ! He will never disown us, unless we disown Him. But He goes further : "Go to My brethren, and say to them : I ascend to My Father and to your Father, to My God and your God." O risen Heart of Jesus, how shall we ever fathom the depths of Thy tenderness ! He has signed the title-deeds in blood, and now He reads them over to us : " My Father and your Father." He places us on an equality with Himself. What if a prince should say to a beggar, " You are my brother," and speak of his father as if he were indeed the father of the poor beggar also ? And yet we are worse than beggars; for generally they are more grateful and loving to their benefactors than we are ; and is not Jesus the King of all kings ?

*3rd Point.*—Consider how we may glorify the risen Heart of Jesus calling us His brethren. Can we not do so best by endeavouring to act as the children of a king should do. We must not disgrace the noble rank to which we are elevated. Our Brother has ascended to our Father; He is preparing mansions for us in the King's city. Oh, let us talk of them, think of them, long for them, and endeavour to become worthy of them! When shall we learn to think of heaven as our home?

*Aspiration.*—Risen Heart of my Jesus, give me grace to love Thee as Thou desirest to be loved.

*Form your resolution, and place it in the risen Heart of Jesus. Examen.*

---

## SECOND WEDNESDAY AFTER EASTER.

### THE RISEN HEART OF JESUS APPEARING TO THE DISCIPLES GOING TO EMMAUS.

" And it came to pass, that while they talked and reasoned with themselves, Jesus Himself also drawing near went with them." (Luke, xxiv. 15.)

*1st Prelude.*—Represent to yourself the road from Jerusalem to Emmaus, and the two disciples in sad and earnest conversation. See how lovingly Jesus watches them, and how kindly He approaches them.

*2nd Prelude.*—Pray for grace to listen to the

voice of Jesus, for He often draws near us to converse with us, and we know Him not.

*1st Point.*—Jesus is the subject of their conversation. And He keeps a book of remembrance, in which all holy conversation is written : " Then they that feared the Lord spoke every one with his neighbour : and the Lord gave ear, and heard it : and a book of remembrance was written before Him for them that fear the Lord, and think on His name. And they shall be My special possession, saith the Lord of hosts, in the day that I do judgment : and I will spare them, as a man spareth his son that serveth him." (Mal. iii. 16, 17.) There were many persons who walked home from Jerusalem that evening, but we do not hear that our risen Lord appeared to any of them. No doubt He " gave ear" to their conversation, but we may fear He was not the subject of it. If we desire that Jesus should converse with us, let us often converse of Him ; and if we may not converse of Him with others, let us at least converse of Him in our hearts. He is listening, and when He hears the murmurs of love which our hearts are uttering, He will "Himself draw near."

*2nd Point.*—Jesus often draws near to us ; but we either fail to discern Him, or He finds us so occupied with other affairs that we have no time to attend to Him. We may be very busy doing things for Jesus, and yet scarcely ever think of Jesus. We may be so absorbed in the occupa-

tion we are engaged in, even though it be a good
and holy work, as scarcely to think of Him ofr
whom we are performing the duty. But if we
wish Jesus to "draw near," if we desire to have
Him close to us, if we would have Him remain
with us during our employment, we must not forget His presence, and we must frequently converse
with Him by loving ejaculations, by little offerings.
Jesus is often near us, and we do not discern Him,
because we do not expect to find Him in the common
occurrences of life; and yet, has He not told us Himself that no sparrow falls to the ground without
His knowledge, that the very hairs of our head are
all numbered.

*3rd Point.*—Consider how we may glorify the
risen Heart of Jesus appearing to the disciples
going to Emmaus. Let us try to imitate the example of His tenderness. See how lovingly He addresses Himself to these disciples : "What are these
discourses which you hold, and are sad ?" Many a
one would have passed by when they saw two
strangers in trouble, but Jesus never passes by any
one who is in trouble. He stops to inquire the
cause ; oh, how lovingly and tenderly ! But if He
receives no answer, and if we are so absorbed in
our grief that we cannot speak to Him, He passes
on. Oh, if we would only let Jesus comfort us in
trouble, how happy we should be ! We would begin
to long for trouble, that we might know more of
Jesus. But let us seek to imitate His example
also ; let us learn to be gentle, and loving, and

thoughtful towards others, particularly towards all who are in affliction.

*Aspiration.*—Risen Heart of my Jesus, gentlest Heart of my Jesus, teach me to imitate Thy tenderness.

*Form your resolution, &c.   Examen.*

---

## SECOND THURSDAY AFTER EASTER.

### THE RISEN HEART OF JESUS INSTRUCTING THE DISCIPLES GOING TO EMMAUS.

" And He said to them : What are these discourses that you hold one with another as ye walk, and are sad ?  And one of them, whose name was Cleophas, answering, said to Him : Art Thou only a stranger in Jerusalem, and hast not known the things that have been done there in these days ? To whom He said : What things?" (Luke, xxiv. 17-19.)

*1st Prelude.*—Look at sweet Jesus, and see how tenderly and lovingly He instructs the disciples.

*2nd Prelude.*—Pray that He may also instruct you.

*1st Point.*—Consider the exceeding love of Jesus. He knew—alas! how well—all that had been "done in Jerusalem ;" but He lets the disciples tell their own story, and gently asks them, " What things ?' Oh, what a lesson of love for us !  It is often the greatest comfort to those who are in trouble to tell their story to others—to the sick to mention their

pains, to the afflicted to tell all the little circumstances of their trial ; and do we, like sweet Jesus,
ask them "what things" are making them sad,
and listen kindly and with interest to all they have
to say? or do we not too often think the long
stories of the poor, or of children, or perhaps even
of an aged parent, or a long-suffering invalid, a
weariness and a trouble, and either refuse to listen
to them, or listen with such indifference as to make
them feel our coldness?   Oh, let us learn from our
risen Love how to console others as they desire to
be consoled—how to mortify ourselves by practising
patience, even in listening to what wearies us.   But
if we love Jesus in all, we would never be weary.
Let us look at Jesus listening so patiently, and with
such interest, to all the disciples tell Him, and then
we shall know how to act ourselves under similar
circumstances.

  *2nd Point.*—Consider the words of Cleophas :
" Art Thou only a stranger in Jerusalem ?"   O
dearest Lord, Thou art, indeed, a stranger in Jerusalem, and we seek to be at home in it.   Would to
God, a thousand and a thousand times, that Thou
hadst been treated therein merely as a stranger !
but, alas ! Thou wert treated as a criminal and a
slave.   Thou art a stranger in the city of Thy
chosen people.   Thou art not known in the courts
of David's palace.   Thou art despised in the temple
dedicated to Thy worship.   This city, the type of
that city which is called the Vision of Peace,
knows Thee not ; but we will know Thee, and love

Thee, O dearest Lord, and Thou shalt not be a stranger in the city of our hearts, and we will make a peaceful abode for Thee therein, to console Thee for being a stranger in Jerusalem.

*3rd Point.*—Consider the reply of Jesus. He tells them that He " *ought* to have suffered, and so to enter into His glory." We also must suffer if we would enter into glory, for suffering is the pavement of the heavenly road. He expounds to them Moses and the prophets ; He teaches them, by the law, what they should do; by the prophets, what they should believe. Let us, then, endeavour to glorify His risen Heart by imitating His example, by listening patiently to others, and then instructing them with holy and gentle words, telling them that, if they suffer here, they shall be glorified hereafter, and pointing out to them the blessed example of Jesus, a "stranger in Jerusalem."

*Aspiration.*—Jesus, my risen Love, Thou shalt not be a stranger while I have a heart to shelter Thee.

*Form your resolution, &c.    Examen.*

## SECOND FRIDAY AFTER EASTER.

### THE RISEN HEART OF JESUS APPEARING AS IF HE WOULD GO FARTHER.

"And they drew nigh to the town whither they were going : and He made as though He would go farther. But they constrained Him, saying : Stay with us, because it is towards evening, and the day is now far spent. And He went in with them." (S. Luke, xxiv. 28, 29.)

*1st Prelude.*—Represent to yourself the disciples absorbed in listening to the words of Jesus, and their grief when they find He is about to leave them.

*2nd Prelude.*—Pray to your risen Lord that He may stay with you.

*1st Point.*—When does Jesus prepare to leave the disciples? When they approached the town. He willingly continues His converse with them as they walk by the wayside, but when they come near the town He prepares to withdraw. He knows but too well what kind of reception He is likely to meet with in a town. The learned, and the wise, and the busy ones of earth, are too much absorbed in their pursuits to have leisure for Jesus. It was evening, and many people passed the three travellers, but never noticed them ; yet the form of one "is like the Son of God." But men hurried past them, and little knew whom they passed.

M

And is it not often thus even now? We pass by many a saintly soul, with whom Jesus converses all day long, and never so much as suspect their sanctity. They seem to walk along the road of life like other men—there is, perhaps, less outward show of piety than in others; we see only a certain sweetness, a certain gentleness, a certain exceeding tenderness for others; but we do not even suspect that all this has its source in continual converse with Jesus. Shall we not also seek to walk with Him? Shall we not also entreat Him to converse with us? He only longs to find souls to whom He can impart the secrets of His love, and all He asks is simplicity and a loving heart.

*2nd Point.*—"They constrain Him." That little town is their home, and it is their duty to remain there. Jesus will not forsake us when in the path of duty, however difficult and painful that path may be. But we must constrain Him to abide with us; and if we also live in the town, that is, in constant and distracting occupations, in employments of duty that scarcely afford us a moment's leisure, in anxious cares that of necessity and not from preference occupy much of our thoughts, we must be all the more earnest in constraining our risen Lord to stay with us, as we need His abiding presence even more than those who are free from such distractions.

*3rd Point.*—Consider how we may glorify the risen Heart of Jesus appearing as if He would go farther. Surely we may do so by imitating the conduct of these faithful disciples. Let us also constrain Him. If we do, He will surely "go in with us." We, also, have the same plea as these faithful ones: "Stay with us, because it is towards evening." The evening of life is closing in quickly round us. What are twenty, or thirty, or forty years to eternity? Are they not less than the few brief moments of a sunset in winter? And perhaps we cannot even calculate on so long an evening; perhaps the shadows of age, or ill-health, or suffering are already falling heavily upon us, and it is "towards evening." Oh, let us cry out, with the whole trust of our souls, to our risen Love, "Stay with us, stay with us!" Let us cling to His garments, and hold His feet, so that He *cannot* leave us. Let our cry be from one communion until the next, "Stay with us!" And He will stay; for He desires to remain with us more earnestly, more truly, and more faithfully than we desire to detain Him.

*Aspiration.*—Stay with us, O Lord: Alleluia! Alleluia! For it is towards evening: Alleluia! Alleluia!

*Form your resolution, &c. Examen.*

## SECOND SATURDAY AFTER EASTER.

### THE RISEN HEART OF JESUS MANIFESTING HIM-
### SELF AT TABLE.

"And it came to pass, whilst He was at table with them, He took bread, and blessed and brake, and gave to them." (Luke, xxiv. 30.)

*1st Prelude.*—Represent to yourself the room where Jesus reclines at table with His favoured hosts.

*2nd Prelude.*—Pray that sweet Jesus may often visit you thus, and, reclining in the home of your heart, give you Himself, the living Bread.

*1st Point.*—The faithful disciples not only constrain Jesus to abide with them, they also offer Him hospitality. Alas! even when we have constrained Him to abide with us, do we not too often forget His presence, and not only fail to offer Him the best we have, but sometimes even refuse Him what He asks for? How can we expect to know Him " in the breaking of bread," if we have not entertained Him with the feast of sacrifice? How can we expect that He will manifest Himself to us at table, if we have not carefully prepared for His entertainment? Let us learn from the disciples how to invite Jesus, and how to entertain Him when we have invited Him. They invite Him by earnestness, and they entertain Him by love.

*2nd Point.*—The disciples find Jesus in the ordinary duties of life. If we only sought for Him
as we should do in these duties, how blessedly we
should find Him! Then, indeed, we should truly
know Him in the "breaking of bread;" then our
hearts would be constantly prepared for His presence, because constantly expecting it. What duty
has He not hallowed? what employment has He
not sanctified? If we walk, we may unite our
steps to the steps of Jesus—at Passiontide, to His
suffering steps; at Easter, to His glorified steps;
at Christmas, to His infant steps; and in the long
weeks of Pentecost, to His weary steps. If we
think, we may unite our thoughts to His suffering
thoughts, His infant thoughts, His glorified
thoughts. If we sleep, we may unite our sleep to
His sleep in Mary's arms, His sleep in the boat on
the Sea of Galilee, or to His last sleep on earth.
Why do we not unite our life to His life? It is
our privilege; it should be our consolation and our
only joy.

*3rd Point.*—Consider how we may glorify the
risen Heart of Jesus manifesting Himself at table.
May we not try to do so in two ways? First, by
endeavouring to unite ourself to the like actions
of Jesus in every duty and employment, and by
seeking to find Him and converse with Him in all;
and secondly, by seeking to know Him "in the
breaking of bread." Jesus is our life. He gives
Himself to us in the Sacrament of the altar, and
He has said Himself, "he that eateth Me, the

same also shall live by Me." (S. John, vi. 58.)
This, then, is our life. Oh, let us seek it; let us
love it; let us live on it; and seek more and more,
in receiving it, that we may be incorporated into it,
until, like the apostle, we can say, " I live, yet not
I, but Christ who liveth in me."

*Aspiration.*—Body of my risen Jesus, be my
life.

*Form your resolution, &c. Examen.*

## SECOND SUNDAY AFTER EASTER.

THE RISEN HEART OF JESUS, AS THE GOOD SHEP-
HERD, CHOOSING PETER TO FEED HIS SHEEP.

"He said to him : Feed My sheep." (S. John, xxi. 17.)

1st *Prelude.*—Represent to yourself the grief of
Peter, when Jesus inquires three times if he loves
Him.

2nd *Prelude.*—Pray for grace to show your love
to Jesus by doing all you can for His sheep.

1st *Point.*—The Shepherd has been slain by His
sheep, but He does not love them less; and now
the first thought of His risen Heart seems to be
what He can do for them. He seeks them in the
garden in the person of Magdalen, to console and
reassure sinners; He meets them on the wayside
in the person of His faithful but perplexed disciples,
to strengthen and comfort those who love Him

truly ; nay, He even consults their convenience, and condescends to their weakness, in the person of Thomas, and if they are not within when Jesus calls, He comes again to look for them. O risen Heart of our Love, how shall we love Thee—how shall we thank Thee ! Thou hast given Thy life for us on the cross, and to us in the holy Sacrament ; and yet Thou wilt do even more. Thou art about to ascend to Thy Father and to ours, to show Him the wounds with which Thou wert wounded in the house of Thy friends, as an excuse and a plea to obtain forgiveness for those friends ; and yet Thou wilt not leave us uncared for or unprotected in Thy absence, well knowing how weak and unstable we are.

*2nd Point.*—Consider how our divine Lord makes feeding His flock the very test and proof of Peter's love. Not only does He give him the charge of chief pastor, and authorize him to fulfil its solemn duties, He even goes further, and by his threefold charge impresses on His apostle how near the interests of His sheep were to His risen Heart. Well may we be amazed at such exceeding love. And let us also observe the marvellous tenderness of this Heart of love in the manner of conveying His command. The lambs are the weakest portion of the flock, they need the most careful pasturing and the most constant care ; and we find our divine Lord reiterates the command, " Feed My lambs," to give this portion of His flock in special charge to His vicar.

dear love! They must suffer with them by tender sympathy in all their afflictions of body and soul, by their efforts to relieve them, by weeping when they weep, and rejoicing when they rejoice ; nay, they must even be prepared to lay down their lives for the brethren, should such an unspeakable honour be conferred on them. And this they may do unconsciously, by the long, slow martyrdom of daily toil for their spiritual and temporal welfare.

*2nd Point.*—They who would feed Christ's sheep, either in the noble ministry of the altar, in the humble duties of the convent, or in the busy cares of secular life, may not do or seek their own will. When they were young, that is, before this noble mission was conferred on them, they might "gird themselves" and walk "where they would ;" but now others must gird them, for they must conform themselves, in all things lawful and expedient, to the will of others, that they may more easily win them for the Good Shepherd ; and they must be led "whither they would not," for nature will often shrink from the stern calls of duty, from the daily, hourly claims of obedience, from the exactions of time, that leave no moment's leisure for occupations which would please themselves, from the constant, wearying labour that may not ask, and will try not even to wish for rest.

*3rd Point.*—Consider how we may glorify the risen Heart of Jesus predicting Peter's martyrdom. Let it be by cheerfully accepting our own. There are some happy and chosen souls to whom life is one long suffering—now of body, and now of mind ; now exterior, and now interior; now from the hidden malice of demons, and now from the open malice or unkindness of creatures. For such there is unbounded consolation in our Lord's prediction to Peter. To all—for Christ Himself has told us that *all* who would follow Him must take up their cross—there is instruction and comfort. To such He says, as to Peter, "Follow Me." Some follow His footsteps closely, and are privileged to lift the cross from His shoulders, and help to bear it on their own ; and they leave footprints after them like His—footprints stained with blood. Some follow, yet not so closely, and they must feel the thorns and briars that beset His path. Some follow, yet further off, but the path is not changed ; it is still rough ; and though those who are nearest to Jesus share most deeply in His sufferings, the traveller even on the borders of the royal road, must have some little share therein.

*Aspiration.*—Risen Heart of my Jesus, teach me how to follow Thee.

*Form your resolution, &c. Examen.*

## THIRD TUESDAY AFTER EASTER.

### THE RISEN HEART OF JESUS SHOWING HIMSELF AT THE SEA OF TIBERIAS.

"And they went forth and entered into the ship, and that night they caught nothing." (S. John, xxi. 3.)

*1st Prelude.*—Represent to yourself the clear and beautiful moonlight night of summer time in Palestine, and the disciples toiling hour after hour in their little boat.

*2nd Prelude.*—Pray for grace to labour constantly and fervently, however fruitless your toil may seem.

*1st Point.*—Consider the example of the apostles while waiting to receive the promised Comforter. As yet they were not fitted for their divine mission as fishers of souls; so in all humility and peace they continue in their lawful calling. What a lesson to our impetuosity and false zeal! Had we received a commission like theirs, we should have supposed every moment lost which delayed its execution. How different to the calm and often slow designs of Providence! There is no time in eternity; and it is always eternity to God and the angels. There is no haste in eternity, for the will of God is always being accomplished. Let us learn to occupy ourselves calmly and peacefully in the most ordinary duties and employments. There are no great or little duties in eternity, for all are acts of love; and the intensity of the love with which each is performed, is the measure of its greatness. A saint, by love and pure intention, might perform a greater act, by lifting a straw from the ground, than we could do by writing a treatise on spiritual subjects.

*2nd Point.*—Consider the patience of the apostles. We are so eager to finish our employment, so dissatisfied if we do not succeed immediately; but they fish all night, and catch nothing, and yet we do not hear that they broke their nets by impatience, or threw them away in despair. If they had done either of these things, they would have had no nets to draw in the miraculous draught. What an instruction for us! Do we not too often measure our profit by our success, forgetting that if we spend the whole night fishing, in obedience to God's command, and find that in the morning we have nothing, we are, nevertheless, just as rich as if we had brought shoals to land? Let us remember also that if we break or spoil the nets of our intention, we may lose the great draught which is still in store for us.

*3rd Point.*—Consider how we may glorify the risen Heart of Jesus showing Himself at the Sea of Tiberias. Let us endeavour to do so by following the example of the disciples: first, by persevering steadily in the path of duty, whatever trials or discouragements we may meet; and secondly, by not giving way to dejection, when our best efforts end in failure. Jesus is standing on the

shore watching us.    Perhaps He is only prolonging the trial, to give us a richer reward.    However
it may be, it is His will, and that is enough for
the soul who loves her risen Lord.    If Peter says, "I
go a-fishing"—that is, if our superiors, in God's providence, appoint or even suggest any duty for us—let
us say, promptly and cheerfully, "We also come with
thee;" and let us neither grieve our sweet Lord,
or weary our superiors, by complaints of failure or
disappointment.    There are no failures when we
do God's will, and we are only disappointed because our motives are imperfect.

*Aspiration.*—Risen Heart of my Jesus, teach me
fervent love and trust.

*Form your resolution, &c.    Examen.*

---

## THIRD WEDNESDAY AFTER EASTER.

### THE RISEN HEART OF JESUS STANDING ON THE SHORE.

"But when the morning was come, Jesus stood on the
shore: yet the disciples knew not that it was Jesus."
(S. John, xxi. 4.)

*1st Prelude.*—Represent to yourself the Sea of
Tiberias, the little boat sailing peacefully thereon,
and coming nearer and nearer to the shore, and
your risen Lord standing on that shore waiting for
its arrival.

*2nd Prelude.*—Pray that you may see Jesus waiting for you on the eternal shore, when the journey of life is over.

*1st Point.*—When morning was come, Jesus stood on the shore. He had watched the disciples all that night, though they knew it not. He had seen their faithful but fruitless toil, and now He is prepared to reward it richly. How calm and beautiful that morning is! The sun has not yet risen, but the hills which surround the lake are already glowing with its coming light, and the waters purpled with the reflection of its coming beauty. Another morning will come, O Christian soul. The night of life will have passed away, like a dark cloud, over the hills of eternity, and the brightness and light of that eternity will be already reflected on the troubled waters of life; and Jesus will stand on the shore—the golden shore—waiting for you; waiting to reward your long and patient toil, your hours of suffering, your years of care; waiting to invite you to the nuptial feast which He has Himself prepared. Who that hopes to see Jesus "waiting on the shore" in the eternal morning, would grieve or concern themselves for what passes during the brief night of time?

*2nd Point.*—Jesus stood on the shore. How beautiful He looks! How lovingly He adapts Himself to every circumstance in the life of His beloved ones! In the garden, He appears as the gardener; on the roadside, He appears as a traveller; and now He stands so patiently on the shores of the lake, that the disciples know not that it is Jesus, and perhaps think it is some poor fisherman, waiting for his companions.  Jesus is fishing for their souls, and they know it not.  Alas! how often our dear Lord is fishing for our souls also, and we do not know Him!  He is watching us during the night; during the night of sin we can catch nothing ; during the night of imperfection we seem to make but little progress; but Jesus is on the shore watching us, praying for us, helping us, strengthening us ; and if we only toil on faithfully and fervently until morning, we shall surely obtain our reward.

*3rd Point.*—Consider how we may glorify the risen Heart of Jesus standing on the shore.  Surely it will be by a constant remembrance of His presence, by a firm faith that He is always watching us, always interested 'in us, always seeking to do us good.  The night is never so long but the morning cometh ; and if Jesus also comes with the morning, how blessed will that morning be !  Let us often think of it, long for it, and desire it ; and when wearied by sin and sorrow, dejected by trials and crosses, fainting under heavy burdens long borne, and fruitless toil long endured, let us think of Jesus waiting for us on the eternal shore, and love on, and suffer on, until the morning dawns.

*Aspiration.*—Risen Heart of my Jesus, O come for me also in the morning.

*Form your resolution, &c.    Examen.*

## THIRD THURSDAY AFTER EASTER.

### THE RISEN HEART OF JESUS COMMANDING HIS DISCIPLES TO CAST THE NET.

" He saith to them : Cast the net on the right side of the ship, and you shall find." (S. John, xxi. 6.)

*1st Prelude.—The same as the last meditation.*

*2nd Prelude.*—Pray for grace promptly to obey all divine inspirations and commands.

*1st Point.*—Consider the words of Jesus : " Cast the net." We also must · cast nets for our risen Lord : nets of prayer—oh, how rich a treasure we may receive thereby!—and nets of love ; for it will suggest a thousand devices and skilful plans · for catching souls; and those who are caught in the net of love, remain more faithful and are likely to prove more fervent than others. Shall we not commence casting these nets for Jesus to-day? If we are only in earnest, we shall find many opportunities. One net is always at hand, the net of prayer. Do we cast it into the ocean of the divine Heart as frequently and as fervently as we ought ? That ocean contains boundless treasures, but we must use this net to draw them forth. Sinners are perishing ; let us cast the net of prayer into the Heart of Jesus, and we may save thousands. The

N

Church is tried, and its holy Vicar is bowed to the earth with care and grief; let us cast a net for him also, and obtain him help and strength. The young are thrown into scenes of danger and temptation, the faith of many is endangered; let us cast a net for them also. We see a sister, a friend, in trial of body or mind, dejected, suffering; let us cast a net for her in the same Heart of love. We see a soul advancing rapidly in perfection, doing great things for God, edifying others by patience in suffering or in labour; let us cast special nets for such, that they may give God yet greater glory. In every place, in all circumstances, every moment of the day, and in our wakeful hours at night, we may cast these mystic nets in the divine Heart, with the certain assurance that we *shall* find.

*2nd Point.*—Consider where Jesus commanded the net to be cast. "Cast the net," He says, "on the right side of the ship, and ye shall find." If we do not cast on the right side, we shall not find. Oh, let us cast on the side of Jesus, not on the side of self; on the side of grace and loving intention, not on the side of our own interest. The net will never break, however numerous the fishes we bring to land, if our intention has been pure. And it is not difficult to have a pure intention. God only asks us to prefer His interests to our own; and, after all, His interests are ours. If we always pray with a sincere desire that God's will may be done, even though it may be His will to give a direct refusal to what we ask for, we shall gain by our asking and our intention is evidently pure.

*3rd Point.*—Consider how we may glorify the risen Heart of Jesus commanding His disciples to cast the net. We may do so by obeying this command ; and we can cast these nets in the midst of the most distracting and anxious occupations, on the bed of sickness, alone, and in company with others, by short and fervent ejaculations for some special intention. Jesus is watching us on the shore ; our little bark will soon land beside Him ; then the net will be drawn to shore, and the fishes counted. What joy will be ours if we find here, the soul of some unhappy murderer, of whose crime thousands talked, but for whom few or none had prayed, and though we knew it not on earth, our supplications have obtained for him the grace of true contrition ; here, the souls of the faithful departed, whose entrance into glory we have hastened ; here, the souls who were preserved from many mortal sins by our instructions or prayers ; and here the saintly, far more saintly than we could ever hope to be, who have obtained through us new graces and brighter crowns. Sweet Jesus, we are coming to Thee every day and hour nearer and nearer. Oh, may we bring great nets full of treasures, to lay at Thy blessed feet !

*Aspiration.*—Heart of my risen Love, teach me to love Thee truly.

*Form your resolution, &c. Examen.*

## THIRD FRIDAY AFTER EASTER.

### THE RISEN HEART OF JESUS RECOGNIZED BY THE DISCIPLE OF LOVE.

"That disciple whom Jesus loved said to Peter: It is the Lord." (S. John, xxi. 7.)

*1st Prelude.*—Represent the disciples hauling in the net heavy with the fish taken at the command of Jesus, and the disciple of love recognizing first the God of love.

*2nd Prelude.*—Pray for such fervent love as will enable you always to recognize Jesus.

*1st Point.*—The disciple of love first recognizes the God of love. Oh, how quick, how keen, are the instincts of love! It sees at a glance what others discern but slowly; it hears the Master's voice, however distant from the object of its desire; it knows the Master Himself in the gloom of morning and in the shades of evening, when others only see a stranger on the shore. Do we thus promptly discern Jesus? If we do not, may we not fear it is because our vision is dimmed and clouded by sin, and is not yet perfectly enlightened by love? The saints always see Jesus in all things, because they are so full of love. Oh, let us pray for love, for burning love, that we also may discern Jesus!

How different life would be were our vision thus purified !

*2nd Point.*—Consider the different conduct of the disciples of love and faith. The disciple of love exclaims, "It is the Lord." He is wrapt in a trance of ecstatic joy. "It is the Lord;" his joy is full; he sees Him, he hears Him, he feeds his soul upon that vision of bliss; and thus he remains in the boat, absorbed in his Beloved, without power to move or speak save only as that Beloved wills him to do. Love only desires the contemplation of the object of its love. It is perfect; it seeks but one. It is calm, strong, silent; for it lives in the eternal strength, in the eternal peace. But faith, beautiful also in its perfection—faith casts itself into the sea. It must come to Jesus; it must see Him, touch Him, speak to Him. And so in God's Church: love remains in the boat of the cloister of contemplation, and wears its life away in desires of Him who stands waiting for it on the eternal shore; and faith springs out upon the ocean, battling with the waves, and doing great, noble, and heroic deeds for its Lord; bringing to His feet many a soul who would have perished in the same waves, had it not ventured in to their rescue. Oh, happy faith ! Oh, happy love ! One may reach the shore in the boat, and the other in the waves, but both shall surely find themselves safe in the arms of Jesus, and together rejoice with Him over the souls won by prayer or work.

*3rd Point.*—Consider how we may glorify the

risen Heart of Jesus recognized by the disciple of
love. Let it be by going faithfully to Him, either
in the boat or on the waves. All we desire is to
glorify His risen Heart, and this we can best
accomplish by devoting ourselves with our whole
soul to our calling in life. It matters not to us
whether it be active or contemplative ; let us leave
the choice to the Master ; we only want to do His
will, not our own. Once we are sure of His will,
let us continue steadily in our vocation. John remained in the ship, and Peter in the sea, until they
both came to land, and the "other disciples"
dragged the net with fishes ; for there are souls
who live between the active and the contemplative life, who do glorious work for God and the
Church, who drag the net with fishes, praying and
working at the same time, now half in the water
and now half in the boat, but always making for the
shore ; bringing in the fish which Peter has caught,
and helping him to bear the burden of the care
which Jesus has laid on him.

*Aspiration.*—Risen Heart of my Jesus, teach me
to love my vocation, and to fulfil it faithfully.

*Form your resolution, &c.    Examen.*

## THIRD SATURDAY AFTER EASTER.

### THE RISEN HEART OF JESUS PROVIDING A FEAST FOR HIS DISCIPLES.

"Jesus saith to them : Come and dine." (S. John, xxi. 12.)

*1st Prelude.*—Represent to yourself Jesus lovingly preparing a feast for His disciples.

*2nd Prelude.*—Pray that you may be worthy to be invited to the eternal feast.

*1st Point.*—Consider the invitation of Jesus : "Come and dine." If we labour for Jesus, He will prepare a feast for us. Does He not offer us a feast every day, if we would only partake of it— the feast of His own blessed Body and Blood? He intends this to be our refreshment after every labour, our strength for every undertaking. If we have toiled all night, and are weary, oh, let us "come and dine" in the morning ! What should we think of any of the disciples who had refused the feast which Jesus had prepared for them?—had preferred the fish which they could procure themselves, to the fish which Jesus had ready laid on the coals? Yet do we not often act thus, preferring the vile and miserable pleasures of our senses to the Feast which Jesus offers us.

*2nd Point.*—One day Jesus will also say to us,

"Come and dine." Already He is engaged in preparing the feast: "To him that overcometh, I will give the hidden manna." (Apoc. ii. 17.) We are invited to the feast; it is prepared for us. One thing only is necessary on our part; we must "overcome." We must either remain faithfully in the boat, or battle with the waves that often threaten to overwhelm it. We must "overcome" all that would render us unfit to take our places at that feast. O my God, what a feast will it be! If our risen Lord took such pains to prepare a feast for His disciples after one night's toil; if He provided not only food but fire, not only necessaries but even comforts, what will He not prepare, what has He not prepared, for the eternal feast! Here, our rejoicings are mostly tinged with sadness, because all we love are not present; there, none whom we love will be absent, because we shall only love those who love Jesus. Already the trees are planted by the waters of life, on whose fruits we shall feed. What matter the privations of time, when eternity shall bring us such repasts!

*3rd Point.*—Consider how we may console the risen Heart of Jesus inviting His disciples to dine. Let it be by listening more attentively to His invitations to approach the Sacrament of His love, and· by preparing more fervently and faithfully for the eternal feast. We must labour to enter into His rest; we must prepare our garments to sit at His feast. Oh, how little all earth's cares and trials will seem, when we are seated at the eternal banquet! Angels will minister to us, and the Lord of angels will serve us : "Come and dine." O sweet Jesus, we are coming, we long to come ; we are nearing the shore every hour, and we can almost see Thee waiting for us upon the beach, "standing" on the shore; for Thou wilt not " sit down" at the right hand of the Father, until the last soul has landed safely.

*Aspiration.*—Risen Heart of my Jesus, feed me on Thyself in time, and with Thyself in eternity.

*Form your resolution, &c. Examen.*

---

## THIRD SUNDAY AFTER EASTER.

### FEAST OF THE PATRONAGE OF S. JOSEPH.

#### THE RISEN HEART OF JESUS RELEASING S. JOSEPH FROM LIMBO.

" You now indeed have sorrow, but I will see you again, and your heart shall rejoice ; and your joy no man shall take from you." (S. John, xvi. 22.)

*1st Prelude.*—Represent to yourself the descent of Jesus into limbo, and the joy with which S. Joseph beheld our Lord.

*2nd Prelude.*—Pray that your sorrows may be turned into joy, like those of the great patriarch.

*1st Point.*—The resurrection was peculiarly S. Joseph's joy. His life on earth had been one constant sorrow ; and though he was spared the deep

anguish of witnessing the passion, we may not
doubt that one so dear to God had his share in
it in some other way. All his connexion with
Jesus seemed to bring him sorrow. Even his
joy at the divine birth must have been oversha-
dowed by his fears and anxieties ; and he had not
the same personal connexion with Jesus as Mary.
He was only the Child's reputed father ; Mary was
His real mother. Thus, Joseph had not the special
joy of paternity; for though Jesus called him father,
it was not as He called Mary mother. But Joseph
had all a father's anxious cares. Perhaps we
scarcely estimate the burden which must have
fallen on that great saint ; and what so difficult to
bear, what so trying, as constant, anxious care!
When we remember that the care of S. Joseph
must have been in some measure proportionate to
the cause of that care, we may form a better idea of
his trials.

*2nd Point.*—Consider the joy of S. Joseph in
the resurrection. It was the completion and crown
of the joy which commenced the moment he beheld
Jesus in limbo. On earth he indeed had sorrow,
but Jesus had said : " I will see you again, and your
heart shall rejoice ; and your joy no man shall take
from you." "I will see you again." Joseph saw
Jesus for the last time as he lay in the agonies of
death ; he sees Him now in all His heavenly glory.
Now his joy is secure ; no man can take it from him.
When he was on earth, fear of his fellow-men was
one of the heaviest portions in his burden of care—

fear of Herod, fear of Archelaus. But no Herod or Archelaus can trouble him now. His joy no man shall take from him ; it is an eternal joy ; it is a boundless joy.

*3rd Point.*—Consider how we may glorify the risen Heart of Jesus delivering S. Joseph from limbo. Let us offer fervent thanksgiving for the graces bestowed on this great saint, and place ourselves with entire confidence and great devotion under his protection. We can glorify Jesus by honouring his reputed father, by promoting devotion to him, by speaking of his glories ; and we can also obtain great graces thereby for our own souls. Jesus rewards His servants in proportion to the sufferings they have endured for His love : how abundant, then, must be the reward of S. Joseph ! how great the power of one so near to God ! Joseph protected Jesus when on earth ; and Jesus will now protect the clients of Joseph in heaven, where, according to a pious tradition, our risen Lord made His reputed father a sharer in His resurrection and glory, by raising his body from the tomb after He had risen Himself.

*Aspiration.*—Heart of Jesus, I adore Thee ;
Heart of Mary, I implore thee ;
Heart of Joseph, kind and just :
In these three Hearts I put my trust.
*Form your resolution, &c. Examen.*

# FOURTH MONDAY AFTER EASTER.

## THE RISEN HEART OF JESUS GRANTING US THE GRACE OF BAPTISM BY THE RESURRECTION.

"Christ also died once for our sins, . . . . being put to death indeed in the flesh, but enlivened in the spirit. In which also coming He preached to those spirits that were in prison: which had been some time incredulous, when they waited for the patience of God in the days of Noe, when the ark was a building: wherein a few, that is, eight souls, were saved by water. Whereunto baptism being of the like form, now saveth you also, . . . . by the resurrection of Jesus Christ." (1 Pet. iii. 18-21.)

*1st Prelude.*—Represent the ark, and the difficulty with which a few souls were saved therein.

*2nd Prelude.*—Pray for grace to be faithful to your baptismal privileges.

*1st Point.*—Consider the reasons for which baptism is compared to Noe's ark : 1. Because it saves from the universal deluge of sin ; 2. Because all who enter therein are in a place of safety; 3. Because all who enter are not of necessity saved. Have we ever thanked our risen Lord sufficiently for the grace of baptism ? Have we compared our condition, humbly and thankfully, with the condition of those who are unbaptized ? Have we ever imagined what it would be never to see the face of God, even if we were saved ? There are two stupendous graces for which we are seldom sufficiently thankful, just because they seem to come to us as a matter of course in the order of Providence in our regard—we forget that Providence has not vouchsafed them to millions; and these graces are baptism, and receiving the Body of Christ. Have we ever thought or pictured to ourselves what a soul must feel which has been saved, and yet has never received Jesus sacramentally? If a soul could die, surely when it knows what it has lost by not having received Jesus sacramentally, its sorrow would be sufficient to deprive it of life. May not the knowledge of what has been lost, and, alas! in many cases, wilfully, be a purgatory of the keenest anguish?

*2nd Point.*—The efficacy of baptism is one of the fruits of the resurrection of Jesus. The apostle says: " Baptism now saveth you also (that is, as water saved the souls in Noe's ark), by the resurrection of Jesus Christ." Baptism is a new life. It imparts new powers to the soul; it gives it a new existence. It raises the soul from death, even as resurrection raises the body. Hence the special resemblance of baptism to the resurrection. Baptism requires that we should live a risen life, and Jesus has obtained the grace to enable us to do so by His resurrection. Baptism is a grace of probation, because we may fall and perish eternally, even after we have been admitted into the ark; but the resurrection is a grace of final recompense, so that after the resurrection we can sin no more.

*3rd Point.*—Consider how we may glorify the

risen Heart of Jesus for His love in instituting
the sacrament of baptism. Surely we may do so
best, first, by fervent thanksgivings for this inestimable favour, and by doing all in our power
to obtain this grace for those who might otherwise
be deprived of it; and secondly, by endeavouring
to walk worthy of our vocation. We know how
of old the newly-baptized wore white garments at
Eastertide, as an outward symbol of their inward
purity. Oh, let us take care that our garments
are very pure and white also, and free from every
stain of sin ! Our risen Lord makes many visits
during the great forty days. Oh, let Him find us
in all our baptismal purity ; or if there are spots
upon our robe, let us wash them out carefully in
tears of love.

*Aspiration.*—Risen Heart of my Jesus, I thank
Thee for the grace of my baptism.

*Form your resolution, &c. Examen.*

## FOURTH TUESDAY AFTER EASTER.

### THE RISEN HEART OF JESUS TEACHING US HOW TO DIE TO SIN.

"That we being dead to sins, should live to justice."
(1 Pet. ii. 24.)

*1st Prelude.*—Represent the glorious form of your risen Lord instructing you in these words.

*2nd Prelude.*—Pray for grace to die to sin, and to live to justice.

*1st Point.*—Consider what it is to be dead to anything. The expression is used to convey the idea of the most perfect indifference, of acting as if that person or thing no longer existed; and this is the state in which we ought to be in regard to sin, by virtue of our divine Lord's resurrection. We have entered on a new life, and the pleasures, cares, and occupations of our former life should no longer affect us. We would not commit sin if we did not take pleasure in it, and we would not take pleasure in it if we were dead to it. We sin because we prefer or find more pleasure in doing something which God wishes us not to do, than in doing what He wishes. Perhaps it is one of the saddest thoughts about sin, that it shows our preference, more or less deliberate, for something which God does not like— nay, even for something which is utterly abhorrent to Him, and an outrage on His majesty. What should we think of the love of a friend who constantly preferred his own inclination to ours, even at the expense of our feelings and our honour? Let us stand under the cross for a moment, even at Eastertide, and see what our preference for sin has cost Jesus. How we should abhor the place, the persons, the circumstances in any ways connected with the murder of a friend; and who ever had a friend like Jesus? Even now, in all His resurrection glory, He bears the marks and tokens of what this preference of ours has cost Him; and all He asks is that we will prefer it no longer. Jesus has died for us, and He only asks us not to prefer that which has caused His death, and which will certainly cause our death also, if we persevere in our wilful choice.

*2nd Point.*—We must do more than die to sin, we must live to justice. Consider the difference between the activity of life and the torpor of death. We must not only fly from sin and abhor it, we must also fly to Jesus, cling to Him, love Him, serve Him with the whole ardour of our souls. See what it is to live to justice. How quick and sensitive are the feelings of the living body; how active its movements, how firm its step, how bright its eye, how noble its bearing! Are we thus quick, and firm, and active in our life of justice? Is our life vigorous? If it is, the effects of its vigour will soon manifest themselves. We shall cling to that life with such tenacity, as to dread all that might destroy or weaken it. We shall produce flowers and fruit, for vitality manifests itself thus.

*3rd Point.*—Consider how we may glorify the risen Heart of Jesus teaching us how to die to sin. Until we receive the incorruptible body of the resurrection, there will always be some insidious disease hovering about us, like a beast of prey, watching for the moment when it can best weaken and destroy our life. Now we can glorify Jesus immensely by our watchfulness against this enemy; and this very watchfulness, moreover, is absolutely necessary for our safety. How careful we are, if predisposed to any bodily infirmity, to avoid what might increase or bring on us the danger we dread. Are we as careful of the special infirmity of our spiritual life? And even as what would prove hurtful to one constitution may be beneficial to another, and they who are anxious for the preservation of their lives consult their physicians, and act by his advice, without troubling themselves as to what others do; so in the spiritual life we should consult our physicians, our spiritual guides and superiors. Happy for us if we follow their directions with half the care and docility with which the bodily physician is obeyed.

*Aspiration.*—Risen Heart of my Jesus, may I live for Thy love alone.

*Form your resolution, &c. Examen.*

## FOURTH WEDNESDAY AFTER EASTER.

### THE RISEN HEART OF JESUS TEACHING US TO BE DOERS OF THE WORD.

"But be ye doers of the word, and not hearers only, deceiving your own selves." (S. James, i. 22.)

*1st Prelude.*—Represent your divine Lord in all His resurrection glory, and listen to His instructions.

*2nd Prelude.*—Pray for grace to be a faithful doer of the word.

*1st Point.*—Our risen Lord has said, " Not every one that saith to Me, Lord, Lord, shall enter into the kingdom of heaven ; but he that doeth the will of My Father who is in heaven, he shall enter into the kingdom of heaven." (Matt. vii. 21.)   Nay, He even tells us that many will say they have prophesied in His name, and in His name cast out devils, and done many wonderful miracles ; but even to these He will say, " Depart from Me, I never knew you."   Oh, words of fear—words to be meditated on constantly, prayerfully, and with many tears ! What if He should say to us also, "I never knew you," even though we had prophesied in His name, discoursed wisely of spiritual things, talked much about sanctity, perhaps instructed many, perhaps even obtained a reputation of holiness from those who only knew us exteriorly, for we can seldom deceive those with whom we live ! And yet we might do all this, and more, and Jesus might say at the last great day, "I never knew you."

*2nd Point.*—"Be ye doers of the word." If we are doers, we shall have little time to be talkers; and the doers of the word will be indeed accepted by our Lord at the awful judgment-seat. If we are doers, we shall not take pleasure in long and unnecessary conversations, even about spiritual things. Alas ! are there not even religious who would prefer spending hours conversing with the poor, to laborious work for them or their sisters ? Are there not persons who employ much time in reading religious works, who can scarcely perform an act of charity to those with whom they live, if it costs them the smallest personal inconvenience ? It is so easy to talk, so easy to read, so easy to write ; but when we come to *do*, then self-love cries out ; for we can seldom be faithful doers of the word, even in the most ordinary circumstances of life, without self-sacrifice.

*3rd Point.*—Consider how we may glorify the risen Heart of Jesus teaching us to be doers of the word. Surely we may do so best by faithfully obeying this loving precept. There can seldom be a mistake about actions. We may talk very piously about obedience, and yet seek our own will in everything ; we may profess great devotion to our blessed Lady, and yet grieve her every day. Our actions alone can prove our sincerity. If we are willing to relinquish an employment, in which we fancy we are doing great things for God, at the voice of obedience, or even at the implied wish of our superior, then we are doers of the word. We may hope that we speak only for God, when we are equally willing to be silent for Him. But if we are discontented at change of place or employment, if we begin to criticise the motives of our superiors in appointing us to or withdrawing us from certain duties, we may be assured we are only hearers of the word, however well instructed we may be in it.

*Aspiration.*—My risen Lord, make me a faithful doer of Thy will.

*Form your resolution, &c. Examen.*

---

## FOURTH THURSDAY AFTER EASTER.

### THE RISEN HEART OF JESUS TEACHING US HOW TO AVOID SELF-DECEIT.

" Deceiving your own selves." (S. James, i. 22.)

1*st Prelude.*—Behold your risen Lord with a countenance full of love, teaching you all that is necessary for your salvation.

2*nd Prelude.*—Pray most fervently that you may know yourself even as He knows you.

1*st Point.*—Consider the result of being hearers of the word, and not doers : " We deceive our own selves." How we dread being deceived by others! What a horror we have of those who deceive us! How mean and contemptible we think them! Alas! may we not need to exercise a little of this dread and a little of this contempt, towards ourselves? There is no deceit can do us so much harm as self-deceit. Sooner or later we may find out if others deceive us; but when we deceive ourselves, self-love holds on the bandage of deceit so tightly, that it is indeed difficult to remove it. Besides, it is always painful to us to find out we have been deceived by any one; it touches our pride too nearly; and when we are the culprit ourselves, pride is even more keenly roused. Hence a person long under the influence of self-deceit, has a thousand excuses, a thousand good reasons for all they do or omit. Woe to the superior or the friend who attempts to lift the veil! They are prejudiced against them, or they are not sufficiently spiritual, or they are indifferent to their feelings, or they cannot see things in a "right light," or "some one" has misrepresented their actions. Anything or everything will be urged by the poor self-deceived soul, as a plea for its most manifest imperfections. Oh, if there is one prayer that we should utter, from the depth of our souls, far more fervently than another, it is this: "O my God, let me not be deceived or a deceiver."

*2nd Point.*—Perhaps one of the greatest blessings of the religious life, is the protection it affords a person *against themselves.* In the world we may deceive others as well as ourselves; in religion we cannot do so, because God imparts special graces and lights to those whom He appoints to guide us. The only fear, then, for a religious, is that she may refuse to submit to the opinion of her guides as regards her spiritual state; and if she does not do this openly, she may fail in the absolute submission of her judgment and conduct, which is necessary for perfection. Self-deceit is as busy in the cloister as in the palace; but if a soul is really desirous of perfection, however imperfect, she has greater security in religion. The only safety for all earnest souls, is a firm conviction that her superior *must* be right; not because she loves her, or because she is thought wise or gifted, but because she is the one person appointed by God to teach her how to do His will, how to be a *doer* of the word.

*3rd Point.*—Consider how we may glorify the risen Heart of Jesus teaching us how to avoid self-deceit. Surely we can do so most effectually by a firm determination not to be guided by our judgment, or to trust ourselves in anything. Even the most fervent and perfect souls are not free from danger. There are degrees in self-deceit as in every spiritual disease; and this disease is so peculiarly dangerous, that we should check even the faintest symptoms of it. Even when souls are advanced in perfection, temptations against obedience may be sent as a special trial from God. Happy are they who obey through all, even unto death!

*Aspiration.*—Heart of Jesus, obedient unto death, grant me the grace of true obedience. .

*Form your resolution, &c. Examen.*

---

## FOURTH FRIDAY AFTER EASTER.

### THE RISEN HEART OF JESUS TEACHING US BY A SIMILITUDE.

"For if a man be a hearer of the word and not a doer: he shall be compared to a man beholding his own countenance in a glass. For he beheld himself, and went his way, and presently forgot what manner of man he was." (S. James, i. 23, 24.)

*1st Prelude.*—Behold Jesus standing and teaching you by this similitude, even as He taught His disciples by similitudes.

*2nd Prelude.*—Pray for grace to learn all that Jesus purposes to teach you in this meditation.

*1st Point.*—Consider the peculiar appropriateness of this similitude. When we hear or read spiritual instructions, the object of those instructions is to enable us to see ourselves, to teach us "what manner of man" we are. We all know, by experience, how completely we forget our exterior appearance the moment we leave the mirror in which we have seen it reflected. We can recall the countenance and personal appearance of others when they are absent from us, with the greatest facility; we often do so

almost unconsciously, when we think of those we
love; but no possible effort of memory can enable us
to recall our own features, except in the vaguest manner.  The same, unhappily, occurs too often when
we have seen ourselves spiritually.  We listen with
the greatest pleasure and satisfaction to a sermon,
to the instructions of a retreat, we read spiritual
books with avidity ; but, in half an hour after, we
prove that we have forgotten them practically, by
committing the very faults or imperfections we have
just condemned.  We behold our spiritual countenance, and then go our way, and straightway forget
what we have just seen.  Oh, well may the apostle
say, that he who is a doer of the word, and not
a forgetful hearer, shall be blessed in his deed !

*2nd Point.*—There are many who readily hear
the word, but, alas ! how few are as earnest in doing
it !  We think, because we like what we hear, because we are fond of listening to instructions, and
of reading pious books, that we are very devout
and very perfect.  Alas ! have we not unhappily
seen those who thus deceived themselves, who
talked well and listened well, who patronized piety,
but seldom practised it humbly, faithfully, and in a
spirit of self-sacrifice ?  They see themselves for a
brief moment in the glass of instruction, but they
soon forget practically what they beheld therein.

*3rd Point.*—Let us consider how we may glorify
the risen Heart of Jesus teaching us by this similitude.  Surely it will be by careful self-examination
as to how we hear the word.  Do we receive it

with joy for a time? Are we only interested or entertained by what we hear at the moment, and then do we forget it afterwards? Were we occupied in thinking how well an instruction suits others, and how much good it ought to do them, or in saying humbly, God be merciful to me a sinner, and forgive me all my failures and omissions in this matter? Do we try to take away a steady practical resolution from our meditations and retreats? One purpose of fulfilling a duty more perfectly, or of subduing an evil propensity constantly, is worth all we can say and think of what we hear.

*Aspiration.*—Risen Heart of my Jesus, teach me to be a faithful doer of Thy word.

*Form your resolution, &c. Examen.*

## FOURTH SATURDAY AFTER EASTER.

### THE RISEN HEART OF JESUS TEACHING US TRUE RELIGION.

" Religion clean and undefiled before God and the Father, is this: to visit the fatherless and widows in their tribulation : and to keep oneself unspotted from this world." (S. James, i. 27.)

*1st Prelude.*—Represent your risen Lord as it were replying to your question when you ask Him in what true religion consists.

*2nd Prelude.*—Pray for grace to understand and to practise what He teaches.

*1st Point.*—Have we not often longed to know in a few words what would make us saints—how our lives might become holy and acceptable to God? What can be plainer and more simple than the instruction of the apostle? It consists of two easy precepts—charity towards others, and purity in ourselves: "Religion clean and undefiled." Let us consider all that is contained in these simple words. There are no by-ends, no double motives in this religion. It is a very plain road, and a very straight one. Perhaps its difficulty is its simplicity. But to the loving little ones, who live only for their risen Lord, it is easy and attractive. They have no self-seeking in their charities. They prefer serving the "fatherless and the widows;" they have a holy predilection for the most desolate, the most neglected, the most repulsive; and in all this they only seek God; it is "before God and the Father" they work and walk. The fatherless and the widows may be forgotten by others, but Jesus never forgets them; the fatherless and widows may be overlooked by others, but Jesus never overlooks them. Oh, how we should love to devote ourselves to such, when an inspired apostle has specially mentioned charity to them as the proof and test of our religion being "clean and undefiled"!

*2nd Point.*—"And to keep ourselves unspotted from the world." "Unspotted." Yes, we must try to go to God without even a spot on our garments; and it is indeed difficult to walk through the muddy and defiled paths of earth without contracting many stains. Alas! would to God we only spotted ourselves; would to God there were not sometimes dark and deep defilements on those robes, which it has cost Jesus so much to purify for us. What, then, shall we do, if this spotless purity is indeed required from us, which is so difficult to obtain? Blessed be God, we are not left without a remedy. The fresh Fountain in which our garments were first purified, is still open. We have only to "wash ourselves and be clean;" and even if our "sins be as scarlet, they shall be made as white as snow; and if they be red as crimson, they shall be white as wool." (Is. i. 16-18.)

*3rd Point.*—Consider how we may glorify the risen Heart of Jesus teaching us true religion. Let us endeavour to do so, first, by faithfully practising the injunction of showing charity to others, especially to the fatherless and widow—"Judge for the fatherless, defend the widow" (Is. i. 17); and secondly, by keeping ourselves "unspotted from the world." We must learn to despise the maxims and to avoid the practices of the world; we must live in direct opposition to its customs and doctrines. The master of the world is the enemy of our Master: how, then, can we love it and love Him? Above all, let us seek to keep our garments pure and white, by constantly washing them in the blood of the Lamb, by fervent acts of contrition for the least fault, and by never allowing a stain to become deeper, as it surely will, if not washed away immediately. Why should not our garments be always unspotted, when one little act of contrition, one little ejaculation of love, may purify our imperfection immediately?

*Aspiration.*—Wash me, and I shall be whiter than snow.

*Form your resolution, &c.    Examen.*

---

## FOURTH SUNDAY AFTER EASTER.

### THE RISEN HEART OF JESUS TEACHING US HOW TO RECEIVE THE WORD.

"With meekness receive the ingrafted word, which is able to save your souls." (S. James, i. 21.)

*1st Prelude.*—Imagine you see Jesus teaching you as He taught His disciples.

*2nd Prelude.*—Pray that you may profit by His instructions, especially by receiving them in the manner He directs.

*1st Point.*—Consider the manner in which our risen Lord desires us to receive His word—with meekness. How much is implied in this ! Meekness is more than gentleness, more than docility ; it includes both, and surpasses both. A meek person seems to the world a contemptible person, because meekness is more thoroughly opposed to the spirit of the world than any other virtue. The world can afford to admire patience, because it sometimes appears heroic ; it can endure humility, because it likes to see others consider themselves beneath it; but it simply despises meekness.   And yet meekness is the special virtue of the Heart of Jesus.   He distinguishes it also from humility; for He says, " Learn of Me, for I am meek and humble of heart, and you shall find rest to your souls." Yes, the meek truly shall have rest.   What can disturb or disquiet a meek soul ?   Not injuries, for it seems scarcely to perceive them ; not contempt, for it considers all contempt its due ; not humiliations, for it receives them with calm love ; not trials or afflictions, for it is too closely united to the Heart of Jesus to be moved by them ; not the loss of all things, for it possesses a land which will more than compensate for all.

*2nd Point.*—Let us consider, first, if we possess this meekness, and secondly, if we receive the word with meekness.   A soul that receives the word with meekness, receives it without questioning, and obeys it peacefully.   A meek soul hears only to obey.   It is enough for her to know that God or a superior has spoken ; she does not commence to question the how or the why, her meekness saves her from this.   A meek soul obeys in great peace. We lose our peace when we question, and argue, and hesitate, either in thought or word ; but the meek soul walks on calmly before God, she only wants to know the surest way to Him ; and when she is told that way, she has no by-ends or self-seekings to prevent her from walking in it.

*3rd Point.*—Consider how we may glorify the risen Heart of Jesus by this meekness. The ingrafting of the word may be a painful process. The term ingrafted implies that the word is not natural to us; therefore, we receive something against our nature when it is ingrafted into us. This must cause us pain; but the meek soul bears the pain without a struggle, and so suffers far less than the impatient soul, which complains, and, perhaps, resists. Let the world despise meekness as it will, what can it matter to the Christian soul, when meekness is the characteristic virtue of the Heart of Jesus? "Receive the ingrafted word, which is able to save your souls." Alas! how many fail to receive the word, because they have not meekness! They are too proud to hear meekly, and as they refuse to hear, they cannot know how to obey; and thus they may perish eternally, because they have not heard aright. Let us pray to our risen Lord for the grace of receiving the word with meekness, that we may indeed bring forth fruit thereby to eternal life.

*Aspiration.*—Risen Heart of Jesus, make my heart like unto Thy Heart.

*Form your resolution, &c. Examen.*

## FIFTH MONDAY AFTER EASTER.

### THE RISEN HEART OF JESUS TEACHING US TO FORGIVE ONE ANOTHER.

"Bearing with one another, and forgiving one another, if any have a complaint against another. Even as the Lord hath forgiven you." (Col. iii. 13.)

*1st Prelude as yesterday.*

*2nd Prelude.*—Pray that you may learn from this instruction how to forgive and bear with others.

*1st Point.*—Consider the two things which our risen Lord requires us to do : first, to bear with one another; and second, to forgive one another— two distinct precepts, and yet closely connected in practice. Our resurrection life requires that we should " put on, as the elect of God," those virtues and graces which are contrary to our natural dispositions ; and, perhaps, there are few virtues to which we are less inclined than that of " bearing with one another." Forgiving is often comparatively easy, but bearing implies the constant endurance of a burden, whether light or heavy ; and this constant endurance often forms the keenest part of the trial. There are very few persons who are not a trial to others in some way : one person tries us by their manner, another by their words, another by the

difference of their tastes or dispositions; but however we may be tried, the precept still continues
the same: "Bear with one another." One great help
towards bearing with others, is to consider that they
must also bear with us. How much long-suffering
and patience we expect towards ourselves, and how
little we are willing to manifest towards others!
If we could only realize that we give others quite
as much to bear with from us as they give
us to bear with from them, we should certainly be
more considerate, do more than bear.

*2nd Point.*—But we must also be willing to forgive: "Forgiving one another," says the apostle, "if
any have a complaint against another." We must
forgive not only when there are slight grounds of
injury, but even if we consider ourselves seriously
aggrieved: "If any have a complaint against
another." If we would only try to persuade ourselves that the little provocations and annoyances
we receive from others, and which make up the
sum of what we have to "bear with" from others,
were seldom, and they really are seldom, intentional,
we should find it much easier to obey this injunction; and does not our own experience teach us
how often we may give pain unintentionally?

*3rd Point.*—Consider how we may glorify the
risen Heart of Jesus giving us this lesson to practise. Surely it will be by forgiving and bearing as
He has forgiven and borne with us. No human
being can ever have been tried by another as He
has been tried by us. Where should we be now if

He did not "bear" with us every day and hour of our lives. Oh ! let us ask Him to give us grace to imitate His infinite charity. And what shall we say of His forgiveness? Can we ever forgive as He has forgiven, however freely, generously, and frequently we may pardon those who injure us? Surely, if we had no other motive for forgiving those who wrong us, than the one motive of pleasing Him who has forgiven us with such unbounded generosity, we would put no limits to our charity, and rejoice in opportunities of exercising it, could we find them without sin in others.

*Aspiration.*—Heart most forgiving, teach me to forgive.

*Form your resolution, &c. Examen.*

## FIFTH TUESDAY AFTER EASTER.

### THE RISEN HEART OF JESUS TEACHING US CHARITY.

"But above all these things have charity, which is the bond of perfection." (Col. iii. 14.)

*1st Prelude.*—Reflect how Jesus loved to teach His disciples charity, and consider how He practised it Himself in its utmost perfection.

*2nd Prelude.*—Pray for grace to follow His example in every circumstance of your daily life.

P

*1st Point.*—"But above all these things have charity." How noble a grace is charity! The apostle had already told the Colossians to "put on works of mercy, benignity, humility, modesty, and patience;" to bear and to forgive, even as Christ had forgiven; and now he places charity above them all, and says, "Above all these things have charity." Perhaps we shall never understand in this life what charity really is. All we can do is to pray frequently, fervently, and unweariedly for this great grace and gift of God, and by frequent acts of this virtue dispose ourselves for obtaining the fruit of our prayers. If we wish to be "cinctured with the golden cincture of love," we must practise acts of love. Repeated acts form a habit; and if we make repeated acts of the love of God, and perform constant acts of charity towards others, we cannot fail to "grow in love as dear children."

*2nd Point.*—Consider why the apostle calls charity the "bond of perfection." It is surely because it unites and supports all other virtues. It is the crown of virtues, the queen of graces. Our sanctity will be proportioned to our love, because our sanctity consists in the manner in which we perform the most trifling or the most important of our daily actions, and love is the measure of our reward and of our success. We cannot too often impress on ourselves this important truth: It is love which makes our actions acceptable to God; it is love which makes them little or great in His sight. What is done with much love is a great act, because it proceeds from a great motive; what is done with little love is a trifling act, however important it may appear to ourselves and to others. God wants our love : alas! that we should ever refuse to give it to Him.

*3rd Point.*—The fruit of this charity is peace—the "peace of Christ." Oh, what can we ask for or desire on earth more than peace! And our peace will be proportioned to our charity. If we love God perfectly, we shall not be disturbed or distressed by exterior things, and there will be peace in our hearts—the sweetest peace—the peace of a good conscience. If we love our neighbour perfectly, we shall have peace, for we will neither give offence or take it. Are we not "called in one body" to this very peace? Oh, let us seek it, let us pray for it, let us labour for it; and as surely as it is said, "he that seeketh findeth, and to him that knocketh it shall be opened," so surely shall we obtain this inestimable gift of peace in proportion to our earnestness in asking it.

*Aspiration.*—Heart most loving, love me into all love.

*Form your resolution, &c. Examen.*

## FIFTH WEDNESDAY AFTER EASTER.

### THE RISEN HEART OF JESUS TEACHING US TO BE THANKFUL.

"And be ye thankful." (Col. iii. 15.)

*1st Prelude.*—Represent to yourself the love and devotion with which your sweet Jesus gave thanks on many occasions to His eternal Father, especially when He thanked Him for making known His will to little ones, and hiding it from the wise and prudent.

*2nd Prelude.*—Pray fervently for the grace of a thankful spirit.

*1st Point.*—Consider the words : "And be ye thankful." It is an express precept, conveyed in as forcible terms as the injunction to bear, to forgive, to be holy, or to be patient. But have we ever considered thankfulness as a duty ? Do we ever examine our conscience, to see if we practise this duty ? or do we not rather pass it by, as an unimportant office, with perhaps no more general meaning than that we should return thanks formally after meals? But this is not "being thankful." The words of our meditation imply a state of thanksgiving : "And be ye thankful." A thankful heart is always making thanksgivings ;

they come spontaneously from it, and thankfulness
is generally proportioned to love; so that when we
see a person very much given to thanksgiving, we
may be tolerably sure their love is very deep.
How we complain if those on whom we confer
favours are not thankful to us! And we like them
to show their thankfulness in their words and
their manner; we are by no means content that
they should be very grateful without saying anything about it; but we like to hear and see the
expression of their gratitude. Alas! is not this
one of the many cases in which we exact from each
other what we ourselves are very unwilling to give
to God?

*2nd Point.*—But it is our own interest to be
thankful. God does not require our thanks,
neither does He require our love or our service;
nevertheless, He commands us to love Him, to
serve Him, and to thank Him. It ought scarcely
to have been necessary to say, "Be ye thankful."
Oh, surely souls for whom God has done so much,
ought to overflow with thanksgiving—thanksgiving
for creation, thanksgiving for redemption, thanksgiving for the grace of the sacraments, thanksgiving
for all the special mercies of our own lives, thanksgiving for our spiritual privileges, thanksgiving for
our vocation. The more we acknowledge our daily
mercies with gratitude, the more God will do for
us. He acts towards us in the order of grace, as
we act towards others in the order of providence.
We are naturally inclined to bestow most on those

who appear most grateful for what we give them. We like to see others grateful for little things ; we think it shows a good disposition, as it surely does; and, in the same manner, our heavenly Father likes to see us grateful for little things, since love often shows itself most kind and tender in trifling gifts.

*3rd Point.*—Consider how much we may glorify the risen Heart of Jesus by thankfulness. The one end of our lives ought to be to glorify His adorable Heart; and we can scarcely glorify Him more than by thanksgiving. If we are thankful souls, we shall be happy souls ; for when we thank God for anything; He returns our thanksgiving with a look of love, and thus makes our souls so full of joy, that we scarcely know how to bear it. Love makes the soul very sensitive of the least token of kindness from her Beloved ; thus a loving soul will constantly receive and acknowledge little favours and mercies of the most tender and thoughtful kind, which will be either withheld from, or unperceived by, a less loving soul. But there is a higher degree still in thankfulness, and a degree to which few attain. " I will bless the Lord at all times," says the royal prophet. Oh, how happy and how blessed are they who thank God, who are thankful, even in the deepest, darkest anguish of soul, as well as in the little daily vexations of life ; and if we truly love, could we be otherwise than thankful, however deep our affliction, since we know that all which is sent by Love is love, and is for our eternal good ! Ought we not to be as thankful for mercies that come in disguise, as for those which are more apparent and agreeable, but not more real?

*Aspiration.*—Glory be to the Father, and to the Son, and to the Holy Ghost.

*Form your resolution, &c. Examen.*

------

# FIFTH THURSDAY AFTER EASTER.

## THE RISEN HEART OF JESUS TEACHING US HOW TO PERFECT OUR ACTIONS.

" All whatsoever you do in word or in work, all things do ye in the name of the Lord Jesus." (Col. iii. 17.)

*1st Prelude.*—Imagine you behold our divine Lord Himself giving you this direction.

*2nd Prelude.*—Pray earnestly for grace to live thus entirely united to Him.

*1st Point.*—Consider the words of our meditation : " All whatsoever you do." There is nothing, then, however trifling, which we not only may, but even ought, to do for God. " All " is to be done for Him, " whatsoever " it may be. Our words and our works are both to be consecrated to Him, to be done in the name of the Lord Jesus—not in our name, taking the glory and credit to ourselves; not in our own name, consulting our own will and inclination; not in our own name, suiting our employments to our own ease and convenience; no, we are to do all, whatsoever it may be that occupies us, in the name of the Lord Jesus. Now, this implies, first, great humility, and secondly, great love. We like to do things in our own name, to get the credit of them. Alas! even in the most trifling matters, how jealous we are, and how our pride is touched, if another is supposed to have any share in, or obtains any praise for what we have done; and, miserable as it is to say it, must we not acknowledge that we even seek to rob God of this very honour which we cannot bear to be deprived of ourselves, and take the credit of what we could never have accomplished without His assistance?

*2nd Point.*—But it also requires great love to do "all things whatsoever we do" in the name of the Lord Jesus. The more we love, the more willing we shall be to sacrifice ourselves for the service of those we love; and unless we have a true spirit of self-sacrifice, we cannot do all in the name of the Lord Jesus. We must sacrifice our pride, we must sacrifice our convenience, we must sacrifice the intense desire we all have to do things our own way; and in addition to all this, we must do it "from the heart, as to the Lord, and not to man." Oh, how much is implied in these words, "do it from the heart"! There is no hesitation, no sloth, no indifference in heart-service; and for whom should we work from the heart if not for Him who has opened His sacred Heart so wide to receive and treasure all we do for His love?

*3rd Point.*—Consider how we may glorify the risen Heart of Jesus by fulfilling this precept. Let us reflect how few there are comparatively, even of those who bear the name of Christian, who thus constantly, faithfully, and unweariedly do all for the Lord Jesus. We know how a faithful servant is valued, who is always devoted to his master's service; and will not our Lord also value those who thus devote themselves to Him? Will He be less generous than an earthly master? nay, will He not far exceed all our hopes and desires by His munificence? Oh, let us again renew our purposes of loving and serving Him, of doing all whatsoever we do for Him and in union with Him. Let us sleep for Him, and in union with His sleep; let us rise for Him, and in union with His rising; let us take food for Him, in union with His condescension in taking food to support His human life; let us work for Him, and in union with His unwearied labours. So shall our lives be truly sanctified, and our risen Lord truly glorified.

*Aspiration.*—Risen Heart of my Jesus, I unite my life to Thine.

*Form your resolution, &c. Examen.*

⁂

## FIFTH FRIDAY AFTER EASTER.

### THE RISEN HEART OF JESUS TELLING US OF THE REWARD OF THE INHERITANCE.

"You shall receive of the Lord the reward of inheritance." (Col. iii. 24.)

*1st Prelude.*—Represent your risen Lord as the purchaser of a royal kingdom, conferring on you what it has cost Him so much to obtain.

*2nd Prelude.*—Pray for grace to live as heirs of such an inheritance should do.

*1st Point.*—Consider how carefully the heir of a great estate is educated ; what pains are taken to fit him for the important position he is to occupy ; how much consideration he receives from others, in consequence of his future prospects ; how he is taught to avoid all that might be beneath his dignity, to despise anything which is of less value or importance than his own inheritance. Consider, also, what we should think of the heir of a kingdom who spent his time in his father's stables, with his servants, instead of profiting by all the assistance given him to fit himself for his future rank. Alas ! and are we not also heirs to a kingdom far surpassing the most noble ancestral estate that earth can boast ? are we not heirs to the very wealth of

God? And how do we occupy our time, and in what manner are we fitting ourselves for our future position? Life is our time of nonage; it is the period during which we are educated for heaven—educated so as to fit us for our place near the royal throne of the Majesty of heaven. What if we should find some who enjoyed far less advantages than we do, and yet were sooner ready for the summons to their Father's court, and who adorned it more?

*2nd Point.*—Consider from whom it is we are to receive this reward. It is from the Lord; from Jesus, who has bought it, and who gives it. How did He buy it? Oh, we know but too well; for we see a large open wound in His hand, as He presents us with the title-deeds of our future property. Can we ever forget what this inheritance has cost Jesus? But do we value it as we ought to value what has cost such a price? If our love is cold and our faith weak, so that we cannot estimate thereby all that is prepared for us, at least let us try to estimate the value of the inheritance by its cost. Oh, how valuable that inheritance must be for which a God has given His Blood! But it is also spoken of as a reward—the reward of inheritance. What Jesus has purchased for us so dearly, He gives as a reward, as if we had done anything deserving of reward. A person who merits a reward, in a certain sense has a right to it; and Jesus wishes us to have a right to this reward, so He confers His merits on us also. Thus He gives us a double gift—the gift of the inheritance, and the merit to obtain it as a reward.

*3rd Point.*—Consider how we may glorify the risen Heart of Jesus bestowing this inheritance on us.  Surely it will be by showing how much we value it, and how deep our gratitude is for it ; and we can only show this by our daily earnest, faithful preparation for our heavenly home.  How many and what careful preparations we would make if we knew we were going to reside for a long time in a distant country !  how indifferent we should be to all temporary inconveniences or trials !  how anxious we should be to learn the language and the customs of our future home, to learn all we could of its inhabitants !  And yet, do we spend one quarter of the time or thought in preparing for an eternal home, which we would give freely and without hesitation to temporal arrangements ?  How it must grieve the heart of our risen Lord when He sees us so indifferent to His love, so unthankful for His amazing goodness !

*Aspiration.*—Heart of my Jesus, teach me how to prepare for the heavenly Jerusalem.

*Form your resolution, &c.    Examen.*

## FIFTH SATURDAY AFTER EASTER.

### THE RISEN HEART OF JESUS LOVING THE CHURCH, HIS BRIDE.

"For no man ever hated his own flesh : but nourisheth and cherisheth it, as Christ doth the Church." (Eph. v. 29.)

*1st Prelude.*—Represent your risen Lord to yourself as a spouse more beautiful and more loving than any of the children of men.

*2nd Prelude.*—Pray that you may be as faithful to your spouse Jesus as He has been to you.

*1st Point.*—How shall we ever return love for love to this God of love ! If anything could convince us how much He loves us, surely the words of our meditation should do so ; at least, let us learn from them how anxious our Lord is to prove that He loves us, and how difficult it is to make us believe it. Have we ever considered how little we really believe that Jesus loves us ? We believe it as a matter of faith, as something that *must* be true ; but, alas ! we do not believe it with the warm, ardent, impetuous affection of those who require little to convince their faith, because their love is so abundant. If any of our fellow-creatures died a cruel death to save us from a similar fate, how we would treasure his memory, speak of his generosity, and believe that none ever had or ever

could love us as he had done ! If he had left rela-
tives after him on earth, how we would devote ourselves to them, how we would sacrifice ourselves for
them, how we would occupy ourselves thinking in
what manner we could repay them in some measure
for what had been done for us ! And has not Jesus
done all this for us, and more? and how do we
repay Him in the persons of those whom He has
called His brethren, of whom He has said, that He
will count as done to Himself even the most trifling kindness shown to them? Have we not even
a cup of cold water to give to the brethren of Him
who has died for our love?

*2nd Point.*—" No man hated his own flesh : but
nourisheth and cherisheth it, as Christ doth the
Church." O our Life, our risen Love, teach us
how to love Thee. And have we ever dared to
think that Thou couldest hate us, that Thou art
obliged thus to try and convince us of Thy love?
Do we not often act as if we thought at least that
Thou didst not care much for us, did not concern
Thyself much about us? Do we not act thus
whenever we mistrust Thy providence, or murmur
at the trials which Thou dost send us? "He
nourisheth and cherisheth us." He nourishes us
with Himself; He unites us to Himself more
closely and tenderly than ever bride was united to
bridegroom, and this does not satisfy His love;
He not only nourishes us and supports our life, but
He condescends yet more, He cherishes us. Do
we know what the words mean? Do we under-

stand them? do we believe them? God cherisheth *us—us*, miserable creatures, whom He can hardly persuade to believe that He loves us. He cherisheth us; not as we would cherish a plant or a bird, or even a dear friend; no, His love passes yet further, has yet deeper depths; He cherisheth us as His own flesh; and He tells us we *are* His flesh, and this is the reason why He nourishes and cherishes us: "Because we are members of His body, of His flesh, and of His bones." (Eph. v. 30.)

*3rd Point.*—Do we need any more consideration and any more inducements to love Him with a boundless love, to trust Him with a boundless trust? Shall we not try from this moment to show Him that we do love Him? There are few trials more painful than when a friend, who has done much for another, receives only coldness and ingratitude in return; and yet this is the reward we give our sweet Lord for all His love. But from this hour let us begin to meditate more on His love, and thus our own will become enkindled; and to practise constant acts of the tenderest and most thoughtful charity to others for His love, and thus the flame will be kept alive.

*Aspiration.*—Heart of my only Love, have mercy.
*Form your resolution, &c. Examen.*

# FIFTH SUNDAY AFTER EASTER.

## ROGATION WEEK.

### THE RISEN HEART OF JESUS DESIRING US TO ASK IN HIS NAME.

"Amen, amen, I say to you : if you ask the Father any-thing in My name, He will give it you. Hitherto you have not asked anything in My name. Ask, and you shall receive : that your joy may be full." (S. John, xvi. 23, 24.)

*1st Prelude.*—Represent to yourself the love and tenderness with which your divine Lord gave this instruction to His disciples.

*2nd Prelude.*—Pray for grace to ask aright, and to ask fervently, for all you want.

*1st Point.*—While Jesus was with the disciples they could ask Him personally for all they needed ; but now that He is about to leave them, He is anxious that their confidence should not be lessened. Like the father of a family who is about to die, He provides with the most tender and sedu-lous care for all His children. None are overlooked, none are forgotten ; and like the most loving of fathers, He makes special provision for the weakest and most helpless, confides them to the care of their stronger brethren, and lest they should grow weary of the charge, He makes it a point of love to Him-self that the " little ones " should be " fed," the "sick" ministered unto, and the "poor" clothed and comforted. But He knew that the little ones and the poor, and the elder brethren, would all need many things when He was away from them ; and so He tells them what they are to do in every difficulty : " Amen, amen, I say unto you : if you ask the Father anything in My name, He will give it you."

*2nd Point.*—See how large our liberty is—if you ask the Father *anything.* Oh, ask now, ask now !—ask the Father anything in the name of Jesus, and He *will* give it. They are the words of Jesus, our Spouse, our risen Love ; would He mock us with empty sound, would He give us great promises, which after all meant nothing? Oh, no ; let us not be so mistrustful, so unloving. Ask, ask anything, in the name of Jesus, and the Father *will* give it to you. It is Rogation Sunday, a day of asking, a day of prayer ; ask, then, all day long, and all day long you shall receive. It will not require any great persuasion on our part to get what we want from the Father : " for the Father Himself loveth you." And even Jesus does not need to ask Him to give us what we ask, because " He loveth " us ; and love only desires to be asked, that it may pour forth all its treasures on the objects of its tenderness.

*3rd Point.*—Consider how we may glorify our risen Lord by obeying His command to ask. We must ask in His name, for His sake, for His honour, for His glory, not for our selfish ends or interests, but for Him alone.  And yet His interests are ours; and the more we ask for Him, the more we shall get for ourselves: "Ask, and you shall receive, that your joy may be full."  Souls who are constantly engaged in prayer, must always be full of joy.  What gives us more pleasure and satisfaction, than to get something we wish for very much!  How success raises our spirits!  We have asked some one to grant us a special favour, and they comply with our request, and we do not know how to express our thanks or our gladness.  But the Father always grants our requests.  How full, then, are they of joy, who are always asking and always receiving—of joy, not of an earthly joy, which often ends in sorrow, which wearies and overpowers the soul, but of joy such as the angels feel when they rejoice in heaven for one poor sinner brought home to the fold.

*Aspiration.*—Ask, and ye shall receive : Alleluia ! Alleluia !  For the Father Himself loveth you : Alleluia !  Alleluia !  Alleluia !

*Form your resolution, &c.    Examen.*

## ROGATION MONDAY.

### THE RISEN HEART OF JESUS TEACHING US TO PRAY FOR EACH OTHER.

"Dearly beloved, pray one for another that you may be saved. For the continual prayer of a just man availeth much." (S. James, v. 16.)

*1st Prelude.*—Imagine you behold your divine Lord appearing now to one of His disciples and now to another, as the great forty days are passing away, and He longs with such tender love to strengthen and fortify them for their work.

*2nd Prelude.*—Pray that your risen Lord may also visit you, and teach you how to pray and what to ask for.

*1st Point.*—Consider the remarkable affection with which the apostles usually commence their instructions to us. Now they say, " dearly beloved ;" again, " my little children ;" again, be ye followers of Christ as " dear children." Let us also learn how to address those whom we wish to instruct, and how earnestly we should ask the favour of their prayers. " Dearly beloved, pray one for another." Do we pray for each other as constantly, as fervently, and as faithfully as we ought ? The precept is general ; we cannot exclude ourselves from it The apostle does not say, let those among you

who are distinguished for sanctity pray for the rest;
let the rich pray for the poor, or the poor pray
for the rich ; no, the precept is inclusive : "Pray one
for another." Each must pray for all. And is it
not a common excuse which we make to ourselves
for not fulfilling this duty, that we want prayers
more than others ? Perhaps we do. We may be
the most unworthy in our convent, the least devout
in our household ; but the precept still continues
unaltered : "Pray one for another."

*2nd Point.*—But we are also told what we are
specially to ask for others : "Pray one for another
that you may be saved." How can we tell in what
mysterious way the salvation of one person may
depend on the prayers of another? And even if the
salvation of others is not concerned, may not their
sanctification in some degree be furthered by our
petitions? If our charity were more thoughtful and
loving, if we were less interested about ourselves
and more anxious for God's glory, we would pray
more for others; and the more unworthy we think
ourselves, the more we would pray for them. If
we see a friend or a sister absent from Mass through
sickness or duty, we would make an intention for
them, asking our Lord to give them the double
merit of the Mass, and of the absence from it; we
would offer it for them, asking Him to accept it
as if they were present, believing in our hearts
that they glorify Him far more by their absence
than we do by our presence. What do we desire
or wish for but His glory ? and if we are so full of

imperfection ourselves that we do not glorify Him as we should, can we have a greater joy than to assist those who do glorify Him to glorify Him more ?

*3rd Point.*—Let us begin now to devote ourselves to praying for others in honour of the risen Heart of Jesus. It may be that those for whom we pray will be enthroned in glory, so far above us that we shall scarcely see the light of blessedness which will surround them. Is not this a reason why we should try to increase that light, why we should rejoice that God is so glorified? And we may be assured we shall not lose by our devotion. If our risen Lord sees that for His love we would rather pray for others, who may glorify Him more, than for ourselves, who glorify Him so little ; that we would renounce for them, or rather for Him, what is most precious for us, our Mass or our Communion, He will look on us with no ordinary tenderness, and it may be so flood our hearts with sweetness and consolation, that we shall scarcely know how to bear our joy.

*Aspiration.*—Heart of my Jesus, may those who love Thee most love Thee more !

*Form your resolution, &c. Examen.*

## ROGATION TUESDAY.

### THE RISEN HEART OF JESUS TEACHING US THE EFFICACY OF PRAYER.

"If he shall continue knocking, I say to you, although he will not rise and give him, because he is his friend; yet because of his importunity he will rise, and give him as many as he needeth." (S. Luke, xi. 8.)

"For the continual prayer of a just man availeth much." (S. James, v. 16.)

*1st Prelude.*—Represent to yourself the subject of the parable from which the text is taken : a friend at midnight knocks at the door of his friend, and obtains all he asks, *after a refusal*, because of his importunity.

*2nd Prelude.*—Pray that you may have grace to persevere continually in prayer, even when your petitions seem to fail of their effect.

*1st Point.*—Consider the instructions and examples of the Epistle and Gospel for the Rogations. "Elias," says S. James, "was a man passible like ourselves: and with prayer he prayed that it might not rain upon the earth, and it rained not for three years and six months. And he prayed again: and the heaven gave rain, and the earth brought forth her fruit." Here is an example of the efficacy and lawfulness of prayer, even for temporal things. Do we, who are God's consecrated spouses, and therefore specially bound to pray for His people, do we pray thus fervently, at the seasons set apart by the Church for this purpose, that God may bless and increase the fruits of the earth? Do we pray thus, especially for the sake of the poor, on whom the effects of a bad harvest or a bitter spring falls most heavily? If either in judgment or in mercy our prayers are not heard, we may be at least satisfied that our dear Lord will accept and bless our love for those who are so dear to His sacred Heart. No doubt the saints have obtained, and can obtain, from God, what He is obliged to refuse to our unworthiness ; but surely an inspired apostle would not have quoted the example of Elias to the faithful in general, if it was not possible, or even probable, that we could also obtain in our measure similar favours.

*2nd Point.*—Consider the parable of the Gospel. A friend asks at midnight for bread. The time was most inconvenient. But no time is inconvenient to God ; it is never midnight in heaven. The friend who comes at midnight is refused because the door is shut ; but the golden door of divine mercy is never shut, and Jesus will not only listen, but even stoop down from His throne of glory, to hear the lowest whisper of our prayer. Oh, with what love He relates this parable to His disciples ! How He tries to *convince* them of His love ! how He seems to lower Himself to a familiar comparison with one of His creatures, and says at last : "Although he will not rise and give him, because he is his friend; yet because of his importunity he will rise." But Jesus is our Friend, and He will give us all we need because He is our Friend, only we must show Him we are in earnest by our importunity.

*3rd Point.*—Consider how we may glorify the risen Heart of Jesus teaching us the efficacy of prayer. Why does He take so much pains? why does He use so many similes and such familiar explanations? Is it to excite our hopes, to urge us to ask, and then to disappoint all our expectations? Alas! do we not often act and think as if this had been our Lord's motive? Oh, let us try to kindle our love, to inflame our hope, to increase our faith. Let us consider well what pains Jesus has taken to encourage us to pray, and learn from hence how great must be the efficacy and the value of prayer. The apostle says, " Pray without ceasing ;" and assuredly, if we obeyed this precept, we should obey that which follows, and "in all things give thanks." (1 Thes. v. 17.) The prayerful soul will be a happy soul and a rejoicing soul. She has asked her Father for what she needs. If He gives she is full of joy, because what she receives has come from Him, and she may treasure what He sends; if He refuses she gives thanks and rejoices, because she knows He has refused what would have been bad for her, and granted her in its place something that will benefit her infinitely more than her utmost hopes could imagine.

*Aspiration.*—Heart of my Jesus, grant what Thou willest, and refuse what Thou willest not.

*Form your resolution, &c. Examen.*

---

## ROGATION WEDNESDAY.

### THE RISEN HEART OF JESUS TEACHING US WHAT OUR FATHER WILL GIVE US WHEN WE PRAY.

"If you then being evil, know how to give good gifts to your children, how much more will your Father from heaven give the good Spirit to them that ask Him?" (S. Luke, xi. 13.)

*1st Prelude.*—Represent to yourself the love with which our divine Lord gives this instruction to His disciples.

*2nd Prelude.*—Pray for grace that we may not only know, but also understand His words.

*1st Point.*—Consider the exceeding love of Jesus. How anxious He is to convince us of what we ought to believe, if we believe in God at all! Are we like heathens or Christians, when we act as we do about prayer? But our dearest Lord bears with us and loves us, and knows our weakness, or how could we bear with ourselves? First He teaches His disciples the prayer of prayers, and then, knowing how often we would say that prayer, and when it was not answered as we desired, think hard thoughts of the loving Father to whom it was addressed, He teaches us by a parable that we must continue praying if we wish to be heard, and assures us by a promise that if we ask we *shall* receive, and if we knock it *shall* be opened to us. But this is not yet enough for the love of His divine Heart, and He uses the comparison of the love of the creature to convince us of the love of the Creator. " And which of you if he ask his father bread will he give him a stone? or a fish, will he for a fish give him a serpent? or if he ask an egg, will he reach him a scorpion? If you then being evil, know how to give good gifts to your children, how much more will your Father from heaven give the good Spirit to them that ask Him?"

*2nd Point.—How much more?* Can we tell *how much more?* can we imagine *how much more?* can we know *how much more?* Never while we are on earth ; only let us try to believe it, and if we cannot believe to *act* as if we believed. " If you then being evil "—if sinful, selfish creatures, whose love for their children is so imperfect, if they will try to do their best for them—if they at least will not give them what is useless, or hurtful, or poisonous— "how much more will your Father from heaven give the good Spirit to them that ask Him?" See how He lowers Himself to us. He does not say, How much more will God, who is so great and powerful, give you all you want? but "how much more will your Father from heaven?" If your father on earth will do so much for you, how much more will your Father in heaven do? He uses the word father to convince us of the tenderness and reality of this relationship, and the confidence which it ought to give us when we pray. What would our Father refuse when our Brother pleads?

*3rd Point.*—Consider what it is that our Father specially promises to give—the good Spirit. What do we need more, what gift should be more acceptable to us, more helpful for us? If we were led, and guided, and taught by that Spirit in all things, how different our lives would be! The Father has promised to give, the Son has promised to send, and the Holy Ghost has promised to come. The Three Persons of the ever-blessed Trinity are united to help us. And what is still needed? Oh, how sad it is even to think it, and yet must we not acknowledge that it is true? The Father has promised to give, but we are not always willing to accept; the Son has promised to send, but we are not always willing to receive; the Paraclete has promised to come, but we are not always willing to welcome His visit. Now at least let us pray in earnest for this good Spirit, and prepare in earnest for His coming.

*Aspiration.*—Eternal Father, I beseech Thee give me Thy good Spirit.

*Form your resolution, &c. Examen.*

## ASCENSION DAY.

### THE HEART OF JESUS GLORIFIED ASCENDING UP TO HEAVEN.

"While they looked on, He was raised up : and a cloud received Him out of their sight." (Acts, i. 9.)

*1st Prelude.*—Represent to yourself the ascension of Jesus, and the looks of love and sorrow with which our blessed Lady and the apostles gaze upon our ascending Lord.

*2nd Prelude.*—Pray for grace to ascend to heaven in spirit to-day, and to learn thus to despise all earthly things.

*1st Point.*—Consider the glories and triumphs of our ascended Lord. Now, indeed, His sufferings are rewarded, and His humiliations are His eternal crown ; and yet His ascension is only manifested to a few, for the great day of triumph is yet to come—the day of triumph and of fear, when all men shall behold His conquering majesty. It is so also with our Lord's most chosen servants. A few may witness, and almost envy, the happy death of some holy soul, who has been despised for renouncing the world, or embracing the true faith ; but the vast multitude neither know of, or care for, their blessedness. The poor man or woman, who has suffered for long years a martyrdom of want and pain, dies also, and angels take the soul in triumphant jubilee to heaven ; but the world goes on as it did on the day of our dear Lord's ascension, and misses the saintly and the poor as little as it missed Him. But the day will come when the world will be compelled to acknowledge them in shame and fear, when they shall receive a reward and a glory beyond all their hopes.

*2nd Point.*—" A cloud received Him out of their sight." Even the apostles were not privileged, while on earth, to see the triumph of their Master. The courts of heaven were ringing with Alleluias as they never rung before. The angels overflowed with gladness. The torrents of joy which ever pour forth on them from the bosom of the eternal Father, poured forth in new oceans of unbounded light and love. But even the beloved disciple, as far as we know, at that time only saw the cloud which took Jesus out of his sight. And all that we can now see or know of heaven may be compared to this cloud. If we had even one glimpse of its brightness, perhaps we could no longer remain on earth. Happy for us if we raise no clouds of our own—no clouds of sin, or imperfection, or coldness—to hide heaven yet more from our gaze.

*3rd Point.*—But there are some souls whom our Lord tries specially, by hiding heaven from them. They are sometimes the very last persons to whom we should suppose He would send such a trial. There is not only a cloud, but a dark cloud before their eyes, when they try to gaze up after their ascending Lord. But heaven is not less bright because our eyes are clouded, either by our imperfections, or as a special trial of our love. Let us trust when we cannot see, and our trust will add to the very joys we find it so hard to realize. The disciples would rather have had the sensible presence of their Lord on earth, but He told them it was better for them that He should go to the Father. We would prefer consolations and spiritual satisfactions, yet is it not better for us also to have trials and desolations? But whether our path be in darkness or in light, let us join our voices with the angelic choirs to-day. Let us forget ourselves in Him. It is enough that He is glorified, that He rejoices, that He can suffer no more; and as we cannot open a window on the most burning summer day without feeling some little breath of air, so we cannot open the window of our hearts in generous thanksgiving, without receiving therein some little breeze of consolation, however dry and desolate they may be.

*Aspiration.*—Ascending Heart of my Jesus, plead for me with the Father.

*Form your resolution, &c.    Examen.*

# FRIDAY AFTER ASCENSION DAY.

## THE ASCENDED HEART OF JESUS TEACHING US CONFIDENCE.

" Having, therefore, a great high priest that hath passed into the heavens, Jesus the Son of God: let us hold fast our confession.   For we have not a high priest, who cannot have compassion on our infirmities : but one tempted in all things like as we are, without sin." (Heb. iv. 14, 15.)

*1st Prelude.*—Represent to yourself the throne of God, and Jesus, the great High Priest, standing before it pleading for you.

*2nd Prelude.*—Pray earnestly to Him, by His tender love, that He will obtain for you all He knows you to need.

*1st Point.*—Consider how the ascension of Jesus has become the special ground of our confidence : " Having, therefore, a great High Priest that hath passed into the heavens, Jesus the Son of God : let us hold fast our confession." The Jewish high priest could only enter once a year into the holy of holies to make atonement for the people ; but our High Priest stands there continually, and as God, pleads with God for us ; as Man, feels as man for us.   Is there anything we desire to have ? the High Priest will ask it.   Is there any suffering which seems so great that we can scarcely bear it ? the High Priest understands it.   He has passed into the heavens, not to rest for all eternity in the bosom of His Father, not to enjoy the glories of His triumph, not to forget all He has suffered; but to plead unceasingly, unweariedly, for the children of His love, the children whom He has loved so much, but who love Him so little.

*2nd Point.*—Consider the compassion of this High Priest. Who could have such compassion for us as He who has died for us? The Jewish priest entered into the holy of holies with the blood of a slain victim, but that blood cost him nothing. He offered it for the people, but his interest in them was merely the general interest, and more or less devout intention of his office. He offered this blood for his "own ignorance" as well as for the ignorance of the people. He was but human, and could but compassionate human miseries according to the limited knowledge and still more limited love of a creature. But Jesus enters not the earthly holy of holies, but into heaven itself. His is not a ministry which is offered once in a year; it abides for ever. He brings blood, but it is His own Blood, for He is Himself both Priest and Victim; and in presenting Himself, He presents the sacrifice.

*3rd Point.*—Consider how we may glorify our High Priest Jesus. Surely it will be by unbounded confidence in the tenderness and efficacy of His intercession. There is no trouble which we may not bring to Him, whether it be a trouble of body or of soul, which He has not felt, and which He does not understand. He understands and feels for our sufferings more than we do ourselves. All He asks is that we should come to Him, and that we should trust Him. Oh, let us hasten to surround the throne of our ascended Lord. The more applicants He has, the more pleased He will be. He will not send His royal guards to drive away the crowds that importune Him on the day of His triumph; nay, rather will He send those guards to invite them nearer, to encourage their petitions, to further their speedy access to His person. O sweet Jesus, we come, we come—we come to besiege Thy ascended Heart, we come to surround the throne of Thy ascended glory; and we ask Thee to offer Thyself, our Priest and Victim, to the eternal Father, for all our needs.

*Aspiration.*—Heart of my conquering Jesus, conquer in me all that displeases Thee.

*Form your resolution, &c. Examen.*

## SATURDAY AFTER ASCENSION DAY.

### THE ASCENDED HEART OF JESUS THE ANCHOR OF OUR SOULS.

"We have an anchor of the soul, sure and firm, which entereth in even within the veil ; where the forerunner Jesus is entered for us." (Heb. vi. 19, 20.)

*1st Prelude.*—Represent the heavenly kingdom, and behold Jesus entered therein as your fore-runner.

*2nd Prelude.*—Pray that you may attain to that blessed kingdom, by casting your anchor therein now.

*1st Point.*—Consider the words : " An anchor of the soul." We know the use and value of an anchor : the ship is safe when it has cast its anchor. Are we, then, casting ours, or have we cast it? The " hope set before us," this is the spiritual anchor of our souls ; and this anchor, if we only use it aright, will save us in every danger. We may be tempted to sin, but the hope set before us of eternal bliss will prove too strong for the desire of present gratification. We may be inclined to sink down weary with our daily strife, but one glance at the hope set before us will nerve us for every trial. We may be overwhelmed with sorrow and depression, but the hope set before us will keep us from being utterly cast down. Let us seek, then, to know the value and the use of our anchor. Let us use it in all the storms of sin, temptation, trial, and perplexity, which at times threaten to destroy our little bark. Five minutes in heaven, and they will be all forgotten ; or if remembered, they will only increase our joy. The anchor is sure, because its safety depends on the word of a God ; the anchor is firm, because it is cast upon the truth of a God. Let nothing grieve us overmuch, let nothing move us. Cast the anchor of hope into the Heart of Love, and all things shall work together for our eternal well-being.

*2nd Point.*—But we not only possess an anchor to secure us, we have also a forerunner who is preparing for us. When the great ones of this earth are about to visit a distant land, they send messengers and forerunners, to see that all things are prepared for them. It is the duty of these forerunners to remove every difficulty in their way, to provide all that is necessary, and to make such arrangements as will tend to their comfort and convenience, when the royal travellers reach the end of their journey. And has not our Forerunner Jesus done all this and more for us ? Has He not opened the way to our country ? Has He not prepared the way to our country ? Has He not gone before us, to make everything ready for our arrival? O Jesus, O our Life, our Love, Thou hast done all this, and more ; and yet we, in our misery and ingratitude, can scarcely exert ourselves to follow Thee, or convince ourselves of the glories Thou art preparing for us.

*3rd Point.*—Consider how an earthly prince would love a forerunner who had sacrificed his very life to prepare the way for him. But do we love Jesus thus? And in our case the King has made Himself the Forerunner to His people, the God to His creatures, the Master to His slaves. Let us consider, then, how we can best love and glorify our Forerunner Jesus. Surely it will be by our fidelity in hastening after Him with all the speed we can command, and our careful and exact observance of every direction which He has left us for our journey. He knows its dangers and its snares. He knows the blessedness He is preparing for us. Let us use the anchor of hope to keep us steady when dangers threaten, and to enable us to believe in the joys to come.

*Aspiration.*—Jesus, be the anchor of my soul.
*Form your resolution, &c. Examen.*

## SUNDAY IN THE OCTAVE OF THE ASCENSION.

### THE ASCENDED HEART OF JESUS SENDING THE PARACLETE TO HIS DISCIPLES.

"When the Paraclete cometh, whom I will send you from the Father, the Spirit of truth, who proceedeth from the Father, He shall give testimony of Me: and you shall give testimony, because you are with Me from the beginning." (S. John, xv. 26, 27.)

*1st Prelude.* — Behold Jesus addressing these words to His disciples, when He made His last exhortation to them.

*2nd Prelude.*—Pray for grace to understand and to profit by this instruction.

*1st Point.*—Consider the office of the Paraclete, as described by our divine Lord: "He shall give testimony of Me." Now, to give testimony, implies that there has been a necessity for evidence. Alas! did not our blessed Saviour foresee but too plainly how soon this testimony would be needed? Even His own chosen ones would soon forget the lessons He had taught and practised, and they would need to receive testimony of Him. Do we listen to this testimony? Do we desire this testimony? Do we pray for this testimony? Do we profit by this testimony? The Spirit of truth alone can teach us truth; but do we not too often prefer the spirit of the world, with its utter falseness and deceit? We cannot be guided by the two spirits; it is as impossible as it is to serve two masters. And even as we may sometimes serve the one and sometimes the other, and thus destroy our temporal peace, and risk our eternal peace; so we may also, unhappily, waver between the two spirits, and listen to that which gratifies nature, instead of listening to that which mortifies and subdues it.

*2nd Point.*—But we are also to give testimony; and unless our testimony be that of the Spirit of truth, it will neither benefit ourselves nor others. We shall require courage to give testimony of Jesus, for the world is full of false witnesses, who bear false witness against Him now, even as they did when He was in the world. Happy for us, if we never join our voices to theirs; happy for us, if our testimony is always given for Jesus and for truth. We give testimony by our actions. This is the most important testimony; this is a testimony which none can mistake. Those who live together in close union of heart, will generally be found to act in the same manner when placed under similar circumstances. Now, if our hearts are entirely united to the Heart of Jesus, we shall indeed "give testimony" of Him in our actions, for we shall act as He would have acted. We give testimony by our words. The conversation of those who live together also obtains a similarity; they acquire insensibly the same ideas, and so the same manner of expressing their ideas. Oh, how blessed shall we be if we give testimony of Jesus by our words, by speaking as He would speak, by thinking as He would think!

*3rd Point.*—Consider how we receive and how we give testimony. The Paraclete cometh to give testimony. Every Whitsunday is a fresh reproach or a fresh glory to our souls. He cometh, the Lord of life, and light, and love. He cometh, the sent one of our Jesus. He cometh on the mission of Jesus, to do the work of Jesus. But how do we receive Him? Alas! with coldness, with absolute indifference, with scarcely a recognition of His office, or of our duties towards Him. He speaks in our souls, He gives testimony there; but we are too busy with other thoughts to listen to His whisperings. He speaks through our superiors, He gives testimony by their lips; but we are so wise in our own conceits, that we will not condescend to that *absolute* submissiveness which is one of the brightest, surest, safest, quickest roads to exalted sanctity.

*Aspiration.*—Come, O Holy Ghost, and enlighten our senses and our hearts.

*Form your resolution, &c. Examen.*

# MONDAY.

## THE HEART OF JESUS ENTERED INTO REST.

"There remaineth therefore a day of rest for the people of God." (Heb. iv. 9.)

*1st Prelude.*—Represent to yourself the ascension of Jesus, and behold Him entered into rest, reposing eternally after His sufferings and labours on earth.

*2nd Prelude.*—Pray that you also may so labour and suffer here, as to be worthy to enter into rest.

*1st Point.*—Consider, O Christian soul, your ascended Jesus entered into rest. Now, human sufferings can no more grieve His human Heart; tears can no more dim His blessed eyes; groans of anguish can no longer break from His blessed soul; the tempests and storms of earth can no longer toss Him hither and thither. The fiend can never tempt, the lance can no longer pierce, the scourge can never again tear His tender flesh. Jesus is at home; Jesus is at rest; Jesus is glorified. He is with His Father, whom He loved from eternity—from whom He proceeded, co-equal in power and majesty. What matter how we are afflicted, or tempted, or tried, Jesus is at rest; and we can bear anything while we know He cannot suffer. It is a "day of rest," because eternity is one long day. It has no morning, it has no evening. It is called a day of rest, because of its permanence ; for a day is as a thousand years in the eternal kingdom. But rest implies previous fatigue, and fatigue implies labour. If we desire to rest with Jesus, we must labour with Him. Let this thought encourage us in the weariness of human life. Let us consider His labours, that we may be animated and encouraged in our own.

*2nd Point.*—The labours of Jesus obtained for Him (to speak in a human manner) the greatness and completeness of His rest. He laboured by day, teaching, preaching, consoling, attending the sick, blessing the little children, curing the blind, instructing the ignorant. He laboured also with His blessed hands for thirty years, ere He commenced these mental labours ; and He sanctified and ennobled all our bodily and mental labours by His. But His were *labours.* Are we willing also to labour, to work either in body or mind, as obedience may direct, until we are weary, and to work on without complaint, and without relaxing our efforts, *when we are weary ?* This is indeed to labour, and to labour like Jesus. When did He ever plead weariness as an excuse for omitting work ? and we know he was often weary. But Jesus laboured also for our sanctification. Every action of His blessed life was for our sanctification. Do we also labour for our sanctification as Jesus laboured for it? Do we make it our great object in life, and this not merely for the sake of being holy, but to glorify God by our sanctification?

*3rd Point.*—Consider for whom it is that this rest is prepared: "There remaineth therefore a day of rest for the people of God." For the people of God—for the children of His love—for the brides of His heart. O happy day! O blessed day! O day of release from bondage! O day of eternal jubilee! O day of surpassing and unending joy! Our night may be long, our labours may be heavy, our road may be rough—what matter; one hour with our God will make up for it all; one moment's enjoyment of that rest, will more than compensate for the weariest and longest life of labour.

*Aspiration.*—Heart of my Jesus, I would rest in Thee until Thou takest me to rest with Thee.

*Form your resolution, &c.   Examen.*

# TUESDAY.

## THE HEART OF JESUS CROWNED WITH GLORY AND HONOUR.

"But we see Jesus, who was made a little lower than the angels, for the suffering of death, crowned with glory and honour." (Heb. ii. 9.)

*1st Prelude.*—Behold your ascended Lord crowned by His eternal Father, with such glory and honour as surpasses all human thought.

*2nd Prelude.*—Pray that you may so suffer with, and for Jesus, as to be crowned with Him also.

*1st Point.*—Consider the words of the apostle, and see how Jesus has obtained this crown : "We see Jesus, for the suffering of death, crowned with glory and honour." He is perfected by suffering, He is crowned for enduring death. "For it became Him, who had brought many children into glory, to perfect the Author of their salvation, by His passion." (Heb. ii. 10.) What a subject of meditation ! Jesus perfected by His passion, and crowned by His death. Do we need anything further to convince us of the value and efficacy of suffering ? We in our measure must also bear our passion, if we would be perfected ; and we, too, must die, if we desire to be crowned.

*2nd Point.*—Let us consider how suffering perfects the soul.  It perfects it by cutting off its imperfections, and by preparing it for new graces. We must each endure our " passion."  Those souls whom Jesus loves most, will be called to endure the greatest suffering.  Souls whom He designs for any special work, are generally prepared for it by special suffering.  A day, an hour, comes when they ascend their Calvary ; there they are crucified, some for a longer, and some for a shorter space.  Their souls or their bodies, and often both soul and body, are wrenched and torn with such anguish, that even when the trial has passed away they still have "the marks of the nails."  The whole course of their lives is changed.  The marks of the nails are never healed till death ; and thus they go through the world, full of suffering and full of love, the recipients and the dispensers of God's choicest graces.

*3rd Point.*—But let us think also of the reward. We may not be privileged to endure this special crucifixion, this passion, which leaves its marks upon the favoured soul for life ; but in our measure we must have and seek suffering.  Our passion may be limited to the ordinary trials of life, which fall far less heavily on some than on others, and to the daily strife with self, a " passion" which all must endure until death.  Let us look at the end, whatever our spiritual condition may be.  If we have been called to endure a special crucifixion, we may be assured of a special crown.  If we are bearing the marks of the nails which then pierced us, we shall soon see those marks radiant with light and glory. And even if our sufferings are less acute, our reward will be glorious—we shall share in the triumph of Jesus. He will make us share the merits of His passion, to brighten and increase our glory. Let us, then, learn how to love and treasure our sufferings, whether great or trifling, thinking of Jesus crowned with glory and honour, for the suffering of death.

*Aspiration.*—Not to love as now, and to suffer as now, but to love more, and to suffer more.

*Form your resolution, &c. Examen.*

---

## WEDNESDAY.

### THE HEART OF JESUS SUFFERING DEATH FOR US.

"That through the grace of God He might taste death for all . . . And might deliver them, who through fear of death were all their lifetime subject to servitude." (Heb. ii. 9, 15.)

*1st Prelude.*—Behold Jesus accepting death upon the cross for us all.

*2nd Prelude.*—Pray that, by virtue of His death, you may be delivered from all undue fear of death.

*1st Point.*—Jesus not only suffers for us, He dies for us also. He tastes death for us all. We tasted the cup of sinful pleasures, and therefore we are condemned to taste the bitter chalice of death. Jesus knew in His sacred Humanity how bitter that chalice is. The sin looked pleasant and attractive, the cup which we tasted so eagerly seemed full of pleasure. Alas! we knew not, we thought not of the bitterness of the chalice which we should be compelled to drink. But Jesus, who came to suffer because we had indulged ourselves—Jesus knew what that chalice was, and how we should shrink and tremble when we were compelled to accept it; and so He tastes it, and by tasting it He removes half of its bitterness, and only leaves just enough to remind us that it is a punishment.

*2nd Point.*—We must all die; and who can think of death without fear? But fear is now tempered by love. The Judge before whom we must stand is also our Father, and the Son of our Judge is our Advocate. The trembling soul is borne to judgment by the angels, who minister but the command of Jesus. It fears; but the angels whisper words of hope and confidence, for they know how dear that soul is to their Lord, and death only opens to it the portals of eternal life. But if we desire to know how much we owe to Jesus for delivering us from the fear of death, let us consider what death would have been had He not died to save us. Let us imagine for one moment what we should have felt, had we known for certain that temporal death would be the precursor of eternal death. Then, indeed, there would have been bitterness, and anguish, and fear—fear, oh, how deadly and terrible!

*3rd Point.*—Consider what death is now to those who have an humble confidence of salvation—such confidence as the Christian soul may and ought to have. It is a momentary pain, followed by eternal joy; a passing darkness, the vestibule to eternal light; a little moment of awful trust in the mercies of God, and the first step to the eternal fruition of those mercies. Let us think of death with love, and long for it with calm and holy patience. It is a trial; it is a punishment; unless we felt it, it would be neither trial nor punishment. But let us learn to feel it, and to think of it as Jesus would have us feel and think; let us often accept its fears from His hand, in anticipation, and with perfect trust: then will He love to show us how He rewards submission to the punishment we have deserved—how He prizes and treasures confidence in His love.

*Aspiration.*—In my agony, sweet Jesus, have mercy upon me.

*Form your resolution, &c. Examen.*

# THURSDAY.

## THE HEART OF JESUS TEACHING US THAT WE MUST DIE IN ORDER TO RISE AGAIN.

"That which thou sowest is not quickened, except it die first." (1 Cor. xv. 36.)

"And if the Spirit of Him that raised up Jesus from the dead, dwell in you; He that raised up Jesus Christ from the dead, shall quicken also your mortal bodies, because of His Spirit that dwelleth in you." (Rom. viii. 11.)

*1st Prelude.*—Represent to yourself the manner in which the sower casts the grain into the earth, and then waits in faith and patience until it germinates.

*2nd Prelude.*—Pray that the quickening Spirit may so dwell in you, that when you are cast into the earth, it may abide in you and raise you up again.

*1st Point.*—The seed must die before it germinates : "That which thou sowest is not quickened, except it die first." The grain is cast into the ground ; it is covered over, and we see no more of it for a time. By degrees it dies, but the little germ within begins even then to live. We "sow not the body that shall be," for it dies ; but God gives a body to that little grain, which is of the substance of the grain which died. Thus, death

brings forth life, decay produces fruitfulness, barrenness begets fecundity ; and the dead seed lives
again, another, but a fair, fresh, and beautiful self ;
and all this because it has been cast into the
ground, and has died there. Thus our sweet Jesus
teaches us even from material things. By the differing brightnesses of the stars, He makes us know
the differing glories of the saints ; and by the
death and resurrection of the seed, He teaches
us how we shall die only to rise again more
gloriously.

*2nd Point.*—Consider how we are quickened. It
is "by the Spirit that dwelleth in us." That
divine Spirit is the germ of life which will re-
animate us. How sacred and how holy are the
bodies of the faithful who die with that quickening
Spirit within them! Oh, let us pray to that
blessed Spirit, let us ask Him to abide with us and
in us, more and more! If He "dwells in us," then,
indeed, will our resurrection be glorious and triumphant. His presence will be the vital spark of our
souls. He will preserve us from corruption, and
allow that only to die which would be a hindrance
to our resurrection.

*3rd Point.*—But we must pray that this death may
begin even now. Oh, let us ask the Spirit of Him
that raised up Jesus from the dead, to raise us up
also ! Even now this death must begin mystically.
The more perfect this mystic death, the less painful
the actual death. If we have been long dead to
the world, it will give us little pain to part from

it ; if we have been long dead to ourselves, we
shall think far more of Him to whom death will
bring us, than of our fears of dying.   Let us beseech
this blessed Spirit to come now and abide in us ;
to prepare us now for that eternal quickening, by
slaying within us all that would prove a hindrance to it.

*Aspiration.*—Come, O Holy Ghost, and enkindle
in us the fire of Thy love.

*Form your resolution, &c.   Examen.*

## FRIDAY.

### THE HEART OF JESUS SENDING US THE HOLY GHOST AS OUR TEACHER.

" For whosoever are led by the Spirit of God, they are
the sons of God." (Rom. viii. 14.)
  " Likewise the Spirit also helpeth our infirmity." (Rom.
viii. 26.)

*1st Prelude.*—Represent to yourself the two
subjects of meditation—a soul *led* and a soul
*helped.*

*2nd Prelude.*—Pray earnestly that you may be
led and helped by this blessed Spirit.

*1st Point.*—Do we ever sufficiently consider how
necessary the guidance and help of the Holy Spirit
is for our sanctification ?   Let us make our meditation to-day and to-morrow, on the eve of this

great festival, as in some sort considerations and examens on this all-important subject. When our divine Lord left the world to go to the Father, He sent the Holy Ghost to teach us and to give us peace. And this Holy Spirit has come, and He works even now the blessed work; but, alas! we are so utterly heedless of His working, that we all but frustrate the designs of the Heart of our Beloved. How different our whole lives would be, if we had more earnest practical devotion to the Third Person of the ever-blessed Trinity! We marvel much how those who associated with our divine Lord when on earth, could have failed even for a moment in conscious remembrance of His Divinity, in trust of His power, or could have doubted His love. We think had we been privileged to live with Jesus and to know Him, that our faith, and love, and submission would never have wavered, that we *could* not have forgotten that He was God, and that we would have acted always on this belief. Alas! can we hope it would have been so, when we are thus utterly forgetful of the abiding presence and the constant mission of the Holy Ghost?

· *2nd Point.*—Are we constantly praying for the full amount of guidance and help which that blessed Spirit is only anxious to give us? Let us consider our conduct in this matter during the last year, the last month, the last week. When temptations came, did it even occur to us to invoke the Third Person of the blessed Trinity, whose office is to " help our infirmities"? Alas! perchance we

never even thought of it. We prayed for the
divine assistance in some general way—well for us
if we even did this ; but can we say that we sought
the special help and grace of the Holy Ghost? Oh,
let us not be like those poor heretics, who think
when our Lord said His Body that He meant only
bread ; for are we not, at least in some measure,
like them, when we do not act as if we believed
what He has Himself declared, and what the
Church teaches us to believe, that He has sent the
Holy Ghost to abide with us, to abide in the
Church with the distinct office of teaching, and
consoling, and strengthening it ? .

*3rd Point.*—Unless we meditate on the office of
the Holy Ghost so as to acquire a distinct and
supernatural knowledge of His mission, we can
scarcely profit by it. If we do not know that it is
by Him we should be led, we are not likely to ask
Him for guidance ; if we do not know who is to
help us, we are not likely to look to Him distinctly
and specially for help. Let us begin now to have
more confidence in this blessed guide. Perhaps
the reason we have failed so often in temptation,
and have been so unsuccessful in our efforts to
acquire virtue, has been simply because we do not
use the special means appointed by the Heart of
Jesus to attain these ends. A more practical recognition of the office of the Holy Ghost, would
obtain two great graces : first, we should have a
deeper reverence for all superiors, from the
Church's head to those immediately appointed to

guide us, knowing that the Holy Ghost speaks to us in and through them; and secondly, we should run in the path of perfection like giants, for we should have the help and guidance of God Himself. This help we shall receive only in proportion to our earnestness in asking it; and if we do not strongly convince ourselves of its necessity, we are not likely to ask as constantly and as perseveringly as we ought.

*Aspiration.*—Come, O Holy Ghost, and fill our hearts with the fire of love and the strength of virtue.

*Form your resolution, &c. Examen.*

## WHITSUN EVE.

### THE HEART OF JESUS SENDING US THE HOLY GHOST AS OUR COMFORTER.

" I will ask the Father, and He shall give you another Paraclete, that He may abide with you for ever. . . . . He shall abide with you, and shall be in you." (S. John, xiv. 16, 17.)

*1st Prelude.*—Represent Jesus addressing the disciples for the last time, in words of ineffable tenderness.

*2nd Prelude.*—Pray that you may receive this great gift to-morrow in all its fulness.

*1st Point.*—Jesus knew, when He was leaving His disciples, how much they would suffer when

He was absent from them. He knew human nature as none other knew it; He felt for all its weaknesses as none other could feel. He knew that the loss of a friend is seldom fully realized until he is taken from us : and what friend was like Jesus? If the apostles were grieved, they had only to go to Jesus, and His very look comforted them ; if they were in any perplexity, they had only to go to Jesus, and His counsel guided them. But now Jesus was going away, and they, with all their grief, scarcely knew what they were losing. But Jesus knew, as He knows now, what we lose and suffer when those we love go home before us ; and Jesus never could bear to see any one in trouble, so He provides beforehand for the affliction He foresees. O my sweet Jesus, teach me to love Thee as Thou lovest me.

*2nd Point.*—Jesus had been the Comforter of the apostles, but now, as He is going away, He says, "I will send you another Comforter;" and this Comforter is not only to abide with them, He is also to abide in them. He has nothing to do with the world, for the world has its own comforters, miserable as they are ; and, moreover, this Comforter is the "Spirit of truth," and the "world cannot receive Him," because it is guided and governed by the spirit of lies ; it cannot "see" Him, because it is blinded by the spirit of darkness ; it cannot know Him, because it is ignorant of His mission and His power. But this Spirit has come to us, and it abides with us, so that we know Him and see Him in proportion to our earnestness and love in receiving Him.

*3rd Point.*—Let us consider how we may avail ourselves of this stupendous gift. When we are in trouble, do we ask this sweet Spirit to comfort us? Alas! is it not often the very last thing we think of? and yet Jesus tells us expressly that He asked the Father to send us this Comforter, that we might have "another" when He was gone. We say no one knows our troubles as well as ourselves; but there is another who knows them better—the Comforter who *abides* with us. Why do we not ask Him to comfort us? We seek comfort from friends, from human pleasures, from everyone and from everything, except the Comforter, and then we marvel that we are left desolate. Oh, let us make one strong resolve, and utter one burning prayer this blessed Whitsun Eve, that henceforth we may seek guidance and comfort from the Paraclete on every occasion, and that we may receive the guidance and the comfort which God gives us so lovingly through our superiors as His special gift. Let us resolve to practise a more constant, faithful, and earnest devotion to the Third Person of the ever-blessed Trinity, and our lives will become far better than they now are.

*Aspiration*—Come, O Holy Ghost, enlighten the Church, and enkindle in us the fire of Thy divine love.

*Form your resolution, &c. Examen.*

## WHITSUNDAY.

### THE HEART OF JESUS SENDING US THE HOLY GHOST WITH HIS SEVENFOLD GIFTS.

#### MEDITATION ON THE GIFT OF WISDOM.

"Give me wisdom, that sitteth by Thy throne . . . . For if one be perfect among the children of men, yet if Thy wisdom be not with him, he shall be nothing regarded." (Wisdom, ix. 4, 6.)
"The wisdom of this world is foolishness with God." (1 Cor. iii. 19.)

*1st Prelude.*—Represent to yourself the eternal Wisdom, the Third Person of the blessed Trinity, enthroned in heaven, where, from all eternity, He has dwelt, but now descending, with the impetuous flight of love, upon Mary and the assembled disciples.

*2nd Prelude.*—Pray that this blessed Spirit may descend upon you to-day in all His fulness and in all His love.

*1st Point.*—From all eternity, the Third Person of the blessed Trinity had been enthroned with the Father and the Son. But He also would have His share in the salvation of the human race, that race which has been loved so much, and which has loved so little. Jesus had promised the Paraclete, and the Paraclete longed to come, not only because

Jesus had promised His coming, but also because He desired to come. What an amount of ingratitude, contempt, and indifference, that blessed Spirit must have foreseen and accepted! From the world it might have been expected, but from the Church at least He might have hoped for love and thankfulness for His mission. But what practical recognition is there now of His office and His presence? Where is the profound submission to His least whisper in the voice of the Church through which He speaks? Where is the constant, prayerful *seeking for*, and dependence upon, His guidance, in the individual Christian?

*2nd Point.*—Let us at least endeavour to meditate attentively, during this week of graces, upon His sevenfold gifts, that we may the better profit by them. And, first, let us meditate on the gift of wisdom. How high and noble it is! It sitteth by the throne of God. Oh, let us cry out with our whole heart, to-day, " Give me wisdom, that sitteth by Thy throne." Sitting is a sign of judgment and authority; this is the office of the Holy Ghost, and by it He enables us to judge as God judges. It enthrones us, as it were, beside Him. We look down upon earth, and see as the angels in heaven. It teaches us what is truly wise and what is really foolish, and it enables us to act upon our knowledge. We may be very perfect " among the children of men," our opinion may be sought and applauded, our wisdom commended; but if the wisdom of God is not with us, we shall " be nothing regarded." Consider how necessary, how essential it is to have this wisdom. How earnestly we should pray for it! The world has its own wisdom, but it is foolishness before God ; and yet, do we not too often prefer the world's folly to God's wisdom ? True wisdom has only one end, and it sacrifices all for that end. The wisdom of the world has countless ends, and for these ends it demands many sacrifices.

*3rd Point.*—The fruit of this wisdom is peace. Peace is the beatitude of heavenly wisdom, and spiritual consolation its special reward. If we have only one end in view, and if that end is God, we shall never be disturbed, our peace will be continual and abiding. We shall leave the world to disquiet itself as it will about the follies which it counts wisdom; we know of only one wisdom, and that is foolishness to the world. The world considers it the very consummation of wisdom to obtain riches, honours, and pleasures ; we know that to despise them is the sublimest wisdom. Oh, consider how great a gift it is to judge of all things as God judges, to estimate things as God estimates them, and thence learn the majesty of this gift of wisdom. Consider how blessed it is to act as God would act, and thence learn how holy is this wisdom. Consider what it is to be calm and unmoved in all adversity, and thence learn what a treasure is this wisdom.

*Aspiration.*—" Give me wisdom, that sitteth by Thy throne."

*Form your resolution, &c.   Examen.*

# WHIT MONDAY.

## THE HEART OF JESUS SENDING US THE GIFT OF UNDERSTANDING.

" Hearken to me, my son, and learn the discipline of understanding: and attend to my words in thy heart." (Ecclus. xiv. 24.)
" But we have the mind of Christ." (1 Cor. ii. 16.)

*Preludes as on Sunday.*

*1st Point.*—We believe by faith, and we are enlightened in our belief by the gift of understanding. The gift of understanding is, as it were, the " words of Christ in our heart," teaching and explaining to us what we should avoid and what we should do. This gift is especially necessary in studying holy Scripture, and hence those who are out of the Church misunderstand it, and explain it falsely. But its greatest practical importance concerns us in the daily exercises of our spiritual life. Hence the apostle says : " Wherefore become not unwise, but understanding what is the will of God." We know, alas ! but too well, how easily the most enlightened persons may be deceived, whose understanding is merely human ; even those who are spiritual do not always follow the will of God in all things, and this because they do not understand

it.   Oh, let us pray with our whole heart for this
blessed gift!

   *2nd Point.*—Consider the different kinds of ignorance from which this gift delivers us.   It delivers
us, first, from that ignorance which prevents us from
distinguishing between what is true and what is
false.   The world is full of false principles and
false maxims, and the world is entirely guided by
them.   How earnestly should we pray for a heavenly understanding, that we may not be led
astray by the example and the opinions that surround us!   But even in spiritual things there are
true and false maxims.   There are the operations
of nature and grace—of God and of the devil; and
unless we are filled with the gift of understanding,
we shall often be led astray, if not to our ruin, at
least to our serious injury.   Secondly, there is the
ignorance which prevents us from discerning between good and evil, so as to understand when a
virtue carried to extreme may become a vice, and
the reverse.   Here, again, the gift of understanding
is our only safety.   It will make us know that the
discretion of our superiors is our surest guide, and
that what they forbid, however good it may seem,
is an evil at least for us.   Thirdly, there is the
ignorance which prevents us from discerning what
is beneficial and what is injurious.   Practices of
piety which may suit one person, may be absolutely
injurious to another.   Circumstances may occur
which may so alter our line of duty, as to make
what would be good and expedient at one time,

evil and pernicious at another. Here, also, we need the gift of understanding.

*3rd Point.* — Understanding is a discipline : "Hearken to me, my son, and learn the discipline of understanding." We must restrain our feelings and our imagination, we must discipline our thoughts and actions, if we desire to be guided by the gift of understanding. Oh, how blessed are they who, with wisdom to enlighten them, possess understanding to guide them, and having the "mind of Christ," always act according to His holy will ! Let us remember how necessary this gift is for us, and how important it is that we should pray earnestly to obtain it.

*Aspiration.*—"Make me to understand the way of Thy justifications." (Ps. cxviii. 27.)

*Form your resolution, &c. Examen.*

# WHIT TUESDAY.

## THE HEART OF JESUS SENDING US THE GIFT OF COUNSEL.

"For who among men is he who can know the counsel of God? or who can think what the will of God is? For the thoughts of mortal men are fearful, and our counsels uncertain." (Wisdom, ix. 13, 14.)

"And be not conformed to this world; but be reformed in the newness of your mind, that you may prove what is the good, and the acceptable, and the perfect will of God." (Rom. xii. 2.)

*Preludes as on Sunday.*

*1st Point.*—The gift of counsel regards the direction of our particular actions. It is a light by which the Holy Ghost shows us what we ought to do in the time, place, and circumstances in which we find ourselves. It is, as it were, a practical and detailed instruction of how we may best fulfil our daily duties. Who does not need this blessed gift? How shall we distinguish between the counsels of human prudence and the counsels of divine wisdom, unless we are guided by it? How holy and beautiful is the conduct of those who are guided by the gift of counsel! They walk calmly heavenwards. There are no returns upon the road, no straying into side-paths, no precipitate eagerness, involving long delay in the end. " The good, and perfect, and acceptable will of God," is always chosen and always followed.

*2nd Point.*—Our natural activity is perhaps the greatest impediment to obtaining this gift in its highest perfection. There is no haste in heaven, and yet there is no delay. When shall we learn the blessed medium? When shall we learn to mortify our natural eagerness by restraining ourselves when inclined to act with undue precipitation, and to mortify our natural sloth when tempted to undue delay? If we run before God's providence, the graces He has prepared for certain times are not ready for us, because we have anticipated them; if we delay unwisely, circumstances change, and what perhaps would have been right and necessary to-day, becomes wrong, or at least unadvisable, to-morrow. Hence the need we have of the gift of counsel.

*3rd Point.*—We should pray earnestly that all superiors may be endowed richly with this gift, and especially we should ask it for our own superior. It is true the counsels and commands of superiors are always God's will for us; but if we have failed in our duty, and have not prayed as we ought for them, God may allow them, however holy they may be, to give us advice or directions which will be less advantageous to us than those which we might have received had we been more prayerful. But above all things we should pray for a profound humility, if we desire this gift. God hides His secrets from the wise; His counsels would appear

foolishness to them: why, then, should He cast pearls
)efore swine ?  We need counsel in speaking, counsel in acting, counsel in difficult circumstances; and
if we are only earnest and faithful, we shall surely
obtain it.

*Aspiration.*—"Thou art my helper, O Lord; make
no delay." (Ps. lxvi. 6.)

*Form your resolution, &c.   Examen.*

## WHIT WEDNESDAY.

### THE HEART OF JESUS SENDING US THE GIFT OF FORTITUDE.

"He hath strengthened them that were fainting in
patience." (Ecclus. xvii. 20.)

"Brethren, be strengthened in the Lord, and in the
might of His power." (Eph. vi. 10.)

*Preludes as on Sunday.*

*1st Point.*—S. Teresa has said that there is
nothing the devil dreads so much as a resolute
soul.  It is but saying, in other words, that there
is no gift so advantageous in our combats with him
as the gift of fortitude.  Oh, how earnestly we
should desire and pray for this gift !  Weak, irresolute, trembling souls are overcome even by the
shadow of danger, while the brave-hearted walk
fearlessly on, and scarcely even notice the lion in
their path.  But there is a natural hardihood, as

utterly opposed to this gift as timidity, and most souls are inclined to either one extreme or the other. A few moments' careful examination would show us to which we are most inclined, and consequently how we should act so as to avoid the danger on either side. Perhaps the timid and irresolute are safer than the bold and self-confident.

*2nd Point.*—Consider how the gift of fortitude strengthens us, first to do, and secondly to suffer. There is scarcely an action in the day, especially if we have been consecrated to God in religion, in which we do not require to exercise the gift of fortitude. We need it in the morning, when the summons to rise finds us weary and desirous of a longer rest; we need it at office and meditation, when pleasant fancies or reflections about coming occupations seem almost to insist on occupying our thoughts; we need it when repugnances arise to this employment or to that; we need it when obedience appoints a duty which we do not relish, and when we see another appointed to an office or occupation which we would naturally desire to fulfil; we need it—oh, how often!—in the little daily trials of our calling, in the little temptations more frequently than in the great ones, which all who are striving in earnest after perfection must encounter. Oh, if we had more fortitude, we should not only run but fly in the path of perfection, and we should find the flying easier than the running, although it is this very love of ease which we seek

T

to gratify, by not exerting ourselves to master the obstacles to this holy flight.

*3rd Point.*—Consider how the gift of fortitude enables us to suffer. There are certain circumstances in which we need fortitude to enable us to suffer, more than fortitude to enable us to act. When a trial has pressed upon us for years, then we need fortitude to bear it bravely and uncomplaining. When we are deprived for a length of time of all spiritual consolation, and we neither enjoy God here or feel as if we should enjoy Him hereafter, then indeed we require fortitude to enable us to walk by faith, as if sight were granted to us. When we are exhausted and wearied by constant labour or bodily infirmity, then we need fortitude to work on through weariness, and in spite of it. Let us consider well how much and how constantly we need this blessed gift, that we may pray for it with an earnestness proportioned to our need.

*Aspiration.*—" In Thee, O Lord, have I hoped : let me never be confounded." (Ps. xxx. 1.)

*Form your resolution, &c.    Examen.*

## WHIT THURSDAY.

### THE HEART OF JESUS SENDING US THE GIFT OF KNOWLEDGE.

"We cease not to pray for you, and to beg that you may be filled with the knowledge of His will, in all wisdom, and spiritual understanding: that you may walk worthy of God, in all things pleasing: being fruitful in every good work, and increasing in the knowledge of God." (Col. i. 9, 10.)

*Preludes as on Sunday.*

*1st Point.*—A perfect knowledge of God will be at once the source of beatitude and beatitude itself. The more we advance in this grace, the more perfect will be our spiritual life. We may illustrate this to ourselves by considering how intimacy with our fellow-creatures results in knowledge of them, and how knowledge, if they are worthy of our affection, is consummated by love. We do not concern ourselves much about the sorrows and joys of those of whom we know little; but how anxious we are in proportion to our intimacy or relationship. The more we know God, the more likely we shall be to "walk worthy of Him;" our knowledge and our works will increase in a blessed circle, the one promoting and advancing the other. Our love here is limited to our knowledge, and because we only "know in part," and see "through a glass in a dark manner" (1 Cor. xiii. 12), we do not love as we shall love when our knowledge is perfect, and our vision unclouded.

*2nd Point.*—But although the gift of knowledge or science assists the understanding in discerning and comprehending obscure truths, and thus increases our knowledge of God, it also assists us in our spiritual life, by teaching us how to perform acts of virtue, by enlightening us as to the state of our souls and the secret movements of our hearts, and by showing us how we may use creatures for our advancement, and avoid them when they would be prejudicial to it. Blessed are those souls to whom God gives largely of this gift ! They love because they know, and they know because they love. Their path heavenward is clear and direct. Humility and purity of heart are their characteristic virtues. They are humble, because, by the light of this blessed gift, they know God and they know themselves—how, then, can they be proud ?— they are pure of heart, because their knowledge of God teaches them how much He loves this purity ; and in proportion as they seek to purify themselves their knowledge increases, for God ever imparts Himself freely to the pure of heart.

*3rd Point.*—Consider how earnestly we should pray for this gift. Self-knowledge is one of the most important elements in the spiritual life. How many scarcely know themselves at all, perhaps because they have never asked for this blessed gift ; there are so many imperfections, so many little self-seekings, so many ends, which are not purely for God, in our daily life. But when God imparts this gift to a soul, she sees at a glance—almost as we see an object without a distinct mental recognition of its existence—what has been the imperfect end, the self-gratification, which had all but marred her action; and she sees this with such peace, that it causes her neither scruple nor disquiet, only it increases her love to Him who bears so lovingly with her; and with one little sigh of contrition and look of love, she renounces the im. perfection by a mental act, and continues her occu. pation in the Heart of her Beloved with a pure intention for Him.

*Aspiration.*—" Blessed art Thou, O Lord : teach me Thy justifications." (Ps. cxviii. 12.)

*Form your resolution, &c. Examen.*

## FRIDAY IN WHITSUN WEEK.

### THE HEART OF JESUS SENDING US THE GIFT OF PIETY.

"Be ye therefore followers of God, as most dear children : and walk in love, as Christ also hath loved us, and hath delivered Himself for us, an oblation and a sacrifice to God for an odour of sweetness." (Eph. v. 1, 2.)

*Preludes as on Sunday.*

*1st Point.*—The gift of piety is the very soul of devotion. It is an intense filial love of God which leads us to "walk in love, as most dear children." Oh, blessed gift! Oh, precious gift! Gift which the world cannot know or understand! Gift which is bestowed in the richest abundance on the most saintly souls! "Be ye therefore followers of God, as most dear children." Oh, how the heart of the great apostle burned with love as he wrote these words! "Be ye therefore." Wherefore? Because, as he tells us in the preceding words, "God hath forgiven you in Christ." This is the reason why we are to be followers of God, as most dear children. We are very dear indeed to God, for our purchase has cost Him the life and the blood of His only Son. We slew Him, it is true; but for all that God has forgiven us in Christ, and He only seeks now, in return for all His love, that we should be "followers of God, as most dear children."

*2nd Point.*—Consider how loving children follow their parents. They follow them, by imitating their example. A loving child is firmly persuaded that no one is so good or so wise as his own parents, and considers their conduct as the highest model which he can follow. If they have faults, he does not see them, for love blinds him. He follows them, by keeping close to them. A loving child prefers the society of his parents to that of others. He follows them, clings to them, and weeps when he is separated from them. Are we thus following our Father, as "most dear children"? Children may be deceived by their love, and follow bad and imperfect example; but we never can be deceived when we follow our Father. A child may injure his prospects in life by too great attachment to his parents; but the closer we keep to our Father, the more we shall advance our best interests.

*3rd Point.*—The gift of piety will also enable us to "walk in love." How much is implied in these words: To "walk in love, *as Christ also hath loved us.*" How did He walk in love? The apostle tells us: it was by "delivering Himself for us as an oblation and a sacrifice to God." Are we willing to walk thus in love, to sacrifice ourselves for our Beloved, even as He sacrificed Himself for us? To sacrifice ourselves in every detail of our daily life for the brethren, for those with whom we associate, because they are Christ's representatives to us;

this is, indeed, to "walk in. love, *as* Christ also hath loved us." O sweet Spirit, come! Spirit of adoption, Spirit of love, come, and enkindle in our hearts Thy heavenly fire—come and fill us with this blessed gift of piety, that we may indeed "be followers of God, as most dear children"!

*Aspiration.*—"My Beloved to me, and I to Him." (Cant. ii. 16.)

*Form your resolution, &c.    Examen.*

---

## SATURDAY IN WHITSUN WEEK.

### THE HEART OF JESUS SENDING US THE GIFT OF FEAR.

"And grieve not the Holy Spirit of God : whereby you are sealed unto the day of redemption." (Eph. iv. 30.)

*Preludes as on Sunday.*

*1st Point.*—Love is the fruit of knowledge, and fear.is the golden shield which protects love. Consider what a holy, beautiful, precious gift is fear. There can be no deep love without fear. True love must always be based upon reverence, and reverence is but another word for fear. It is said of Jesus, in His adorable Humanity, that "He was heard for His reverence." (Heb. v. 7.) The souls who love most deeply, generally are most full of fear ; but it is the fear of intense reverence, not the fear of slavish dread, for that fear is "cast out by perfect charity." He that feareth with the fear of a servant, is not "perfected in charity" (1 John, iv. 18); but he who fears with the reverence of a child, has attained its highest consummation. Oh, let us pray for this golden gift, and give no rest, by our urgent importunity, until we have obtained it !

*2nd Point.*—This fear manifests itself, when most perfect, in an interior dread of "grieving the Holy Spirit of God." It is the fruit of burning love; and in souls who are far advanced in charity, its manifestations are surpassingly beautiful. They speak in their hearts all day long to Jesus, and Jesus speaks to them; not always with evident sensible consolation, but with a distinctness often accompanied with extreme dryness and darkness, which may perhaps be sent as a balance to this unspeakable favour. They scarcely commit an imperfection, ere it is distinctly pointed out to them ; and the love that burns so strongly within them, excites their fear, and they suffer, as only such souls can suffer, from intense fear, lest they should grieve their Beloved. To such souls there is no fear like the fear of grieving the object of their love ; yet, because of their familiarity with Him, they are often supposed to fear less than those who love less.

*3rd Point.*—This gift also manifests itself in another form, in souls who are not so much led by personal love to Jesus. In them it is simply fear

282 MEDITATIONS FROM EASTER SUNDAY

or awe of God and of His judgments; and such
souls walk very blamelessly before Him, but rather
from the love of fear, than from the fear of love.
Let us pray to-day, as the octave of gifts closes upon
us—let us pray above all things for holy fear : God
will impart the gift to each soul in the way best
suited to promote its perfection. The Spirit is our
" seal unto the day of redemption." Oh, let us
beware how we break or cast from us that blessed
seal ! Let us begin a new life of prayer to the
Third Person of the ever-blessed Trinity ; let us
try to convince ourselves firmly of the importance
of His office, and of the immense importance of
invoking His help daily as our Teacher and our
Comforter.

*Form your resolution, &c. Examen.*

## TRINITY SUNDAY.

### GLORY BE TO THE FATHER, AND TO THE SON, AND TO THE HOLY GHOST.

*1st Prelude.*—Represent to yourself the Church
triumphant in heaven, suffering in purgatory, and
militant upon earth, uniting in prostrate adoration
before the throne of the ever-blessed Trinity.

*2nd Prelude.*—Prostrate with the Church, and
adore the Eternal Three.

*1st Point.*—What can we do to-day, but lie in
prostrate adoration before the throne of God ! We

have meditated on the love of the Father, in the weeks preceding Advent; on the love of the Son, from Advent to Whitsuntide; and on the love of the Holy Ghost, during the blessed octave which has just closed upon us; and now it only remains for us to anticipate our beatitude, to live in anticipation of our first day in heaven, and cry out if our our love can speak, *O beata Trinitas.* All day long the glorious chime is surging up into heaven; the angels hear the voices of men, and unite with them; the suffering souls in purgatory cannot think of pain; they cry also, *O beata Trinitas,* and pine yet more deeply for the vision of God.

*2nd Point.*—The weeks that follow Trinity Sunday seem like the weeks of eternity, if we could fancy the divisions of time to exist there. They pass on in calm, even measure. We honour the saints as their festivals come and go, or we praise the white-robed army of martyrs; but our hearts are not wrung as they are in Lent, when we think of the passion, nor do we weep as we must in Advent, because sweet Jesus is coming to suffer. Our occupation in these long weeks should be devotion and praise; not devotion of words, if that can be called devotion, but devotion of acts of our whole lives and being to the blessed Three. Oh, if we could only fathom the depth of the meaning in that word devotion; if we could know the absolute, entire, unreserved sacrifice of self which it implies; and better still, if we could, in the strength of the Holy Ghost, commence now to practise it!

*3rd Point.*—But this should be also a day of reparation—of reparations of praise to the blessed Trinity, for all the blasphemies, the indifference, the insults of the creatures whom He created, redeemed, and sanctified. Can we think of what men owe to God without feeling how deeply we are bound to reparations of praise? We must praise Him also for His own greatness and magnificence, that He is what He is; and we must offer our lives to Him as the best anthem of praise we can bring. Heaven will be eternal praise: perhaps earth would be more like heaven, if we began the employment of thanksgiving here.

*Aspiration.*—Glory be to the Father, and to the Son, and to the Holy Ghost.

*Form your resolution, &c. Examen.*

# A RETREAT

FOR THE

# THREE LAST DAYS OF THE YEAR.

---

## MEDITATION FOR THE EVE OF RETREAT.

### ON THE VISIT OF THE SHEPHERDS TO BETHLEHEM.

"And the shepherds said one to another: Let us go over to Bethlehem, and let us see this word that is come to pass, which the Lord hath showed to us. And they came with haste: and they found Mary and Joseph, and the Infant lying in the manger. And seeing, they understood of the word that had been spoken to them concerning this Child." (S. Luke, ii. 15-17.)

*1st Prelude.*—Represent to yourself the haste and love with which the shepherds go over to Bethlehem.

*2nd Prelude.*—Join yourself with them in spirit, and go over with them to Bethlehem, that you may also find Mary and Joseph, and the Infant.

*1st Point.*—Where can we make our retreat better than at Bethlehem, with the shepherds? All we desire in our retreat is to find Jesus, to know more about Him, that we may love Him more, and by loving Him more, that we may serve Him better. So we will go over to Bethlehem, and spend three days at the crib, studying the life of our new-born King, reading His love in His gentle smile, His tenderness in His outstretched hands, His sufferings in His hard bed ; and we will ask Mary to give us a lodging in the stable for these three days. How happy we shall be if she will comply with our request! Let us also, like the shepherds, animate each other, at least by our prayers, in the performance of this holy intention. The shepherds said *one to another*, "Let us go over to Bethlehem." They all united together in their purpose, and mutually assisted each other, even as we will now unite and assist each other in our retreat.

How the angels must have rejoiced to see them going in haste to adore their new-born King! They will also rejoice if they see us preparing to enter this spiritual retreat with alacrity. What greater joy could we have than to go over to Bethlehem! What greater favour could be granted to us than to spend three days at the crib! How much we shall learn there if we are only docile and attentive ! The world may occupy itself in its gaieties and rejoicings, in its thoughtless mirth, but we have other occupations and interests now. We are going over to Bethlehem. We prefer associating ourselves with the shepherds and the wise men, to joining in the revels of a world which forgets Jesus, and leaves it to the poor and simple to worship Him and remember Him.

2nd Point.—When the shepherds went over to Bethlehem, they left all their worldly cares behind them. We must imitate their example, now that we are about to set out on a journey like theirs. We also have our flocks, our ordinary duties and employments, which we must leave for a time, and, above all, without a thought, if we desire to profit by this visit to Bethlehem. We only watch these flocks during the night of time, but now that a glimpse of eternity is breaking upon us, we must leave them in all haste to follow where the light is leading. We have only watched those flocks for Jesus, but now it is Jesus Himself who is calling us; and we must leave what we have guarded for love of Him, to fulfil the yet higher duty, to obtain the far more exalted privilege, of waiting on Him personally. The angels, that is, our superiors, have "stood by us," and told us the joyful news. How glad, how thankful we are, for we dare not leave our flocks unless obedience called us from them, and now we may leave them in peace, leave them to God and the angels! But let us be sure that we leave them not only in act, but also in thought and intention. We must not occupy ourselves with thoughts of them, or of anything on this earth, save of Him to whom we are going, who has called us so lovingly to come over to Bethlehem.

3rd Point.—Consider what the angels found when they came to Bethlehem : "They found Mary and Joseph, and the Infant;" and we also shall "find Mary and Joseph, and the Infant," when we arrive at the crib. What more can earth give us? What more can we desire? They who possess God, possess all things. They have all joy, for He is the source of joy ; and if we do not receive the full tide of His joy in time, it is only that we may have it all poured forth on us in eternity. They have all wealth, for He is the source of every treasure; and He only-waits to unlock His stores for us, when we shall be where we cannot waste them or use them amiss. Our visit to Bethlehem will teach us so much. We shall begin "to understand the word spoken to us concerning this Child." It is only by living with Jesus, that we can know Jesus; it is only by knowing Jesus, that we can understand Jesus. How much we have yet to learn which we ought to know! How slow are we to understand the deep mysteries of His life, the value of His suffering, the depth of His love! But, like the shepherds, when we visit Bethlehem we shall understand. How happy we shall be if we learn all that Jesus is waiting to teach us!

*Form your resolution, &c.* *Examen.*

---

# FIRST DAY.

## FIRST MEDITATION.

### ON THE POVERTY OF MORTIFICATION.

"And they found the Infant lying in a manger." (S. Luke, ii. 16.)

" For you know the grace of our Lord Jesus Christ, that being rich He became poor, for your sakes; that through His poverty you might be rich." (2 Cor. viii. 9.)

*1st Prelude.*—Enter the stable of Bethlehem, and behold your Infant King.

*2nd Prelude.*—Adore Him with your whole heart, and ask Him to make you rich by His poverty.

*1st Point.*—Once more let us try very earnestly to put away all exterior distractions, to shut our hearts against every thought but the one thought which should occupy us now. We must be alone with Jesus in the stable, if we would learn all He has to teach us. He is speechless as yet, but He will tell us all we desire to know by the gentle murmurs of His love; and the first lesson He will teach us here is about "the grace of our Lord Jesus Christ, that being rich He became poor, for your sakes; that through His poverty you might be rich." Let us then consider the poverty of Jesus, and the cause of this poverty. The poverty of Jesus! How can we wonder that the seraph of earth, the great S. Francis of Assisi, loved to call His Lord "my most poor Jesus"! That poverty of Jesus was the key-note of his spiritual life, and has become the foundation-stone of His seraphic order. A God poor, a God in want, a God cold, a God hungry, a God in a stable, a God despised by His creatures, a God burning with love and not loved in return, a God giving up all things for the sake of His creatures, and only asking them to love Him, and those creatures refusing to love Him. Oh, Jesus is poor indeed. The poorest can get a little love from those around them—can obtain some tenderness to soothe their sufferings ; but Jesus is so poor that He even wants love. Shall we let Him suffer this poverty any longer ? We cannot make the manger softer, or keep out the cold night wind, but we can fill it with love, and Jesus asks no more.

*2nd Point.*—Why is this God so poor? *For your sake.* You were once rich with every blessing a Father's love could give ; you had every blessing of nature and grace ; your Father did all He could to make you happy ; but you sold all your joys, all your treasures, for a little carnal pleasure, for the miserable satisfaction of committing an act of disobedience ; and now you have lost all God gave you, and you have nothing, absolutely nothing, of all the wealth you once possessed ; but that sweet Infant, that dear little Child, cannot enjoy His wealth while you are poor ; and though you deserve nothing but the most cruel punishment for losing all your riches, He prefers being punished Himself, and He not only bears the punishment you deserve for having made yourself a beggar, but He also cannot be satisfied without making you rich. O dear Christian soul, do you "*know*" now the grace of our Lord Jesus Christ? Do you see why He has deliberately chosen poverty to enrich you ?

*3rd Point.*—Consider all the sufferings which this poverty has entailed on Jesus. In choosing poverty, He deliberately chose all the sufferings of poverty. How happy are we if we, like Jesus, have deliberately chosen poverty—if we, like Jesus, welcome all the little trials and privations which that choice involves ! However much we may suffer, we shall never suffer like Jesus. The sufferings of poverty are comparative ; what would be a privation to one class, would scarcely be thought of by another. But if a king became a beggar, and endured all the privations of that state after a life of luxury and ease, how great would be his sufferings! And yet the King of kings has become a beggar; and the only complaint He makes is when He begs for love, and men refuse to give it to Him. O most poor Jesus, we will at least try that Thou shalt no longer suffer this poverty.

*Form your resolution, &c. Examen.*

## SECOND MEDITATION.

### ON POVERTY OF SPIRIT.

"And they found the Infant lying in a manger." (S. Luke, ii. 16.)
"Blessed are the poor in spirit, for theirs is the kingdom of heaven." (S. Matt. v. 3.)

*1st Prelude as in the last meditation.*

*2nd Prelude.*—Pray to your sweet Infant King to teach you this poverty of spirit, by which you may gain a royal kingdom.

*1st Point.*—Pride is the vice most directly opposed to this poverty of spirit which Jesus has come to teach us. Hence, our dear Lord commences and ends His life by giving us a lesson of humility. We might have supposed that those who had lost a kingdom through their own fault, and degraded themselves by the vilest sins, would find but little room for pride; and yet we know that the most holy are the most humble, while souls full of guilt are usually full of pride. We lost the kingdom of heaven by pride, and Jesus is buying it back for us by humility. Poverty of spirit is one of the many and beautiful fruits of the tree of humility; and hence, at this holy season, when Jesus comes to repair the ruin caused by our pride, we should specially meditate on, and endeavour to imitate, His humility. Let us look once more at Jesus lying in the manger. Here we have both an example of exterior poverty of spirit, and of interior poverty of spirit. Exterior poverty of spirit manifests itself in our general deportment. It is easy to know a soul filled with this poverty of spirit by her exterior. How gentle she is! how silent she is! how meek she is! Like Jesus, she lies in a manger, placing herself ever in the lowliest position she can find. Like Jesus, she lies in a manger, choosing suffering as her

U

portion, and preferring the hard, cold wood of mortification to the soft couch of sensual pleasure.

*2nd Point.*—Poverty of spirit inclines the soul to self-sacrifice. We were ruined by our first parents eating the fruit of the forbidden tree. They would not sacrifice their inclinations in this trifling matter to God's will; and, as a just judgment, we, their posterity, have wills naturally opposed to God's will. Hence, until we are so very far advanced in sanctity, that our wills become one with God's will, our spiritual life is a continual struggle between yielding to our own inclinations to evil, and obeying God's will that we should do the duty opposed to our inclination. Our sweet Jesus is even now giving us the example of how we should punish our transgressions, by a punishment corresponding to our fault. He commences His infant life by lying on the hard, cold wood of the manger; He ends it by lying on the hard, cold wood of the cross; and this because we eat of the fruit of the tree: so that the expiation is made to correspond to the crime. Thus, the soul that desires to practise poverty of spirit, will be filled with a holy revenge on self, and seek every means of punishing those evil inclinations by which it has been led astray.

*3rd Point.*—Interior poverty of spirit leads the soul to low thoughts of herself. She imagines that all are richer than she is in the gifts of Jesus, and she tries to hide herself as one utterly unworthy to be seen of men. In truth, her poverty of spirit is so great, that she is absolutely unconscious of it. She is spiritually blind with a blessed blindness to her merit, and knows not the richness of her poverty. We cannot possess the kingdom of earth and the kingdom of heaven. If we are rich here, we shall be poor hereafter; if we are poor here, with a true and holy poverty, then the kingdom of heaven is already ours. "Blessed are the poor in spirit, for theirs is the kingdom of heaven." Shall we not pray most earnestly to our sweet Jesus to teach us this poverty, that we also may possess that kingdom which He has purchased for us by becoming poor?

*Form your resolution, &c. Examen.*

## THIRD MEDITATION.

### ON POVERTY OF DESIRE.

" And this shall be a sign unto you: You shall find the Infant wrapped in swaddling clothes, and laid in a manger." (S. Luke, ii. 12.)
" I have learned, in whatsoever state I am, to be content therewith.' (Phil. iv. 11.)

*1st Prelude.*—Represent to yourself the Infant Jesus, swathed in the poor garments His blessed Mother has provided for Him, and lying in the manger, desiring nothing but to lie there as long as God wills.

*2nd Prelude.*—Pray for the grace of poverty of desire, that you may ask for nothing, and wish for nothing, but what God sends.

*1st Point.*—Poverty of desire is the fruit of poverty of spirit. Those who have been long accustomed to privations, cease to desire comforts they cannot obtain ; how much more should we cease to desire them when we have renounced them with a free will ! Poverty of desire is the perfection of the exercise of the vow of poverty, and a perfection to which few souls attain. We are content to do without the little conveniences and comforts of our former mode of life, but there is a higher perfection than mere contentment. We may be content to do without them, and yet half wish we had them ; and this little wish, which, perhaps, we scarcely see, and, alas ! too often do not notice when we do see it, is indulged until it grows up into a formal desire, and manifests itself in some expression of dissatisfaction. We do not say, even to ourselves, and perhaps pride alone prevents us from saying it to others, that we would like some convenience which our vow of poverty forbids, some better clothing, some more palatable food ; and we think we have kept our vow when we do without it, simply because we cannot get it ; but all the time there is a little secret wish for it, gnawing us like worms, and that wish, if not perceived and generously sacrificed, will manifest itself in some imperfection. We shall never, never know in this world, what we lose by not watching and controlling the hidden motions of our hearts ; and only those who are very faithful know one-half the secret springs from whence they proceed.

*2nd Point.*—But the virtue of poverty of desire extends itself much further. We have made a great advance if we

desire nothing in regard to our personal comfort, if we have
not even a wish, or rather if we generously and promptly
check or mortify every wish for even the least convenience.
But we must advance yet further.  Jesus not only lies in
the manger, content with the food and clothing which His
Mother gives Him, and wishing for no other food or clothing ; He is also content to remain lying in the manger as
long as she pleases to leave Him there.   O my little King,
what lessons Thou dost teach me !   Thy Heart is burning
with a love which all but consumes Thy Infant frame—with
a love which makes Thee long to work and suffer more than
we can possibly imagine ; and yet Thou liest in the manger
in the poverty of desire, as if Thou hadst neither work to
do, nor suffering to endure.    And how restless we are !
How anxious to do this and that, as if all depended upon
our labour—how forgetful that all depends on our doing
God's will, and, like the apostle, learning, in whatsoever
state we are, to be content therewith.

*3rd Point.*— Consider Jesus lying in the manger as our
great model of poverty of desire.   If our plans and intentions were purely for God, we should easily practise this
virtue, but the truth is we seldom act purely for God.
Shall we not commence the new year by endeavouring to do
so ?  There is only one desire which the soul should have who
wishes to practise this poverty of desire in its utmost perfection, and that one desire is to do the will of God.    It is
not God's will we are anxious about, but our own inclination, if we wish to labour when He bids us rest.    Oh, let us
be content to lie in the manger, wrapped hands and feet in
swaddling clothes, helpless and dependant on others for
help, useless to all appearance to others, and only a burden
to them, if sweet Jesus wills it so.    He lay in the manger,
wrapped in swaddling clothes, in all the helplessness of
infancy, to teach us what sublime merit we might have
even for doing nothing and giving trouble to others, when
we were thus occupied, because God willed it so.    He was
loosed from the swaddling clothes, and commenced to work
and instruct others, to teach us what equal merit we may
have for labouring and toiling for His love.    For our perfection, and the glory we give to God, depends not on what we
do, but on the accomplishment of God's will every moment
of our lives.

*Form your resolution, &c.   Examen.*

# SECOND DAY.

## FIRST MEDITATION.

### ON PURITY OF BODY.

"Therefore the Lord Himself shall give you a sign. Behold a virgin shall conceive, and bear a son." (Is. vii. 14.)
"These were purchased from among men, the first-fruits to God and to the Lamb." (Apoc. xiv. 4.)

*1st Prelude.*—Represent to yourself the joy with which the angels contemplated Jesus a virgin, the Son of a virgin mother.

*2nd Prelude.*—Pray to understand the beauty and nobility of this grace of virginity.

*1st Point.*—Consider how exalted is the state which God Himself has chosen. How highly virginity must be prized by God, when He mentions it as the special privilege of His Mother, and confers this grace on the souls dearest to Him. Poverty is beautiful, obedience is beautiful, but virginity is a jewel of surpassing worth. If we would estimate its value, let us ponder on the words of Holy Writ. "These," says the virgin disciple of the virgin Lamb—"these were purchased from among men,. the first-fruits to God and to the Lamb." Thus we have the highest authority for believing that virgin souls are the first-fruits of the most precious Blood. Oh, how dear those souls must be to Jesus! He came to redeem us all, but *first* He purchases special jewels, special treasures. He selects as it were for Himself, and for special nearness to Himself, some of those souls which He has come to redeem. And who are they thus favoured? Virgins, who are to follow the Lamb "whithersoever" He goeth—virgins, who were "purchased from among men." Oh, let us mark these words, and linger over them in adoring love : "Purchased from among men." All are redeemed, all may avail themselves of this redemption; but there are some souls selected, chosen first, by Him who chooseth as He willeth, and those souls are virgins; and in addition to the privilege of their special purchase, they have a special privilege—they follow the Lamb whithersoever He goeth.

*2nd Point.*—The bride follows the Bridegroom. She follows Him because His strong arm will protect her and will caress her. O virgin brides of the virgin Lamb, will you not follow Him also closely?—oh, how closely! But you must follow Him "whithersoever" He goeth. You may not find it difficult to follow Him when He leaves Bethlehem, and goes down into Egypt; you may not find it difficult to follow Him when He comes up from Egypt, and goes to Nazareth; but, perhaps, you will shrink back when He whispers to you that He is going to Calvary. O virgin bride of the virgin Lamb, if you desire to follow Him whithersoever He goeth in heaven, you must follow Him whithersoever He goeth on earth; and there may be many Calvarys which He may ask you to ascend with Him. Will you go with Him? Oh, surely you will, not from the desire of the rewards of Thabor, but from love, pure love; you will go because you cannot choose but follow the Bridegroom "whithersoever" He goeth. You will go because joy without Him would be suffering, and suffering with Him is joy. You remember that you are the "first-fruits" purchased by the Lamb; and as the Lamb payed down the last drop of His Blood as the price of your purchase, so that suffering has become, as it were, your very life, it is a blessed necessity of your spiritual existence to suffer. You are never so happy as when the Bridegroom takes you up with Him on Calvary, for there you obtain glimpses of that nearness to Him, of that eternal embrace of love which will be your beatitude, and the beatitude of all the Blood-bought first-fruits.

*3rd Point.*—The first-fruits were always specially consecrated to God. The Jews were even bound, under the most solemn obligation, to sacrifice the first-fruits to God, or to redeem them by sacrifice. Oh, how holy, how pure, how noble, are the first-fruits purchased by Jesus! Look at your little King in the manger; He came to purchase you as one of His first-fruits. Have you ever considered the honour He conferred on you? Have you ever meditated on the glory He has reserved for you? There are souls who lose themselves in raptures of ecstatic love, when the simple word "whithersoever" falls upon the ears of their souls. Oh, picture to yourself, one little moment, that virgin Lamb walking on that pavement of pure gold, lighting that city with His own light, for He is the light thereof; and picture yourself walking beside Him, going "whither-

soever " He goeth, and see if you have words to tell your
love.   The blessed in heaven see Jesus all day long, and
there is no night there, but the virgins walk beside Him—
walk beside Jesus.   Whithersoever He goeth they go also.
Can you imagine what it will be to *walk* beside Jesus ?
Is there any sorrow that will seem great, when such blessedness may be yours for eternity ? is there any sacrifice that
will seem hard, when you may walk beside Jesus as your
reward ?   And if anything could enhance this blessedness,
it will be the company in which we shall enjoy it.   What
a happiness it is, even in this world, when sisters walk
together in full union of heart and love, sharing their
joys and their sorrows !   How much, then, will the society
of the virgin choir add to the joys of each !
*Form your resolution, &c.   Examen.*


## SECOND MEDITATION.

### ON PURITY OF HEART.

" Blessed are the clean of heart, for they shall see God." (S. Matt. v. 8.)

*Preludes as in the last meditation.*
*1st Point.*—The former meditation will have shown us
how much God prizes purity.   He manifests the value
in which He holds this virtue, by making it the singu-
lar privilege of His blessed Mother that she alone should
be at once a virgin and a mother ; and we have seen that
He rewards those on whom He confers this virtue, and who
are faithful to His grace, by a special nearness to Himself
for all eternity.   Let us now consider how purity tends to
our sanctification, and especially the purity of virginity.
Look into the Heart of the Infant Jesus.   From the manger
to the grave, He knows no love but the love of His
eternal Father, the love of Mary, and the love of His
Church.   His Church is the mystic bride whom He has
come to wed, and He selects from the members of this
bride some more favoured than others, a chosen first-
fruits, and by a choice of predilection He sets them apart
from others, because they are virgins.   Thus we see how
Jesus prizes and honours purity.
*2nd Point.*—Purity promotes our sanctification by bringing us near to God.   In heaven it will bring us near to

Him as our reward, but we must labour for that reward by earnest efforts to obtain nearness to Him here. "Blessed are the clean of heart, for they shall see God." They shall see Him hereafter in some special manner, doubtless, but even here they shall "see God" far more clearly and intimately than others. Who has seen God most clearly in this life? Who has fathomed the depths of His mysteries and the secrets of His love? Has it not ever been those who were most pure of heart? The purest earthly love leaves a faint shadow on the soul, like vapour on a glass, which prevents the image of divine things from entering into it clearly and perfectly. True, the vapour may be dispelled by the ardent flames of love which saints receive and emit; but if we except cases of extraordinary sanctity, the vapour still remains, and more or less dims the soul's perceptions of heavenly things. But this vapour dims not the virgin soul; and in proportion to the purity of her virginity, to the "cleanness" of her heart, she will see God even here below, and know and understand what others only perceive faintly. Thus S. John, the disciple of purity, S. Bonaventure, the saint of purity, S. Thomas Aquinas, the doctor of purity, were specially and singularly enlightened in all heavenly mysteries.

*3rd Point.*—Let us learn how to value the virtue which makes us both like our Lord and singularly dear to Him. We have one only Love, and our Love is Jesus. We plighted our troth to Him at the altar. Like true spouses, we left all to follow our Bridegroom, and that Bridegroom left all to win our poor love. Shall we not be faithful to Him? We never, never can love Him as much as He loves us; but let us try to do what we can. Let us try to love Him as much as we can. Let us be convinced that it is impossible for us to know or understand in this life the privilege He has conferred on us in calling us to be His spouses; but let faith convince us that we shall one day know all, and more even than we can imagine, in the eternal embrace of our Bridegroom Jesus. And even here it may be He will give us some little foretaste of this celestial joy. There are souls who are ravished even here with the melody of His voice; there are souls who even here are clasped in the embrace of His love; there are souls who seem to lose their very being in His—souls whom he has taken up to Calvary, souls whom He has all but crucified in heart-wrung anguish, souls whom He has permitted to taste the cup of human affection, and then dashed it from their lips, not in anger, but in surpassing love, not to deprive them of lawful earthly pleasure, but to inebriate them with the chalice of divine delights—souls whom He will not permit to have any love but His love, souls whom He has loved long before they knew that He loved them, souls whom He seemed almost to drive to the nuptials to which they should have run with joy, and whom He consoles with double tenderness for the grief He has caused them, though that grief was but the prelude of a moment to eternal and unsurpassing beatitude.

*Form your resolution, &c.    Examen.*

### THIRD MEDITATION.

#### ON PURITY OF INTENTION.

"Christ also loved the Church, and delivered Himself up for it: that He might sanctify it, cleansing it by the laver of water in the word of life. That He might present it to Himself a glorious Church, . . . that it should be holy and without blemish." (Eph. v. 25, 27.)

*1st Prelude.*—Represent to yourself the Infant Jesus as the divine Bridegroom, preparing to suffer for His Church, that He may cleanse and purify her by His sufferings.

*2nd Prelude.*—Pray that you may be indeed cleansed and purified from every defilement.

*1st Point.*—But there is another kind of purity which all Christian souls are bound to practise, and this is purity of intention. A soul that acts before God with a pure intention, must be very dear to Him. Now, the first step in this purity of intention is to divest ourselves of self-love. As long as we are filled with self-love, we cannot act with purity of intention, because we act according to the inclination of self-love, which will be always opposed to the will of God. Our sweet Infant Jesus has come both to redeem us and to sanctify us. Fear of hell makes us prize our redemption, and think more of it than of our sanctification. We love God so little, that we think of our safety first, and of His glory last. If we can satisfy ourselves that there is a fair probability of our salvation, we are content, and we take little or no trouble about becoming saints. We forget that our dear Lord came to sanctify us as well as to save us. We forget that He "cleanses His

Church by the laver of water in the word of life, that He
may present it to Himself a glorious Church ; that it may
be holy and without blemish." But we are so utterly
selfish, that we only care for our sanctification as far as it
may be absolutely necessary for our salvation. Oh, if we
loved Jesus more, we would desire so ardently to be like
Him, that this desire alone would urge us cheerfully and
bravely up the steep mountains of sanctity.

*2nd Point.*—Let us consider what this purity of intention
is, which is of such immense importance in the spiritual
life. We may say it is doing everything purely for God
alone ; and when we have said this, it seems easy and
simple, and we think there can be no great difficulty about
accomplishing it. But like all great principles of spiritual
life, it is indeed simple, but the practice is difficult, not
because what we wish to accomplish is difficult in itself,
but because we are so hindered and crippled by our sins
and imperfections, that every step towards perfection is
full of difficulty. And thus it is that this great and most
noble virtue—great, because it brings us so near God ;
noble, because it assimilates our purposes and intentions to
His—is in practice very difficult. But, like all spiritual
difficulties, it becomes easier by practice, until at last the
virtue is almost an acquired habit. Purity of intention is
the very soul of our actions. If we have a bad intention
it makes an action bad, which in itself would be good.
For instance, if we perform an act of charity to another
from a bad motive, the good action is immediately turned
to evil. But how many degrees there are of evil and good
between a deliberately bad motive or intention, and a pure
and perfect one. Let us consider this subject carefully,
and then we may be able to form some idea of the value
and importance of a pure intention.

*3rd Point.*—Unless we have watched our interior life
very carefully and very prayerfully, we shall have no idea
of how imperfect our motives are. Happy for us if we have
ever performed even one action in our lives purely for God
alone ! Happy for us that He in the intensity of His love,
accepts our desire of a pure intention almost as if it were
indeed pure ! How our sweet Jesus loves a soul which is
earnest in her desire of doing all things purely for Him
alone ! What bright lights He will place in her heart, to
show her the imperfections of her motives ! And even if
she forgets this careful self-introspection for a time, and

returns again, or rather is recalled again to it by her Beloved, she finds Him there as of old, still ready to show her the words she has uttered from vanity, the little sentence she has carefully framed to say to some one at some certain time, to remove a bad impression which she fancies they have got about her, or to advance her own merit or qualifications in their estimation. He will show her an imperfection in the motive for which she is about to perform some duty, or He will whisper sweetly to her a little thought which will enable her to perform some action more purely for Him, and with some special and blessed intention suggested by this inspiration. Oh, if we were but as faithful to Jesus as Jesus is to us, how we should walk with Him, and act with Him, and speak with Him, and think with Him all day long—for Him, in Him, because of Him, by Him!

*Form your resolution, &c. Examen.*

# THIRD DAY.

## FIRST MEDITATION.

### ON PASSIVE OBEDIENCE.

"And she laid Him in a manger." (S. Luke, II. 7.)

*1st Prelude.*—Represent to yourself the Infant Jesus just laid in the manger by Mary.

*2nd Prelude.*—Pray that you may learn the grace of passive obedience from this mystery of love.

*1st Point.*—Look once more at the little Infant Jesus. There is no lesson which the Christian soul ought to learn which will not be taught at the crib. Oh, how noble, how sublime a lesson of passive obedience we have here! Let us meditate on it till our very hearts melt away in tears of love and tenderness, and, better still, until we have formed the strongest resolutions to imitate the example of the Babe of Bethlehem. Our sweet Jesus commences His life by an act of passive obedience. He appears as if He

were absolutely helpless, and Mary, His mother, and our
mother also, lays Him in a manger. O sweet Jesus, how
Thou didst sanctify every act of passive obedience at that
moment! What grace Thou didst obtain for us, who are
so restive and so restless, that we weary ourselves and our
superiors with our unholy activity! But we learn from
Thee, sweet Jesus, a lesson never to be forgotten; and
henceforth we will lie down wherever obedience may
place us, and ask not to rise until obedience takes us up
again. Passive obedience is the lowest step in the attainment of this great virtue; but happy are those souls who
advance even thus far in its perfection. The heights of
crucified obedience will never be attained, unless we have
commenced to walk in the lowly valley of passive obedience. And even when we attain the utmost perfection
of obedience, passive obedience, like the key-note of a
chord, will still be needed to complete the divine har-
mony.

2nd Point.—Our blessed Lord's life of obedience may be
divided into three parts. From His birth until the time of
His active ministry, He practised passive obedience; during
the three years which commenced with His long and lonely
fast, and ended with the last supper, He practised suffering obedience; the close of His life was crowned by crucified obedience, endured in submission to His Father's will,
interiorly, in the agony in the garden and the dereliction
on the cross; exteriorly, by the fearful agonies of His passion. At this holy season our Lord specially teaches us the
lesson of passive obedience. He is passive in His obedience
to the will of His eternal Father in all that concerns His
nativity. He accepts the time, the place, and the circumstances, because He has not come to select for Himself, but
"to do the will" of God. He is passive in His obedience
to the will of His blessed Mother, permitting her to "lay
Him in the manger," or to take Him in her arms as she
pleases. Shall we not also learn passive obedience in all
things, spiritual and temporal? The simple reason why we
are not more obedient, is that we have so little faith. If
we believed that all the directions of our superiors were the
will of God for us, and that our sanctification depended on
the accomplishment of His will, we should practise obedience with far greater fervour and exactness.

3rd Point.—But let us now resolve to take Jesus, laid in
the manger by Mary, as our model of passive obedience.

See with what a gentle smile of acquiescence He accepts her will ; see how patiently He lies wherever and however she places Him.  How meek His patience is !  How different from our restlessness, when we are placed in an employment we do not like!  But we have learned a great lesson during our visit to the crib ; and henceforth we will model our practice of obedience on what we have seen there.  We will unite our answers to the summons of the bell, to the requirements of our holy rule, to the directions of our superiors, to the passive obedience of Jesus in the manger.  We will come or go, stay at or leave our employment, in the spirit of passive obedience.  We will have no other object but to accomplish the will of Jesus, and we know this will be manifested to us, so that we cannot mistake it by the bell, and the rule, and the voice.  O sweet Jesus, before we end our three days' visit to Thee, give us a little more faith and a little more love, and our lives will henceforth glorify Thee incomparably more than they have ever yet done.

## SECOND MEDITATION.

### ON SUFFERING OBEDIENCE,

*And how it is perfected by the exercise of the theological virtues of Faith, Hope, and Charity.*

"Arise, and take the Child and His mother, and be there until I shall tell thee." (S. Matt. ii. 13.)

*1st Prelude.*—Represent to yourself the Infant Jesus taken from the manger, where, at least, He had some protection and repose, and awakened from His sleep, to commence His flight into Egypt.

*2nd Prelude.*—Pray that you may learn and love the deep mysteries of suffering obedience.

*1st Point.*—Our sweet Jesus uttered a few words in one of His blessed instructions to His unbelieving people, in which He admits us to the deep secrets of His interior life at Bethlehem : "I came down from heaven, not to do My own will, but the will of Him that sent Me." (S. John, vi. 36.)  Let us look once more at our dear Infant King, and listen to Him while He softly whispers these words in the ears of our hearts.  This is the one simple, the one sublime

object of His birth and His intention, "to do the will of Him
that sent Me." And our blessed Lord will whisper another
secret to us if we will come very close to Him. He will
say : "Dear little child, I think you wish to love Me; I
think you wish to be My friend. I have very few friends,
as you know ; but you wish to be one of the few. Well, you
*shall* be 'My friend, if you do the things that I command
you.' (S. John, xv. 14.) You wish to be very dear to Me
also. Well, 1 am very dear to My Father ; ' l abide in His
love,' because I keep His commandments ; if you wish also
to 'abide in My love,' you must keep My commandments."

*2nd Point.*—lf we desire to "abide" in the love of Jesus,
we must practise constant obedience. Now, it will not be
possible to practise constant obedience, without practising
suffering obedience also. But see what we shall gain by it.
Can we imagine for one moment what it is to "abide in the
love of Jesus ;" to have the ardent, the vivifying fire of
His love poured out on us *without intermission;* to have the
whole depth of the tenderness of His human Heart poured
out upon us at every moment ? And yet this may be ours,
but on one condition—a condition named by our dear Lord
Himself : we must keep His commandments. We must live
in a constant state of suffering obedience ; we must be
prepared to obey when our obedience costs us something.
It will often cost us a great deal to be obedient even in trifles.
The constant recurrence of a duty, however insignificant,
to which we feel some repugnance, is in itself no light cross.
But what a blessed opportunity of practising suffering
obedience ! It is the constant action of the file which wears
down the irregularities on the surface of the metal. The
file of obedience is passing over the golden metal of our
wills all day along ; the pain it causes each time may be very
trifling, but the aggregate pain becomes something con-
siderable. An inspired apostle has already told us that
no comparison can be made between the sufferings of this
life and the rewards of the next, and that however great
the trials of obedience may be, whether by an accumulation
of trifles forming a heavy burden, or by one single act of
more than ordinary difficulty, the merit and reward of
obedience incomparably surpasses any estimate we may
form of its sufferings.

*3rd Point.*—To obey perfectly we need a most ardent
charity, a steadfast faith, and a firm hope. Why do we not
more frequently make acts of faith, hope, and charity, and

try to increase those virtues in our souls. Is it not because we do not sufficiently estimate their importance? It was by "faith" that Abraham, the great father of the faithful, practised suffering obedience, and "went out not knowing whither he went." (Heb. xi. 8.) It was by faith that Joseph also practised suffering obedience in the flight into Egypt, and went out not knowing whither he went. It is by faith that every soul who corresponds to her vocation to religion, "goes out" from the world to the cloister, not knowing whither she goes. By faith she ventures on this new and untried life, obeying the command, the inspiration, which calls her to it, whatever this faithfulness may cost her. It is by hope, and a most steadfast hope, that she perseveres therein, and practises suffering obedience, hoping for the reward which God will give "to them that seek Him." (Heb. xi. 6.) It is by charity that she becomes perfected therein; for in proportion to the greatness of her love, will be the largeness of her faith and her hope. Love prefers suffering in Egypt with the Beloved, to a peaceful life in Jerusalem without Him. Love knows not how to question the will of the Beloved, whether that will occasion her sorrow or joy. Love cannot be content without accomplishing the will of the Beloved with unchanging fervour. Love contains in itself the perfection of faith, "for it believeth all things;" hence it obeys without a question; and the perfection of hope, "for it hopeth all things," and hence it endures without a murmur. O sweet Infant Jesus, give me these three, faith, hope, and charity—of charity the most and largest share, for "the greatest of these is charity."

*Form your resolution, &c. Examen.*

## THIRD MEDITATION.

### ON CRUCIFIED OBEDIENCE.

"And after eight days were accomplished that the Child should be circumcised, His name was called Jesus." (S. Luke, ii. 21.)

"He humbled Himself, becoming obedient unto death, even to the death of the cross. For which cause God also hath exalted Him, and hath given Him a name which is above all names: that in the name of Jesus every knee should bow." (Phil. ii. 8-10.)

*1st Prelude.*—Behold your dear Infant King meekly submitting to the pain which He endures while shedding His Blood for you.

*2nd Prelude.*—Pray that you may understand and practise this most sublime virtue of crucified obedience.

*1st Point.*—There are souls who are called to practise crucified obedience on the very heights of Calvary—souls which have been crushed in the winepress of interior suffering, such as, perhaps, others can scarcely imagine, and which only a chosen few are called to endure. These souls are mostly prepared by this special suffering for some special work, and for some special nearness to their Spouse. God works in the kingdom of grace as He teaches us to work in the kingdom of nature, and labours most severely and constantly with the jewel He destines for some particular place in His eternal palaces ; but though all are not called to this peculiar kind of crucifixion which God sends, and which God alone inflicts, all are called to crucify *themselves :* " They that are Christ's," says the apostle, "have crucified their flesh, with the vices and concupiscences." (Gal. v. 24.) Alas ! have we ever advanced so far as even to drive one nail into our flesh? This is no matter of choice ; this is not a mere practice of devotion, which we may omit or perform as we please ; no, it is a question of salvation, a question of " being Christ's " or not. Shall we not then examine ourselves very carefully, to see if we have even commenced to practise "crucified obedience" ?

*2nd Point.*—Crucified obedience seems specially to refer to the bodily sufferings we inflict on ourselves, to subdue our " vices and concupiscenc." The words of the apostle are very plain : " They that are Christ's have crucified their *flesh.*" Now, anything which causes suffering to the flesh crucifies it. We may not be called to crucify our flesh to the extent to which the saints crucified theirs ; we may not be required to fast until we become emaciated, or to lacerate our bodies until they become full of wounds ; we may not be required to stand in ice until we are frozen, or in the burning sun until we are scorched ; but we must each in our measure crucify the flesh. Now can we do this every day in the little and low degree that our dear Lord asks from us, by practising crucified obedience. We can crucify our flesh by bearing little privations of comforts, little inconveniences of heat and cold, little fatigues of body or mind ; and there is one grand field of self-sacrifice open to us all, the crucifixion of practising real earnestness in our spiritual life. Oh, how much we lose for want of earnestness ! Oh, how we should entreat our little Infant

Jesus to give us the grace of earnestness, as a last blessing, before we leave the crib! We see what earnestness of purpose accomplishes every day in the world. We see how a man advances who gives himself up with his whole heart to his trade or profession; we see what obstacles we overcome by steady perseverance in the attainment of any object. Would to God—oh, would to God a thousand times!—that we were earnest even for one day in the pursuit of sanctity!

*3rd Point.*—Consider what we should gain by this earnestness. Men are earnest to gain a fortune, which they can only enjoy for a few brief years; to gain a reputation, which dies with them; to gain a position in society, which they will lose sooner or later; and we, with the prospect, nay, rather the certainty, of gaining an eternal inheritance, an eternal reputation, an object that no one can deprive us of, we cannot be earnest even for an hour! Oh, how we should pray for earnestness—how we should strive to impress on ourselves the great necessity for it! One half-hour we are fervent, the next half-hour we are cold; to-day we make aspirations of love to Jesus all day long, and strive to purify our intention in every action; to-morrow we scarcely think of Him, and perform our duties as if we were machines, and had no end but to do what we were occupied in doing. This was not the obedience of Jesus. This was not the obedience for which God "exalted Him, and gave Him a name above all names." But we will begin now to imitate His example; we will ask pardon for the past, and commence the new year with great fervour, and what is of still greater importance, with a firm resolution to renew our fervour whenever we find it has failed. We will be obedient even "unto death"—unto the death of every evil, perverse, and imperfect inclination; and then we also shall be exalted where the just shine as stars in the firmament. Then we also shall be saviours of others in our measure, by our prayers and our example; then we also shall receive that eternal recompense, that surpassing glory, that unending embrace of the Bridegroom, which is the sure reward of all who practise crucified obedience by mortification of will and of body.

*Form your resolution, &c.    Examen.*

DEO GRATIAS.

X

# THREE MEDITATIONS

# THE FEAST OF S. FRANCIS OF ASSISI.

---

## FIRST DAY.

### S. FRANCIS CONSIDERED AS AN EVANGELICAL POOR ONE.

"As long as you did it to one of these My least brethren, you did it to Me." (S. Matt. xxv. 40.)

*1st Prelude.*—Consider S. Francis of Assisi seated at table with his mother, Pica, and then rising quickly to give bread and alms to the poor.

*2nd Prelude.*—Pray for grace to imitate this great saint in his love of the poor.

*1st Point.*—Love of the poor is generally one of the first and surest marks of sanctity. Our divine Lord has made it one of the special, if not the very special sign and pledge of love to Himself. Hence we find, in the lives of the saints, that their first impulse, after God has called them to follow Him in the highest paths of the spiritual life, is to give all to the poor. They wish to give *all*, because it is given to Jesus ; and they could not be content with giving Him less than all. Let us ask ourselves is our love of the poor anything like theirs. We can only measure it by our willingness to sacrifice ourselves for them.

*2nd Point.*—Generosity to the poor draws down on the soul the most special graces, even where this generosity has not been practised from very high motives. How great, then, will be the reward of those who practise it for God alone ! Perhaps the first feeling of tender compassion which Francis felt for the poor, was a little impulse of divine grace, the commencement of a full tide of grace.

Had he not corresponded with this little impulse, perhaps the full tide would never have been poured forth on him. Let us learn, then, how important it is for us to follow the least good thought, to do the least good action. Let us examine ourselves, and see if we are prompt in obeying these inspirations. We do not know what we do when we resist the least inspiration. God will withdraw these special precious little lights from us, if we are not faithful to them.

*3rd Point.*—"As long as you did it to one of these My least brethren, you did it to Me." Consider the amazing love of our dear Lord in saying these words : remember that He uttered them Himself. Oh, how happy shall we be, if we are privileged to do the least thing for His least brethren : for the little children, whom He loves so much ; for the neglected, whom He always thinks of ; and for those holy souls who consider themselves the least, but who shall one day rank amongst the greatest. O Francis, our father, our dear father, pray for us. Obtain for us the grace, the honour, to do something, to do many things for the brethren of Jesus ; obtain for us a share in thy love of Him, and of those whom He has loved so much.

## SECOND DAY.

### S. FRANCIS CONSIDERED AS A DISINTERESTED POOR ONE.

"Our Father, who art in heaven."

*1st Prelude.*—Consider S. Francis standing before the Bishop of Assisi, and renouncing even necessary clothing—renouncing wealth, friends, and position ; and saying to his father, "I have called you father until to day ; henceforth I can say, 'Our Father, who art in heaven.'"

*2nd Prelude.*—Pray for grace to imitate the entire renunciation of this great saint.

*1st Point.*—It is easy to renounce what we do not care for. Hence we may often find persons who will make apparently great sacrifices of certain things, but if they are asked to sacrifice the special object of their preference or attachment, they are unwilling to do so. Entire self-renunciation, exterior and interior, at all times, and under all circumstances, this constitutes a saint. S. Francis made his first great act of renunciation before the Bishop of

Assisi. He renounced wealth, giving away even his very garments; he renounced his family ties, declaring that henceforth he would have no father but his Father in heaven; he renounced his position in society, by adopting the clothing and the life of a beggar. Let us pray to this blessed saint to obtain for us the grace of sacrificing whatever God may ask from us.

*2nd Point.*—The sacrifice of S. Francis was disinterested. Many persons will make great sacrifices, will endure great privations, but they only sacrifice what they consider a lesser good to obtain a greater. Men will toil and labour for years in a distant land, and endure constantly the severest pains of hunger and thirst, of heat and cold, of fatigue and exhaustion, to obtain worldly wealth, because they consider the wealth they hope to obtain as of greater value to them than their labour and suffering. They also run the risk of suffering for nothing, for they may not succeed in their object, or they may die before they succeed; and then all their labour is lost. They sacrifice themselves, but their sacrifice is not disinterested; what gives suffering its value is the motive with which we suffer. Hence the most trifling pain which we endure purely for God will obtain an immense reward, while the severest sufferings may be endured for a sinful purpose, and may merit still more severe sufferings hereafter.

*3rd Point.*—Consider how completely disinterested was the sacrifice of S. Francis. He knew not that his name would be one day honoured by the whole world, that his memory would be revered, that he would be tenderly loved as the very dearest of fathers by thousands then unborn; and even had he known all this, it would not have influenced him. He had one motive so sublime that every other motive would have seemed as nothing in comparison. His motive was love; his end was his Beloved. He loved God so much that there was no room in his heart for love of himself; hence his motive was pure, was disinterested. Let us beseech him to obtain a like purity of intention for us in all our actions.

## THIRD DAY.

### S. FRANCIS CONSIDERED AS A CRUCIFIED POOR ONE.

"If we suffer, we shall also reign with Him." (2 Tim. ii. 12.)

*1st Prelude.*—Consider the state of constant suffering in which S. Francis lived during the last few years of his life.

*2nd Prelude.*—Pray that you may have some share in his merits, and the graces he then obtained for his children.

*1st Point.*—Even before S. Francis received the grace of the stigmata, his life was one of continual suffering. He was a crucified poor one. We may be poor ones either by choice or of necessity, and yet not be crucified poor ones. A true and really perfect religious, will be always in some manner a crucified poor one. Let us consider how this is. However great and meritorious the sufferings of the poor, they have a limit; even the poorest may exercise their own will, and gratify their own inclinations, at certain times, and under certain circumstances. But a spouse of Christ, who desires to attain to the utmost sanctity of her holy state, may ascend still higher. To be an evangelical poor one, and to renounce all earthly goods; to be a disinterested poor one, and to prefer others to herself, and choose rather to suffer than see others suffer, and to do all this purely for God alone, such are high attainments; and blessed are they who have ascended thus far on the steep hill of perfection; but Calvary is on the summit, Jesus is there, and the spouse that loves must go even to Jesus.

*2nd Point.*—How can we become crucified poor ones? By imitating our beloved Lord, by following the example of this great saint, whose life comes so near the life of Christ. Surely, in order to become *crucified* poor ones, we must do more than give up all, and bear the inconvenience of poverty; we must *suffer*. Yes, to suffer—this is truly to be crucified poor ones. To go a little beyond what we *must* do in order to be saved, or in order to keep the letter of our holy rule—to bear actual bodily or mental discomfort, or, if such be permitted us, even severe sufferings for others—this is to be crucified poor ones. To give up our own way and will, inclinations and wishes, to others, even when we

think it will injure us, or cause us great suffering—this is
to be crucified poor ones ; this is to live as Francis lived,
to live as Jesus lived.

*3rd Point.*—Let us consider that the perfection of this
crucifixion does not require that it should be instantaneous.
The most painful deaths are slow ones, the most severe
tortures are those which are the most protracted.    The
stigmatization on Alvernia was the work of a moment, but
the preparation for this crowning grace was the work of a
lifetime.     Each sacrifice made for others, each suffering
which we choose to bear, though we might lawfully have
avoided it; yes, and each suffering which we would have
chosen, and which obedience has forbidden us ; each kind
action which has cost us some labour, some self-denial ; each
pain of body or mind borne in secret, each little comfort
which even our poverty might allow, and which to be more
like our Lord we refuse—the pains of cold, or the
oppression of heat, which we would rather bear than inconvenience or offend another—these are the strokes of
the hammer, these drive in the nails.    Blessed, thrice
blessed, they who, when the spear of death drains out their
life-blood, are found thus nailed, calm and peaceful,
fastened to the cross of their Spouse—crucified poor ones,
like this blessed saint !

# MEDITATION

# THE FEAST OF S. FRANCIS OF ASSISI.

---

" Bring my soul out of prison, that I may praise Thy name: the just wait for me, until Thou reward me." (Ps. cxli. 8.)

*1st Prelude.*—Represent to yourself the death of this great saint, as he lies on the ground, surrounded by his children, longing to go to God.

*2nd Prelude.*—Pray, through his merits and intercession, for the grace of a happy death.

*1st Point.*—Consider the last words of the saint : "Bring my soul out of prison, that I may praise Thy name." Truly, life is a prison, where we are held captive from our home and our celestial Spouse. It is a prison, because we are not free to act as we desire. It is a prison, because we are tied and bound therein with the chains of sin, with the infirmity of a weak will. It is a prison, because we are often separated from those whose society we most desire. It is a prison, because we often eat the bread and water of captives, and, like the royal psalmist, water our couch with our tears, and our food with weeping. But do we say also with S. Francis, "Bring my soul out of prison"? Alas! do we not rather love our chains, and delight in the place of our banishment? Do we not often prefer the society of men to that of angels? Oh ! when shall we say truly, "Bring my soul out of prison"?

*2nd Point.*—Consider to whom it is that Francis addresses his prayer. Neither saint or angel, blessed though they be, can help him in the attainment of this desire ; God alone can release from the prison of the flesh. What comfort this should give to every Christian soul ! The Father of eternal love, the God of eternal wisdom, has Himself appointed the hour and the moment of our release from prison. Can we doubt for an instant that that hour and that moment will be the best for us? Let us then begin to prepare for this blessed release. Let us employ ourselves in preparing the garments we shall wear when we go home—in gathering jewels for our celestial crown. This should be the only occupation of our long lives of imprisonment. Oh, how quickly and how blessedly would they pass, were they thus employed!

*3rd Point.*—Consider the reason why S. Francis desires that God would bring him out of prison. "Bring me out of prison," he says, "that I may praise Thy name: the just wait for me, until Thou reward me." Here we cannot praise God as we ought, because we do not know Him as He is; but when we see Him face to face—when our souls are flooded with the glories of the beatific vision—when we know all that we have been saved from, and all that has been purchased for us—oh, then, indeed, we will praise the holy name of our Saviour and our Deliverer! Consider, also, with what joy those who are delivered from prison are received by the just who have gone before. Oh, how tenderly each true religious will be welcomed by the founders of their respective orders! and may we not believe that, since the soul of Francis was ever so tender and affectionate on earth, it is even more so since he has lived for centuries in the possession of eternal love, and that his welcome to his fervent children will be that of the most loving and kindest of fathers? Let us, then, unite in thanking God with great fervour for his deliverance from prison, and pray that he will assist us, by his merits and prayers, at the awful moment of our release from earth.

# FEAST

# THE STIGMATA OF S. FRANCIS.

## (SEPTEMBER 17.)

---

"Henceforth let no man be troublesome to me; for I bear the marks of the Lord Jesus in my body." (Gal. vi. 17.)

*1st Prelude.*—Represent to yourself the wild mountain of Alvernia, and S. Francis praying there with his whole soul to God.

*2nd Prelude.*—Pray for the grace of a like fervour in prayer.

*1st Point.*—Consider what it is S. Francis desires; he asks for suffering and for love. "O my Lord Jesus," he cries, "I ask of you to grant me two graces before I die: first, that I may feel in my body and in my soul, as far as possible, all that you endured in your bitter passion; second, that I may feel in my heart as much as possible of that excess of love by which you were induced to suffer such torments for poor sinners." He wishes to understand the greatness of the suffering, that he may fathom the depth of the love. Hitherto he has been an evangelical poor one, and a disinterested poor one; now he desires to become a crucified poor one. Life is drawing to a close, and suffering appears to him, after the experience of years, and on the verge of eternity, as the greatest favour which a God can bestow. What a lesson for us of the value and efficacy of suffering, from the little pain of body or mind, which passes in a few moments, to the long hours, or months, or years of mental or bodily anguish!

*2nd Point.*—Consider why Francis desires suffering. Is it not that he may become like to his Lord? Long years of seraphic communings with his God have not satisfied his blessed soul. He asks for more; he asks to bear the marks of the Lord Jesus. Not that he ever imagined or desired the favour which was to be conferred on him. Far from it. He desires ignominious suffering; he obtains honourable suffering. He desires to suffer *with* the King; he is privileged, as far as mortal can be, to suffer *as* the King. And we also, have we not asked for the stigmata of the Lord Jesus? Have we not asked to live a life of poverty, humiliation, and contempt? Have we not stretched out our hands and feet, that they may be nailed by the nails of our three blessed vows to the cross of Jesus? And we also may dare to hope, that if we suffer with the King, we shall also reign with Him.

*3rd Point.*—Consider the result of this prayer: "Henceforth let no man trouble me." "Who," exclaims an inspired apostle—"who shall accuse against the elect of God?" Who shall condemn those whom He has justified? Who shall accuse those whom He has acquitted? If the marks of the Lord Jesus are upon us, none may dare to touch us. We are thereby sealed and set apart as His. There is no more "trouble" for the crucified soul; our "passion" has blunted the edge of all other pains. Henceforth the crucified soul knows only one suffering, and that suffering is her strength, her rest, and her joy. O blessed father, O Francis, obtain for us this grace, that we may be so "troubled" with the troubles of Jesus, and pierced with His griefs, that no other troubles or griefs may have power to move us.

# THREE MEDITATIONS

# THE FEAST OF S. CLARE.

———◆———

## FIRST MEDITATION,

*In which she is proposed as a model of fervour in obeying the call of God to embrace a religious life.*

*1st Prelude.*—Represent to yourself the young and beautiful virgin of Assisi, surrounded with all the world could give of wealth, distinction, and happiness, and consider her promptness in obeying the interior inspiration which she received to devote herself entirely to God, and the perfection with which she accomplished her sacrifice.

*2nd Prelude.*—Pray for grace to correspond as promptly with all divine inspirations.

*1st Point.*—Let us consider the promptness with which S. Clare obeyed the interior inspiration to devote herself entirely to God. From her earliest childhood she had sought only how to please Him more each day; every little self-denial with which she was inspired by divine grace was promptly executed. There were no delays, no excuses. She deprived herself of food and of rest for the sake of Christ's poor; and later, under the magnificent apparel which her station in life compelled her to wear, we find that she mortified her body with haircloth. Each day's sacrifice, each day's correspondence with grace in matters which we, alas! too often think trifling, were preparing her for the crowning grace of her vocation. Had she not corresponded with these first graces, would she have received the last? Ah! let us learn from our mother to obey divine inspirations with more fidelity and promptness; let us ask her to obtain for us this grace.

*2nd Point.*—Consider the perfection with which she accomplishes her sacrifices, consider her circumstances before she left the world, and then consider the circumstances in which she placed herself by taking this step. Rich, noble, surrounded with all that earth could give or heart desire, beloved by her family, loving them deeply in return ; was ever domestic happiness more complete? Living a pious, nay, a devout life, practising all the virtues of the cloister; such was the position of the noble Clare de Seiffi. Ah! think you, had she no temptations of home and kindred, no affections to sacrifice, no family to consider. How many would have listened to the temptation to wait until they were older, to wait until this new order was better established. Surely she was pleasing God as she was, benefiting others, and edifying all : what need, then, for this precipitation ? Alas! such is the reasoning too often urged on us by our artful foe ; and how willingly do we listen to it !

*3rd Point.*—The saints are the stars of the celestial firmament, who light us on our way to glory ; but if we do not avail ourselves of their example and intercession, how can we hope for all the graces we require in order to live as they have done? Do we value the rich treasures we have in the saintly founders of our holy order? Are we as devout to them as we should be? Do we endeavour to imitate their example? Do we constantly ask their prayers ? To-day, at least, let us honour our blessed mother. To-day, at least, let us make many thanksgivings to our heavenly Father, for all the graces He has bestowed on her. If we desire to be her true and faithful children, she will most assuredly help us ; and who, except the sweet Mother of Jesus, would be so likely to intercede efficaciously ? She has left us the tenderest, the most maternal of benedictions. She, at least, desired to show us she would never forget us ; and shall we be neglectful or unmindful of her ?

## SECOND MEDITATION,

*In which S. Clare is proposed as a model of devotion to the most holy Sacrament.*

*1st Prelude.*—Behold S. Clare prostrate before the blessed Sacrament, interceding for her native city.

*2nd Prelude.*—Pray that, through her intercession, you may obtain a great devotion to Jesus in the Eucharist.

*1st Point.*—Let us consider the lively faith which our saint had in the most holy Sacrament. On two occasions we find her miraculously delivering the town of Assisi from savage enemies. And what is the means she uses? It is the exposition of the blessed Sacrament. Always trusting with a childlike trust, always loving with a childlike love, we cannot wonder that her prayers met with a ready acceptance before the throne of God. In all trouble, in all necessities, Jesus was her refuge ; and when did Jesus ever fail ? The Moors trusted in their armies, the captains of the Emperor in their valour ; Clare has only Jesus—Jesus hidden, silent, and apparently helpless in the tabernacle. But Clare knows that this silent, hidden, helpless Jesus, who seems to let us do what we like with Him, is still the God of armies, the only sure refuge of the afflicted. Oh, that we had a faith like hers ! Oh, that we, in all our necessities, fled to the tabernacle ! Surely we should oftener have our prayers answered, surely our faith would thus become more lively.

*2nd Point.*—The most holy Sacrament was also the source of all her sanctity, as well as the peculiar object of her devotion. Indeed, we may say that the blessed Sacrament supported both her natural and supernatural life. We are told that her fasts were so continual, as to have exceeded what nature could have borne, unless it were supported by some special grace. How, then, did she live ? What sustained her in the pains of her sickness, the cares of her office, her long vigils, her ceaseless fasts? Truly it was Jesus. He was her daily bread, and her life was a life of ceaseless union with Him, by sacramental and spiritual communions. Behold her in the long silent nights, prostrate in the choir, when all have retired to rest. She can-

not leave her Love, and in her sickness He will not leave
her.

*3rd Point.*—Let us seek to imitate this blessed saint, by
uniting our exterior duties to an interior spirit of prayer and
recollection. Above all, let us continually unite ourselves
to Jesus in the tabernacle. Let us seek consolation, and
help, and support from Him, and He will never disappoint
us ; and if we cannot beautify many altars, or furnish many
churches with necessaries for the divine service, let us, at
least in spirit, make visits of reparation to neglected sanc-
tuaries, and let us show by our manner, and still more in
our hearts, the love we bear to Jesus when in His presence.

### THIRD MEDITATION.

*S. Clare consecrates herself to God at the altar of Mary.*

*1st Prelude.*—Represent to yourself the love and fervour
with which our blessed mother kneels at the altar of Mary,
in the church of the Porzcola, and there consecrates herself
to God.

*2nd Prelude.*—Pray that you may offer yourself to God
with equal devotion and earnestness.

*1st Point.*—Ever since that most glorious moment when
the Word was made flesh in the Virgin's womb, every
good and great work has been either begun or continued
through the Mother of God. The saints who have been
most devout to her, who have been most fervent, those
who have obtained the richest gifts of sanctity, have mostly
acknowledged that they obtained these graces through her
intercession ; while sinners, who could never otherwise
have hoped to enter heaven, have owed their salvation,
under God, to their Immaculate Mother. The order of
Poor Clares began at the moment when Clare pronounced
her vows at the altar of Mary, to the end, say its ancient
chroniclers, that it might evidently appear that the Mother
of God did equally cover with her mantle her first and second order of Franciscans. We, then, should be specially
devout to Mary. May we more and more value her protection, and trust in her intercession !

*2nd Point.*—Consider that S. Clare began her spiritual
life under the protection of Mary, and also ended it under

her manifest and visible care. To-day we commemorate her death; and truly, if ever a saint died in the arms of Mary, it was our dear and gentle Clare. The mantle of Mary had covered her mystically when she began her religious life at the altar of the Queen of heaven, and now, in her dying moments, Mary comes, visibly to many, and covers her child with her mantle; nay, more, she embraces her with the tenderest love. If we also begin our good purposes, our desires of amendment, our resolutions, under the same blessed protection, we may be sure that Mary will guard them and us to the end.

*3rd Point.*—Consider what fervent thanksgivings we should make for the inestimable favour of being under the protection of a saint so devoted to Mary, and so cherished by her. The clients of S. Clare may well hope that their blessed patroness will intercede for them, specially with her whose intercession never fails. But to obtain the special interest of any saint in our behalf, we must endeavour to imitate their virtues. Let us, then, try to imitate the fidelity of S. Clare, in corresponding to the graces God bestowed on her, to imitate her patience in sickness and suffering, and her zeal for God's honour in the adorable Sacrament.

LAUS DEO.

THE END.

www.ingramcontent.com/pod-product-compliance
Lightning Source LLC
Chambersburg PA
CBHW031339070726
47496CB00017B/1282